BEYOND THE BLUE HORIZON

First Published in Great Britain 2015 by Mirador Publishing

First edition: 2015

A copy of this work is available through the British Library.

ISBN: 978-1-911044-20-8

Mirador Publishing
Mirador
Wearne Lane
Langport
Somerset
TA10 9HB

Beyond The Blue Horizon

By

Curtis Moon

Other books by Curtis Moon

The 21st Century Crusaders
Sentimental Journey
Secret Place

CHAPTER ONE

She deftly allowed the soft silk dressing-gown to slip from her slender shoulders to fall to the floor exposing her beautiful slim mature body. Her long legs sauntered smoothly over the body of her handsome young lover before she folded neatly into his ready arms, enjoying the warmth of his lustful intimate embrace. His hand caressed her neck gently and easily, moving up and down sensuously. She felt erotic emotion swiftly welling up inside her. His hands moved slowly to her breasts, stroking each one smoothly touching the nipples softly so that she felt transported to a higher level plane than she had never known before. Suddenly she felt her body becoming moist as her heart beat rapidly in anticipation of what was about to happen, and beads of perspiration began to appear on her forehead. It was so wonderful … so marvellous… so brilliant… so erotic! His hand moved to the lower part of her body causing her adrenalin to begin to flow fiercely then, without warning, a shock ran through her body as her eyes opened widely to the bright light that pierced through a gap in the curtains, causing her to wake abruptly from her reverie utterly alone and desolate in her large comfortable bed. It was yet another dream… a mirage in her mind… in the depths of her sleep… another figment of her frustrated imagination.

Diana Templeton was a woman heading slowly towards middle age who preferred to live her life in a dream world. It would be fair to say that it had overtaken her sanity for she worshipped the remarkable gift that had been especially endowed to her. The humdrum life of boredom in a house that was far too big for her to manage alone offered absolutely nothing in the way of passion, emotion, or even a modicum of tenderness… all interest having been lost to the past. This was accentuated by the fact that her husband, like many others after twenty-three years of marriage, neglected her badly. Indeed, it was far worse than that for he was absent most of the time as a result of his work and had become a conditioned workaholic. She recalled some research carried out that women spoke seven thousand words each day but men only managed two thousand. To her dismay, when she and Charles were alone, the dialogue was negligible. She could not recall any meaningful discussion, debate, argument or decision they had made together over the past ten years. They simply held their silence and very rarely spoke to each other. Subsequently, she began to yearn for night to come so that she could lay full-length in her comfortable bed, with her head lolling on the soft pillow and be allowed to experience such brilliant dreams to relieve the frustration that built up inside her. It was a means of entering another world which was wistful, exotic, erotic and absolutely unreal. The strange part of the matter was that she always enjoyed such pleasant fantastic dreams. There was never any ugliness or situations that distressed her or affected her mind with threats of disaster... only emotional love! As soon as she fell into the arms of Morpheus each night, a new world opened up to her... another world that was wonderful... similar to the theme of the book of the thousand tales of the Arabian Nights.

* * * * *

At the age of forty-three, with a wealthy husband and two grown-up children who had left home, she was relatively free in mind and most adventurous in spirit. She felt that there was something inside her struggling to get out but there was no opportunity for it to do so. As with every other woman she wanted to enjoy life to the full until her husband moved up the promotional ladder at work and refused to allow her to do anything. Each morning, with time on her hands, she would climb out of bed and stand in front of a full-length mirror preening herself for some time, thanking her lucky stars that she had an outstandingly slim figure and a beautiful unwrinkled smooth-skinned face. Such was her outstanding beauty that people who didn't know her believed that she was about fifteen years younger, in her late twenties, and she took great pains not to tell them the truth.

On one particular evening, she undressed, went to bed, and lay between the luxurious sheets solemnly thinking about the future, but it wasn't long before she fell asleep to enter into a fantastic dream where she was magically transported to Morocco in Africa with the vast Sahara Desert stretching out before her. She found herself in a Bedouin tent laying nude in the arms of an equally naked handsome dark-skinned young man... one who was younger than herself who she found to be extremely amorous. In the realm where excitement abounded, she found herself wrapped around his lithe brown body, kissing him gently but firmly on the lips before pushing her tongue into his mouth which thrilled her intensely.

He began to kiss her all over her body with gentle kisses causing her to experience tremendous erotic pleasure. She then moved her body so that the two of them could enjoy a session of pure intimacy. In reality, as her mind wafted through the emotions, her limbs moved up and down under the blankets suggesting that she was undergoing extreme intimate pleasure. The stimulation continued for some considerable time until she gave a series of light gasps and completely relaxed her body. This was the crowning moment of the life she loved to live… enjoying magnificent satisfaction within the confines of her own mind which also seemed to satisfy her physical needs. The exercise was entirely personal and she was not obliged to reveal any details to any other person or offer any kind of explanation to anyone. Certainly it would be impossible to talk to her husband of her great passion… he would never understand what she meant or why she revelled in such a reaction. He was a dull Civil Servant of high-standing within the Government and, apart from being a workaholic, he was often away for weeks on business. No… not only would he fail to understand but he wouldn't care to fathom out the reason. Work was all he wanted to do. His wife took second place in his life. If she tried to explain her nightly intimate clandestine affairs in her nether-world to him, he would eye her with an element of contempt or perhaps consider that she was losing her mind. No… this was her secret… her precious private superb secret which she would never reveal to anyone!

The dream about Morocco stayed firmly in her mind for a very long time and it wasn't too long before she approached her husband, asking him to take her on holiday there.

'Why Morocco?' he demanded with an element of surprise. 'You know nothing about it. What's so fascinating that you want to go there?'

'It's just a whim,' she responded easily, thinking about the young handsome dark-skinned Arab but refusing to give her husband any other reason. 'If you want, you can say it's my birthday present.

He huffed and puffed for a while, examining his diary at length in order to set a date for the vacation.

'I'll have to get clearance for a trip to that country,' he muttered indicating his reluctance to leave his work. 'In any case,' he went on. 'I can only afford to be away for one week. You know how my work builds up.' He turned over some more pages in his diary and then gave a grunt. 'I can go one week before the end of June!'

As far as he was concerned, it was extremely difficult to find time to spend on a frivolity such as a vacation but, regardless of any date in his calendar, it was always difficult for Charles Templeton to find spare time away from his duties. Nonetheless, they went ahead and Diana booked the holiday but she recognised that there would be no lascivious or intimate relationships with any young handsome dark-skinned Arab when she arrived there. Despite her boredom and distress at home, she was still compos mentis, capable of defining dreams from reality although it sometimes peeved her to have to do so.

CHAPTER TWO

The day of their departure soon arrived and they made their way to the airport to board the aircraft which took off without delay. Diana was in her element. She was on an aircraft flying to the place she had seen in her dreams. However the journey was not without incident. A short time before the plane approached Agadir airport in Morocco, the pilot announced that a simoom was in force in the area and that all passengers needed to secure their seat-belts as he expected a very bumpy landing. When the aircraft descended on to the runway, the fierce wind blew so strongly that it swerved at an angle ramming one of its wings into another plane parked nearby. The aircraft then slewed violently off the runway causing the passengers to scream as it rendered off its course. As it happened, the damage was relatively limited and the aircraft managed to resume its progress towards the main building, albeit the portside wing had been slightly dented. When the door of the plane was opened, Charles Templeton stood on the gangway to disembark and stared outwards at a sea of sand being blow about by the strong wind. As he did so, it ripped open his jacket and swept away the pens and papers which were located in his inside pockets, distributing them into oblivion.

'My goodness!' he remonstrated staring bleakly as he looked for them on the open runway. 'What an awful forceful wind!'

The stewardess standing close by smiled weakly. 'The simoom

is a hot sand-laden wind in North Africa,' she informed him. 'It normally lasts for three days.'

He nodded wistfully climbing down the stairway to suffer a rain of sharp sand which whipped against him. He and his wife raced into the main building to face an immigration officer who held out his hands for their passports.

'Tell me,' asked Templeton in earnest, 'How long does it take for this simoom to die down?'

'It has been here for three days long,' replied the immigration officer in clipped English. 'It will not last for more than a few hours at most.'

'Thank Heavens for that!' muttered the Civil Servant dryly with an element of relief in his voice. 'The last thing we want on a holiday is to suffer a damned continuous sandstorm.'

'But it will still remain quite hot,' concluded the officer, returning their passports to them.

The Templetons left the airport clutching their luggage and hailed a taxi to take them to their hotel. The cabbie was extremely talkative believing that the more he told them about the place the larger would be his tip.

'Agadir is growing very fast,' he informed them, deliberately taking them the long way round to their hotel so that he could continue his lecture and increase his fee for the journey. 'On February the twenty-ninth 1960, we suffered a great earthquake which killed many people. Fifteen thousand people died in fifteen seconds. There were too many bodies for us to handle so we buried them at the end of town in an enormous grave covering them with cement. Money poured in to help us from all over the world and we used it to make Agadir a beautiful place. Over there you can see the Purple Mountains. Here you can see the beautiful blue sea.'

He ranted on about the town, highlighting its features, until they arrived at their destination. After they had unpacked their suitcases, Diana sat on the edge of one of the twin beds considering her views about the holiday. It was on the cards that Charles would buy newspapers every day and bury his head in the text for hours on end. In order to please her during the week, he would arrange a boat trip around the harbour or book two seats on a tour coach so that they could see the sights. On the latter occasion he would go off leaving her to her own devices. She had to face it that nothing exciting was ever going to happen on the holiday and she wondered why she had influenced him to come. But then she had only herself to blame because she had really known the situation before starting out. What she needed was the presence of a young handsome dark-skinned Arab, like the one in her dreams, to show her kindness, attention, tenderness and love but she realised that such a situation was practically impossible. Not that she would want to carry on in the same fashion as in her dreams with regard to intimacy or adultery. Not so… for she was honest and loyal to her husband and would never consider engaging in some physical intimate activity with another man. Within this context, she continued to torture herself although she knew in her heart that she could rely on the dreams at night to satisfy most of her physical desires.

The holiday began exactly as she had predicted. Charles bought a newspaper at the reception desk of the hotel and buried his head in the pages. He would stay reading it for the best part of an hour at least, deliberating on every political story as he lit his pipe and puffed on it. What a change there had been in the man since she first met him. He had been tall, good-looking and very attentive towards her. He had paid her numerous compliments, bought her chocolates and flowers, took her out for candlelit dinners, and there was a strong physical relationship between them. Of course in those days, he was merely a clerk in one of the Governmental ministries with little hope of glory or rising to elevated heights. Indeed, he did have ambition but work was secondary at that time. However, after a series of promotions, it had taken him over and his attitude towards her changed. He became so wrapped up in his work that he hardly ever saw her, spending some nights and too many weekends in his apartment in London. At one time, she thought that he might be having an affair with another woman, staying with her each weekend but Charles was too dull and too much of a workaholic to be bothered with anyone else of the female sex. Over the past fifteen years, his attention had drifted elsewhere and he forgot to continue buying her chocolates and flowers. There was simply a card and an expensive present on her birthday and just a card on their anniversary. Now, on the holiday which they could have both enjoyed, she was left by herself as usual.

'Are you coming with me to see some of the sights?' she asked pleasantly.

'Plenty of time for that,' he grunted, puffing at his pipe, without taking his eyes off the print. 'We have a whole week here. I think I'll finish reading the newspaper first.'

'But we're on holiday, Charles, surely…'

'Despite what you want to do, my dear,' he interrupted rudely, looking deeper into the newspaper, 'life still goes on in the world.'

She mused that the man was hopeless as a husband, even worse as a companion, and complete forlorn as a lover. Shrugging off his neglect, she regarded it as an opportunity to be adventurous… to find out more about the place and enjoy what it had to offer.

'Well I'm going out,' she told him with a tinge of anger in her voice. 'You do what you want to do. I mean we don't want the world to come to an end, do we?'

Without looking up from his newspaper, still puffing on his pipe, he grunted carelessly. She left the room to descend the main staircase of the hotel, finding it necessary to hold on to the banister as the staircase shifted beneath her.

'There's something wrong with your staircase,' she mentioned to the receptionist at the main desk. 'The stairs keep moving up and down… they're loose.'

'No, ma'am,' came the easy reply. 'The stairs automatically adjust themselves so that if there's another earthquake it will weather the storm.'

* * * * *

Diana left the hotel duly informed and made her way down the well-made road furnished with palm trees on the pavements on both sides. The simoom had faded away to leave the sun shining brightly in a clear blue sky as she walked on slowly until arriving at the main square. The entrance was guarded by a raggedly-dressed man sitting cross-legged on the ground playing a flute, In front of him was placed a large wicker basket containing a cobra. The snake reached up at the rhythm of the music, swaying from one side to the other, its tongue flickering forwards and backwards in its mouth. It had wicked eyes and would not hesitate to surge forward and bite the man if the music stopped. A shiver ran down her spine as she hurried past the musician and his snake to enter the square. It had become very hot and she waved her hand in front of her to blow away the flies as well as the stench of spices being sold as they wafted in her direction. The place was indeed a paradise and the atmosphere extremely pleasant in the hot sun with the vacant sound of the flute in the distance and the cries of the owners of the snack trolleys trying to sell their wares. She noticed that very few people wandering to and fro wore Arab clothing.

After a while, she decided to rest and sat down lightly on a bench seat closing her eyes in the bright sun, basking happily in its warmth. Suddenly, a shadow appeared in front of her cutting off the sun from her body. She looked up to stare into the eyes of a young, handsome, dark-skinned Arab. She blinked twice at the sight of him because he was identical to the man she had seen in her dreams.

'My name's Ahmed.' he told her in perfect English. 'You look rather hot and uncomfortable. Can I be of any assistance?'

Diana had difficulty crossing-over from dream to reality and she tried to adjust her mind to the change. 'Ahmed!'' she uttered almost in disbelief. 'I think I was with you in one of my dreams a short while ago.' She bit her tongue for divulging her secret but it was too late to withdraw the remark.

'Really!' he retorted with interest, smiling as he sat down beside her. 'Tell me about it.'

'I'm not sure that I should,' she laughed, refusing to say anything more about her nightly ventures.

'We've never met before in real life,' he confided amiably, 'and we shall probably never see each other again after today because you will return to wherever you came from shortly. So any secret of yours will go to the grave with me.'

She stared at him obliquely thinking what a wonderful person he seemed to be. 'You must have lived in England to be able t speak the language so well.'

‘I went to Oxford University,’ he explained. ‘Maudlin College. I rowed on the river Isis. But that’s a long story.’

‘You intrigue me,’ she went on. ‘Oxford. Why did you return to Morocco?’

‘It was because of my family,’ he replied with an element of sadness showing in his eyes. ‘My father died and then my mother fell ill. I have two brothers and a sister all younger than myself. They had to be cared for.’ He paused as thought wiping away his past problems to concentrate on his newly-found friend. ‘Now come on,’ he continued firmly, ‘tell me all about your dream. I’m fascinated to hear it.’

Diana allowed the request to cross her mind for a moment trying to come to a decision. He was right. After the week was over, they would never meet again but then she held her ground. ‘No,’ ‘she told him with a twinkle in her eye. ‘I don’t think I will.’

‘Then I can only presume that your dream was exotic in which you and I made love to each other,’ he continued relentlessly.

Her face became slightly red as she blushed at his comment. She considered him to be quite pretentious and it was difficult to let the comment pass. ‘How could you possibly think that?’ she riposted, almost angry that he had identified her weakness.

‘Why else would you not wish to tell me,’ he responded casually. He took her hand and turned it so that the palm faced upwards. ‘Hm!’ he predicted brightly. ‘You are blessed with a long life line. A very long life line. Can you see it?’

She pulled her hand away although she didn’t really want to and stared into his face. They were in the open… in a public place … she could not allow any indiscretion to take place and, in an instant, her loyalty to her husband came to the fore.

‘I don’t want to get involved with you,’ she told him curtly, even though the will to resist began to fade a little. ‘I hope you realise that from the start.’

He seemed surprised at her reaction. ‘Of course not,’ he returned easily. ‘You’re a married lady on vacation. Why should you want to become sexually involved with someone you’ve only just met… someone you don’t know?’

She stiffened at the word ‘sexually’ and it seemed to drive a knife into her heart. ‘That’s right,’ she commented. ‘I don’t know you. I don’t know you at all!’ She paused and sat back on the bench seat as though intending to end the conversation. ‘Don’t you have work to do? I mean I presume you’re employed by someone.’

‘Of course,’ he told her. ‘I’m a lawyer but this is a festival day and the Courts are closed. I’ve given myself the day off.’

'A lawyer,' she repeated, staring at him in admiration. 'How clever! I'm glad you made use of your days at Oxford.'

'Look,' he suggested, standing up in front of her. 'You've probably never seen Agadir before. Let me show you around. We shall be in the open all the time so you have nothing to fear. And I'm very interested in your companionship. I'm not interested in money. I'm not going to rob you. Lawyers are quite well paid here.'

She found herself getting to her feet as though she was in a fantasy. 'You're so like the man in my dreams,' she repeated with a smile lighting up her face. 'It's so uncanny.'

'And what did this man do in your dreams?' he asked hoping to obtain a reply.

'Never you mind!' she retorted bluntly, feeling quite indignant

that he should challenge her on the subject. They walked out of the square and to her concern he began to lead her back to her hotel. 'Where are we going?' she demanded with a worried expression on her face.

He took her arm gently to move her on. 'You've seen the sea before and over there is the dock area which is as dull as ditchwater. You'll go to the casbah climbing the winding road that leads up to it during your holiday so there's no point in taking you there. In any case, it will take too much time to do it. Where are you staying?'

'At the Hotel Sahara.'

'Fine! I shall take you to the woods at the back of the hotel. You'll see some beautiful scenery and lots of trees. A lady of your standing clearly loves gardening and beauty.'

She glanced at him suspiciously wondering whether he had some secret agenda in mind. After all, she didn't know him in the real world. He might be a rogue with ideas of doing something to her that she would not wish to happen. The newspapers were full of such stories about tourists who were raped or murdered when travelling in foreign countries.

'That's where you're wrong,' she told him sharply coming to her senses. 'I hate gardening. My husband and I have someone to do it for us.'

'So there you have it,' he rattled, stopping for a moment in his tracks to summarise her life. 'I see. A lady on holiday with her husband who, after many years of marriage, cares little about her and tends to neglect her badly. Why else would you be alone in a place like this on your holiday. As a result, you take pleasure in dreams. You live in a large house with a big garden and you have a great deal of money. For that reason, you don't need to work. You are in your prime of life… a very beautiful lady in face and body… and you don't really know whether to commit yourself to a lover or not because of the sacred vows you took when you married. How am I doing?'

Diana pulled her arm away from him remaining silent, astonished that he could know so many things about her and her life in such a short time. Was she really so transparent? She had told him nothing about herself. 'You're very presumptuous!' she snapped angrily although she failed to understand where the anger was coming from.

'But I am right, aren't I?'

There was a long pause as they continued past the Hotel Sahara. By now, it was possible that Charles may have finished reading the newspaper and that he was standing on the balcony watching them. However she realised it was a faint hope. What could she say to him if he saw her with a strange young handsome Arab. Such a situation would never happen in her dreams because they were so perfect in safeguarding her despite any salacious activity in which she might become involved. It was a gift designed never to distress her. But now, reality had suddenly come to the fore to face her point-blank, and she wasn't sure how best to deal with it.

Within a few moments they had passed the hotel and came to the dense forest.

'What's the name of this wood?' she asked directly, feeling extremely unhappy at her present plight.

'The Forest of Snakes,' he replied flatly. 'But I do not think you'll find any snakes here.'

She shuddered as she recalled the image of the cobra swaying from side to side at the entrance to the main square and then she decided that on no account would she enter the wood. They sat on a wooden seat nearby for quite some time discussing both his life and hers. Then, he glanced at his wristwatch and to her dismay, he stood up taking her hand at length to kiss her fingers.

'I've got to go,' he said with sadness showing in his eyes. 'I doubt whether we shall meet again and I wish you to have a good life. Try to find as much happiness in any way you can... whatever the sacrifice. Remember... you have only one life. Good bye, beautiful lady. Farewell!'

He took his leave looking back at her before he vanished into the distance. As she watched his departing figure she mused that she was back in dreamland enjoying his company at a different level. She continued to sit on the seat for a further five minutes musing about their meeting. How remarkable... to meet the man she had seen in her dreams. She could hardly believe the coincidence. He even thought in the same fashion although that is where it ended. Eventually, she stood up and was about to return to the hotel when a man wearing a black balaclava over his head emerged from the edge of the wood brandishing a revolver. He wielded it wildly and raced towards Diana pulling her round roughly to face him as he grasped her arm forcibly.

'Gimme all your money and credit cards!' he snarled angrily

in broken English, pushing her in the chest and threatening her with the revolver which he waved about ungainly in front of her face.

Her body became extremely intense at the onslaught as she managed to shake her head slowly. 'I haven't any money on me. My purse is in the hotel and I haven't any pockets. I have no money!'

He paused for a moment to think. This was not the kind of response he expected from his victim and, in view of his determination to rob her, he refused to listen to reason.

'I said gimme your money,' he repeated savagely. 'Hurry!'

'I told you… I have no money,' she persisted beginning to tremble at the notion that he might wound her with the gun or even kill her.

He placed the gun to the side of her head angrily and his finger trembled on the trigger at her refusal. Unwittingly, he pulled the trigger although he had no intention to do so. There was a loud gunshot and Diana fell to the ground with blood seeping out of the back of her head. The assailant stood in shock for a moment and then ran as hard as he could to flee the scene. At that precise moment, hearing the gunshot, Charles appeared on the balcony to look downwards. He saw his wife laying full-length on the ground and stared at her body in disbelief. Then, as the adrenalin surged through his body, he hurried out of the room to get to her, shouting to the female receptionist to call for an ambulance. When he got to his wife, he stood over her body and felt her wrist to determine a pulse. When this proved positive, he removed his jacket and placed it under her head.

'Oh my God!' he cried, shocked at the sight of his wife in such a desperate state. 'This can't be! It can't be!'

Some people passing by crowded around them, curious to know what had happened, but Charles ushered them away, shouting and ranting in a most unlike fashion for him. The ambulance arrived quite swiftly and Diana was transported to the local hospital where she lay unconscious in a coma for six days. When she opened her eyes, her life had changed completely.

'Where am I?' she asked wearily in a muffled tone, closing her eyes as the pain in her head intensified.

'You're in hospital,' confided the nurse waving to a doctor to come and attend his patient.

The doctor moved beside her without delay, a slight smile

touching his lips. 'Mrs. Templeton,' he exclaimed brightly. 'Glad you're awake at last. Nice of you to come back.'

'At last,' she mumbled in the same muffled tone. 'How long have I been here?' She winced at the pain and her hand moved to her head to feel the bandages. 'What's going on?'

'You've been asleep for six days,' the doctor told her. 'You were shot at the back of the head by someone who tried to rob you. Do you remember anything about it?'

Diana shook her head slowly wincing as the pain returned. 'No… I don't remember anything.'

The doctor nodded sagely. 'You may not recall anything for a while.'

'You called me Mrs. Templeton. Is that my name?'

'Yes it is.'

'Does that mean I'm married? I have a husband?'

'He's sitting in the Waiting Room ready to see you right now. He'll be delighted that you've come out of the coma. I'll go and fetch him.' He turned and left the room to find Templeton who was sitting on a seat reading a newspaper. 'I'd like to speak to you about your wife, sir,' he began quietly. The Civil Servant looked up at him from behind the newspaper. 'She is extremely fortunate. The bullet fired at her clipped the edge of her skull, fracturing the cranium. I do not think the bullet touched any part of her brain but a small part of it was exposed. At present, she cannot be moved. She is very confused and suffered a great deal of pain and shock. You can see her now, if you wish.'

Templeton folded the newspaper neatly before standing up and entering the room. He sat down on a chair beside the bed, leaned across, and took hold of her hand.

Diana stared at him blankly. . 'Are you the specialist?' she asked slowly.

He seemed very put out by her reaction. 'I'm Charles… your husband!'

'You're my husband?' she countered staring long and hard at him. Her face screwed up in distaste before she continued. 'I don't know you. I've never seen you before. I doubt that I would choose someone like you to be my husband.'

The doctor entered the room at that moment to clarify the situation for the Civil Servant. 'Do not concern yourself, sir,' he uttered. 'It's quite common for a patient coming out of a coma to be mentally confused. You'll need to give her time to recover properly.'

'What happened?' asked Diana, staring bleakly at the doctor. 'Why am I in hospital?'

'I'll handle this, doctor,' declared Templeton solemnly. 'I'm sure you have other patients to deal with.'

The physician looked at him obliquely, indicating for the nurse to follow him, and they left the room. Templeton gripped Diana's hand more firmly which discomforted her in her present state and she withdrew it smartly. Her mind tried to think past the pain which raged through her head like a knife cutting through butter. What was going on? Why did she have bandages wrapped around her head? And why was she suffering so much pain?

'Don't concern yourself, my dear,' began her husband in a tone that was quite dictatorial. 'Everything will come back to you in time. It's all a matter of time. However, I have a problem staying here with you. I'm desperately needed back at the office. I did say I could only afford to be away for one week on holiday and that's up now. I have to get back to England as fast as possible.'

'On holiday?' she repeated still in a confused state. 'Where am I?'

'You're in Agadir... in Morocco.' he explained tiredly, dagging to get away. For him, this was all a waste of valuable time. 'We came here on a week's vacation.'

'Morocco!' Her mind was completely blank remembering absolutely nothing. She lay quite still in the bed staring at the ceiling as the pain increased in intensity in her head.

'I contacted the British Embassy,' he went on disregarding his wife's incapacity, 'because I shan't be here and they recommended a lawyer who can visit your regularly and report to me how you're getting on. He'll keep in touch with me all the time.'

Diana's eyes moved to the man sitting at the side of her bed. Who was he and what was he talking about? She tried to clear her mind to recall her name but came face-to-face with a complete void.

'What's my name ?' she asked weakly as despair overcame her.

'Diana,' stated her husband briefly. 'Diana Templeton.'

Her eyes became glazed at his reply as the name meant nothing to her. 'Diana... huntress of the moon,' she muttered.

'Ah!' exclaimed Templeton, 'your memory's coming back. That's good. Really good!'

She stared at him bleakly unable to recall any facts about herself, he life, her husband or her whereabouts. It seemed as though she was peering through a mist... so remote... so distant. She groaned as the pain seared through her head again. 'I need something to stop the pain!' she cried out.

Templeton immediately left the room and returned with the nurse who administered a liquid dose of medicine which returned the patient to an element of comfort.

'I'm sorry I have to leave you,' forwarded her husband sadly, 'but my presence is urgently needed in Britain. I have to get back.' He stood up slowly. 'But you will be visited by a lawyer who'll keep me fully informed of your progress.'

He might have not said anything to her as his words had no meaning for her whatsoever. What lawyer was he talking about? Why did he have to be informed of her progress? She didn't even know the man! He was a total stranger to her. Templeton leaned across the bed and kissed her awkwardly on the cheek before leaving the room. As he did so, a man dressed in police uniform entered with the doctor.

'This is the policeman who arrested your attacker,' announced the physician. 'He wants to ask you a few questions.'

'We arrested the man who attacked you, Mrs. Templeton,' began the policeman. 'Do you remember what happened?'

Her head turned towards him as she eyed him up and down. 'I can't even remember my name,' she bleated with tears running down her cheeks. 'What attacker are you talking about?'

The doctor intervened quickly turning to the policeman. 'She's only just come out of a coma. You'll have to come back tomorrow if you want answers to your questions.'

The policeman took a long hard look at Diana and then realised that any attempt to find out about the attack was futile. Ultimately, he nodded to the doctor and left the room.

Diana's mind remained completely blank and she lay in the same condition for two whole days. On the third day, the nurse appeared at the door.

'You have a visitor,' she announced, beckoning to someone waiting outside.

The man entered the room and Diana stared at his face. She failed to recognise him but it was Ahmed and he walked cautiously towards the bed. 'Mrs. Templeton,' he began warmly. 'Destiny has it that we should meet again. I'm sorry that this awful thing happened to you.'

'Meet again?' She looked confused. 'Do we know each other?'

'We met in the public square,' he went on. 'I took you to the Forest of Snakes. Don't you remember?'

She shook her head slowly. .'No I don't. That's the problem. Whatever happened has taken away my memory.'

'I'm really sorry about that,' he apologised although it was not his fault.

'Your attacker has been caught and I've just learned that he hanged himself in prison. Losing his life is punishment enough. But unfortunately it doesn't help you.'

'Hanged himself!' she repeated not knowing how she should feel about the man's demise. 'How terrible!'

'Not so. He deserved to die. The laws are very strict here. If someone resorts to violence, he has to be punished severely.'

She stared at his face trying to recall when they were supposed to have met but nothing came to her. 'I don't remember you at all. Not at all.'

'Well never mind,' he returned sympathetically. 'Your husband has employed me to report to him as to how you're getting on. Let me tell you what little I know about you. You're Diana Templeton, married to Charles, a senior Civil Servant, You have a house in Berkshire with five bedrooms and a large garden. You have two children, a boy and a girl, aged twenty-two and twenty accordingly, who have both left home to lead their own lives. Money is not a problem as you are fairly wealthy. You don't need to go to work. And that just about sums you up. You came on holiday to Agadir and was shot by a man who tried to rob you. Do you have any questions?'

'Oh yes!' she remonstrated forcefully. 'I have lots of questions. It's just that I can't seem to think of them at this precise moment. My mind is a void. I can't remember anything. Why is the man who calls himself my husband not here himself?'

Ahmed smiled at her uneasily. 'There are husbands and husbands,' he replied enigmatically.

'What does that mean?' she asked, confused by his answer.

'Well,' he continued, trying to make his reply as pleasant as possible so as not to upset her. 'Your husband is a senior Civil Servant and he has great responsibilities resting on his shoulders. There are matters to which he must respond quickly as a lot depends on his judgement. So it's not possible for him to be here with you.'

'Don't you think that wives and families are far more important than work?' she retorted angrily. 'Surely he can delegate the work to subordinates for a short while. I mean if he was run over by a bus would the world come to an end? Would it stop in its tracks in confusion? I don't think so.'

'I cannot reply to hypothetical questions, Diana,' he told her informally, using her first name as a sign of endearment. 'All I can tell you is that I'm here to help you in any way I can and to report your progress to your husband.'

'Well as far as I'm concerned, there hasn't been any progress,' she continued dolefully. ‘I still can’t remember anything. So where does that leave you?’

‘There was something you mentioned at our last meeting. Perhaps it might act as a trigger to your memory. You said that you dreamed about me, or someone like me, but you refused to tell me what went on between us in your dreams. Maybe you can dream again. It might bring something back.’

‘Dreams!’ she thought to herself. ‘If only I could enjoy one.’ The words had no meaning to her in her present condition. Her mind was completely blank. There was no emotion, no ideas, no planning, no intent on revenge for the attack by the gunman… absolutely nothing!

CHAPTER THREE

It was almost a week later when the first development occurred. The precious gift endowed to Diana returned to her at last. When she finally fell asleep that night, she began to dream again. It so happened that Ahmed's image appeared to her to start it off. The vision she could see in her mind's eye seemed to be so real. Even though she could not recall anything that happened in the past, his face was exactly the same as she had seen it in previous dreams. As her head moved slightly on the pillow, her mind moved to a wide stretch of the Sahara Desert as she watched the sun go down before entering a nearby Bedouin tent. Inside, she found herself moving towards the outstretched arms of the young handsome dark-skinned man but this time she was fully dressed. They kissed wantonly but all the time there was a strange feeling for the pain she suffered drove right through her head. As her mind was completely blank, she was unable to compare it with the dreams she had experienced before coming to Morocco. Suddenly, the pain in her head seemed to ease and she found herself removing her clothes and pulling off her lover's shirt. On this occasion, there were no inhibitions. Both she and her lover flirted for a few minutes and then he pointed to the straw bed laying on the sand on one side of the tent. In their nudity, they folded their bodies into each other, moving their hands over erogenous areas to stimulate their excitement before entering into an intimate sexual relationship. Then, almost as quickly as it had started, the dream came to a sudden end. Her mind went blank and she opened her eyes to see the moon reflecting its light through a gap in the curtains. She tried to recall the substance of the dream but the essence of it had vanished into infinity. She could remember nothing about it and then the miserable persistent pain shot through her head again. She reached out to take the medication left on the side table to ease it and lay back on the bed in desolation. Tears of frustration started to run down her cheeks. In her opinion, life was never going to get any better. She would ostensibly be an invalid with no mind at all. Furthermore, staying at this hospital would do her no good and a desperate urge which surged across her brain overwhelmed her. She had no idea where she would go and no plan had formed in her mind with regard to her future. Springing into action, she lifted the sheet from her body and sat up on the edge of the bed. She swayed there for a few minutes trying to pluck up courage to place her feet on the floor. The same dull pain went through her head again and she moved forward to stand up. It was as thought the world was about to collapse. She almost fell down as a bout of dizziness overcame her and she managed to climb back on the bed. She paused for a while and then tried again but fell back on the bed with tears continuing to run down her face. She was a prisoner in this hospital with no means of escape, considering that this was the hell in which she would spend the rest of her life. Why was this happening to her? She had done nothing to offend the Gods. Why were they picking on her? Undaunted, she attempted to stand on her feet again but this time she collapsed and fell heavily to the floor. As she lay fully-stretched, unable to move, she cried out at the top of her voice. Was there no mercy in this world? It was fortunate for her that the nurse happened to be on duty and was passing the room when Diana fell. She heard the thud of the

patient's body hitting the floor and then the cry for help, so she hurried into the room to investigate. She helped Diana to her feet and got her back into the bed, calming her and forcing her to swallow some tablets which soon put her to sleep. A little later on, the nurse spoke to the doctor about the incident and he pulled a face at his patient's dilemma.

'She needs someone to be with her during the day,' he responded without knowing how to solve the problem.

'Why don't we send in Mrs. Naylor... the English woman in Dr. Mahmoud's care?' suggested the nurse sagely. 'You know, the one suffering from cancer. She's English and she could keep Mrs. Templeton company.'

The doctor nodded his agreement and asked the nurse to approach the woman to solicit her assistance. It seemed to be the only immediate solution.

* * * * *

On the following morning, Betty Naylor entered Diana's room and sat on the chair at the side of the bed.

'My name's Betty,' she greeted warmly as Diana stared at her in a confused fashion. 'It's a terrible name, isn't it? But that's what it says on my birth certificate. You'd think my parents would have called me Elizabeth or Lisbeth but no... that would be too much to ask. It's plain and simple Betty.'

Diana stared at her bleakly. 'Why are you here?' she asked bluntly.

'To keep you company of course,' came the reply. 'You must be lonely laying in this bed all day and night with no memory at all. The nurse told me all about you.' She shrugged her shoulders and screwed up her lips. 'To tell you the truth, sometimes I feel exactly the same way... all alone with no one to speak to. Worst still, I don't speak Arabic which means I can't communicate with anyone here. But you're in for the long stay and you're British… thank God! Mind you, I'd rather forget most of my memories. I've been mistreated most of my life so there's not a lot worth remembering.'

'Why do you stay here then?'

'That's a long story, dear.'

'This is a hospital,' uttered Diana clearing her throat. 'And you're here.'

'That's right, dear. This is a hospital.'

'What's wrong with you?'

The woman gave a raucous laugh before replying. 'What's wrong with me? The bottom line is that I've got cancer of the pancreas. It's incurable but I've been treated by Dr. Mahmoud, a scientist attached to the hospital. He's brilliant!'

'Dr. Mahmoud?'

'Yes. He's a scientist… not a doctor within the hospital. He has a small laboratory in the annex. He works on a science that uses extracts from flowers and plants to cure people… and I can tell you he's very successful. I'd have been dead two years ago if it wasn't for him. As I said he's brilliant!'

Diana began to show some interest in the woman's plight and she sat up in bed to listen to her. For a moment she felt a savage pain in her head but it passed quickly. 'Doctor Mahmoud,' she repeated slowly. 'Do you think he might be able to help me?'

'I'm sure he can,' replied Betty optimistically, 'but you'll have to get special dispensation from the hospital to come under him. He's a very busy man.' There was a pause as Diana stared at the distant wall vacantly. 'I tell you what I'll do. When you feel ready

I'll take you to him and we'll find out whether he's willing to take you on.'

'Good idea,' responded Diana eagerly, although her mind was practically in a dream.

Betty prattled on throughout the day, delighted to be able to talk at length to someone in English. She was never short of words. They spouted from her mouth like Tennyson's bubbling brook flowing on for ever. Towards the end of the afternoon, despite a torrent of information that her visitor expounded about her life, Diana fell off to sleep. Listening to Betty over a long period of time was more than she could take. Immediately her mind went to Ahmed in the tent in the Sahara Desert and she uttered a moan as the scene was to her satisfaction. After a short while, Betty realised that continuing her dialogue was futile and she left to go to her own room. Sadly for Diana, just as before, the dream ended abruptly and she awoke bleary-eyed before it developed. By now her plight was becoming desperate. She was all alone in a strange hospital in a foreign country and the man who alleged to be her husband had abandoned her. She was visited regularly by a lawyer whom she did not know and a woman suffering from cancer kept visiting her who would not stop talking. The situation was an absolute nightmare. When was it going to end?

* * * * *

The next day, Betty entered the room with a big smile on her face.

'How are you today, dear?' she asked warmly. 'I've just seen Dr. Mahmoud and he's cleared me to leave this damned place. I'm off to England in the next few days. The doctor's in his laboratory so it might be a good time to go and see him.'

With nothing else to do, Diana pulled back the sheet on the bed and climbed out relatively easily. 'Thank Heavens that awful dizziness has gone,' she thought to herself placing her feet firmly on the floor. Then she started to sway a little.

Betty became concerned and left the room to return shortly with a wheelchair. 'Here, love,' she commented. 'Climb into this and I'll wheel you there.

'Okay,' said Diana putting on her dressing-gown and climbing into the vehicle. 'I'm ready to see your quack.' She regretted having made the comment, noticing the effect the lack of respect had on her visitor.

'He's not a quack!' retorted Betty loyally with a tinge of anger in her voice. 'He saved my life!'

Diana shrugged her shoulders aimlessly as Betty wheeled her out of the room into the corridor. They made their way to the far end of the hospital and entered the annex. Betty knocked on the door and entered unannounced. Dr. Mahmoud looked up at them with surprise.

'Dr. Mahmoud,' began Betty earnestly. 'This is Diana Templeton, a friend of mine, who's a patient at this hospital. She was shot at the back of the head by a gunman and it caused her to lose her memory.' He stared at Diana as she sat quite still in the wheelchair. 'I know you're a very busy man, Dr. Mahmoud,' went on Betty unabatedly, 'but she'd like you to take her on as your patient.'

The scientist rubbed one hand across his goatee beard and stared at the two women. 'I would like to do so but my work already fills my day. I cannot take on any more patients at this particular time. I'm sorry but my list is full.'

Betty pulled a face at his response but she refused to back down. 'She's just one more patient, doctor, and you're releasing me so you have space for one more. Surely you can fit her in. I mean she's a patient in this hospital. You don't have to spend time going on visits.'

'I'm sorry,' he told her adamantly. 'I can't take on anyone else at this time. I'm here for twenty-four hours a day as it is. My work would be affected if I became too tired or jaded. I would like to help you but it's not possible.'

Betty pointed to Diana with sadness in her eyes. 'This woman has no memory. She doesn't know who she is or what went on before in her life before she was shot. Can you imagine how she feels laying in a hospital bed all day and night with nothing going through her mind? Please show some mercy!'

He shook his head slowly. 'As I said… it's not possible.

'And that's your final answer.' The words were fired like an arrow from a crossbow.

'I have work to do, Mrs. Naylor,' he added finally hoping to dismiss them quickly. 'Please close the door on your way out.'

The cancer patient felt inflamed at the lack of interest in her plea and she went to the door irately wheeling Diana in front of her. 'Come on! He's not interested. This was a waste of time!'

She pushed the wheelchair back along the corridor, neither of them speaking. Betty was fuming on her failure to convince the scientist to help her newly-found friend. Surely Mahmoud could have added her to his patient list! After all he was losing one patient in Betty Naylor and Diana was in the hospital and unlikely to leave for some time. She considered that their sudden intrusion into the scientist's office had influenced his negative decision when he was having a bad day.

They arrived back at their starting point and Diana climbed into bed dolefully, staring bleakly at the other woman who sat down heavily in a chair. Betty threw her arms in the air with frustration.

'I don't know how he could turn you down!' she snarled bitterly. 'He could have added you to his list. It wouldn't have caused him that much problem. The only reason I can think of is that he doesn't deal with people who've lost their memory. That must be it. People without memories are an enigma to him. That's why he wouldn't take you on.'

'I can't blame him,' uttered Diana sadly. 'I'm an enigma to myself. How could I expect him to treat me? As you said, he's a scientist not a doctor. He can pick and choose whoever he wishes to treat.'

'That's all very well,' Betty went on miserably, 'but I recommended you and he turned you down. It goes very much against the grain.'

The two women continued their conversation for some time although Diana contributed very little.

‘Although I’m discharged, I’m not going ‘til the end of the week,’ Betty told her, showing her a flight ticket to England which she held in her hand. I’ve got to make arrangements for my accommodation in Britain. So you won’t get rid of me that quickly.’

Diana smiled weakly at the information not wishing to comment and Betty left shortly afterwards leaving her friend wanting.

* * * * *

The following morning, Diana pushed her breakfast away from her dismally. She disliked the taste of the cous-cous, especially for the first meal of the day and she was extremely unhappy at being presented only with Moroccan cuisine. Some eggs, ham and bacon would have gone down well but such a whim was not possible under these conditions in a foreign country. Sitting sat back in the bed, she was thankful not to experience any further pains in her head. She still faced the far wall blankly with nothing going on in her memory cells… nothing at all! Visions of the people who came to visit her formed in her mind… her alleged husband, Ahmed the lawyer, Betty Naylor, the nurse and her doctor… but that was all she could remember. It was indeed sheer hell! Then, without warning, the door of the room opened and Ahmed appeared. He approached the bed and looked at the uneaten breakfast.

‘The food here’s disgusting,’ he commented knowingly. ‘I can understand why you refuse to eat it. How are you this morning?’

‘Much the same,’ she responded miserably. ‘Still nothing!’

‘You have to be patient,’ he told her sympathetically. ‘It all takes time.’

‘That’s what everyone keeps telling me… it all takes time! That’s all I have!’

At that moment, Betty Naylor entered the room and looked at the lawyer. ‘You’re the one her husband hired, aren’t you?’ she ventured. ‘The one who reports back to him.’

‘I am, ‘ retorted Ahmed easily. ‘And I’m more than just a hireling. I’m Diana’s friend.’

‘And just how do you make that out?’ challenged Betty staring directly into the young Arab’s eyes.

‘We met before she was attacked,’ he declared blatantly. ‘We walked around Agadir together.’

‘Did you know she was going to be mugged?’ Nothing was going to move suspicion from the cancer patient’s mind.

‘Of course not! I’m her friend!’ he riposted with mock annoyance.

'Well if you really are her friend, can you use your influence on Dr. Mahmoud?'

'Mahmoud? The scientist?' Ahmed was surprised at the request.

'He turned her down yesterday. Refused to add her to his list of patients Left her high and dry. Will you do something about it… please?'

'I'll try,' he promised thoughtfully. 'I'll go and see him now.' He nodded to Diana and left the room without hesitation.

Betty turned to her friend. 'If anyone can swing it… he will. I mean they speak the same language, don't they? I wouldn't give up hope yet, dear, Not yet.'

It was almost twenty minutes before Ahmed returned. The two women looked at him with an element of optimism although Diana doubted that the scientist would change his mind.

'Good news,' echoed the young Arab with delight. 'I've managed to get him to reverse his decision. He will treat you after all. He wants to see you in one hour's time.'

Betty clapped her hands with joy. 'There you are! I knew he'd get Dr. Mahmoud to change his mind. Wonderful...wonderful!

You really are a good friend.'

The three of them stayed together for the next hour until Ahmed reminded her of the appointment. She got into the wheelchair and he pushed her all the way down the corridor to the annex. Mahmoud looked up as she was wheeled into his office and he stared hard at her for quite some time before speaking.

'I have your hospital notes here. You have a total blackout with regard to your memory.'

'That's correct,' she said firmly. 'I remember nothing of the past.'

'How old are you?'

She stared at him bleakly. 'I don't know. No one told me that. I really don't know.'

His attempt to trick her clearly failed and he looked down at

the notes in front of him. 'I have some notes provided by your husband. He says you are forty-three years of age.'

'Am I?' she responded in a dull tone.

'You're married…'

'They told me I was married,' she interrupted sharply. 'and the man who came to see me told me that he was my husband but I didn't recognise him. He was a complete stranger to me.'

Mahmoud looked at her face at length and then closed the cover on the notes in front of him placing them at a corner of his desk. 'Let me have a look at your wound,' he demanded.

He stood up and went around the back of the wheelchair unwinding the bandages carefully to examine her. He stared at the wound intensely, pursing his lips as he did so. 'Hm,' he muttered eventually. 'It would appear that the bullet cut a ridge through your skull breaching it to expose a tiny part of your brain. Other than that, no serious damage seems to have been done. The bone will grow over in due course or the hospital will apply a filler. The reason your memory has failed is because of the shock.'

'The question is will it ever come back?' asked Diana in desperation, hopeful to receive an encouraging answer.

'I should imagine it will in time but you will have to be very patient. It may return suddenly or sporadically,' he told her as he rewound the bandages around her head. 'How long you will ask. Well it's like the proverbial piece of string. It could take weeks, months or even longer.'

'That's not very promising, is it, doctor,' she returned slowly. 'What can you do to help me?

He returned to his chair behind the desk to face her again. 'My work deals with the extracts of exotic flowers and plants,' he informed her seriously. 'Different essences assist in the cure or prevention of certain diseases. I'm not quite certain what to do with regard to loss of memory but I can try some experiments which might help you. The brain is a minefield of activity of which we know so much and yet so little. We understand about axions and dendrites, the thalamus, the cortex and all the other parts of the brain but we're really uncertain about many other things concerning its operation. However, if you're interested in placing yourself under my care, I shall do all I can to deal with your problem in the best way I can. Are you willing to allow me to do that?'

'I have no choice, Dr. Mahmoud,' she told him sadly. 'Do

with me as you will. I just hope that you pull me out of this limbo as quickly as possible.'

'Good!' he declared stroking his goatee beard with his hand. 'I'm going to start by supplying you with the essence of Beotag in the form of tablets. It's a unique plant which grows in North Borneo for which I have great hopes. In addition, I am going to blend it with another exotic plant which will take the form of an experiment. I have never combined the two of them before. Are you willing to take the risks involved?'

'What risks are there?'

'I doubt whether there'll be anything but a few side-effects.'

'I've nothing to lose,' she retorted definitely. 'Use me for your experiment.

He nodded sagely. 'Whether it will help you in your condition is unknown but we can only try.'

'Beotag,' she repeated. 'I've never heard of it before.'

'Nor has ninty-nine per cent of the world's population. It's a very rare plant with unusual qualities that produces fantastic results. I managed to cure Mrs. Naylor of pancreatic cancer when every other doctor told her she had three months to live. She would have passed away over a year ago had it not been for my experiment with that plant.'

'I know. She told me all about it. I just hope you can cure me in the same way.'

'I have great hopes for the additional exotic plant but we shall have to wait for some results in due course. He stood up swiftly ending the conversation nodding to Ahmed to be ready to wheel her outside. 'I will call for you in two days' time for your first application.'

She nodded with hope in her heart and looked to Ahmed to return her to her room. She discussed the treatment briefly with the young handsome Arab as they went along the corridor and in due course he helped her into bed.

'He'll solve the problem, I'm sure,' said Ahmed confidently. 'Dr. Mahmoud's a brilliant scientist with avant-garde ideas. If anyone can help you, he will.'

Hope was all she had as Ahmed bade her farewell. No doubt he would report the incident directly back to the man who alleged to be her husband. Not that he would care for he never visited her at the hospital. She mused that at least there would be no surgical treatment but then realised that, as it was all experimental, the

results might take some considerable time before she was cured. In any case, it was better than just laying in a hospital bed with no memory and no hope at all.

That night, her single dream returned to her. She was in a Bedouin tent with Ahmed. Why she should concentrate on him as her lover was beyond her understanding but it happened again. This time she was partly dressed, laying in his arms and kissing him gently on the lips. His hand moved to the back of her neck and rubbed it gently causing an erotic feeling to well up inside her. She tore off his shirt and then removed her brassiere so that his face could burrow into her breasts. He touched her nipples lightly and her head moved back slightly as emotion began to overwhelm her. She had sexual pleasure in her sights with the young handsome dark-skinned Arab and her hands moved between his legs to excite him. But then, as had happened in her earlier dreams, everything ended abruptly and she found herself wide awake staring at the blank ceiling. Why was this happening when her mind and body told her to succumb to the joy of erotic pleasure? It was so unfair! Every time she came to the point where the intimate sexual relationship came to the fore, it all ended in nothing.

* * * * *

Two days later, Betty Naylor burst into the room almost unable to contain her excitement She dropped her suitcase and walked over to her friend.

'Well, my dear. It's time to go. I'm leaving. All the arrangements have been made for me to live with my daughter in Essex. I'm in full recession with the cancer and I can't wait to leave this hole... if you'll pardon the expression.'

'I'm very pleased for you,' Diana told her with envy in her soul.

'Not as pleased as I am,' came the smart reply. 'I've got a second chance in life.'

'What do you mean?' asked her friend with a puzzled expression on her face.

'I've got another chance to live my life again and I'm going to find a man to share it with. That's what I'm going to do.'

'But what about Mr. Naylor?' forwarded Diana, concerned about the attitude of her companion.

'Mr. Naylor... huh! He ran out on me the moment he thought

I was going to die. I had no life insurance and he was a coward... a bloody coward... if you'll pardon my French. He told me he wasn't going to look after a dying invalid and buggered off. Now I'm going to look for another man... a real man. Someone who'll give me all the love and tenderness I deserve. It's going to be lust and love in that order.'

'Well I wish you luck,' returned Diana with a smile on her face. 'I sincerely hope you find what you want.'

'Sorry to have to leave you in the lurch like this, dear, but needs must when the Devil drives. I'm going to fly back to England tonight and never come back to this lousy place again.'

'Essex, you say.

'Yes... right in the heart of Basildon. There's a lot of good-looking men there. I don't have much money but I'll manage living with my daughter. Who knows, the man I find might have his own house. You never know.' She paused to finalise their brief meeting 'Well I'm off now. I hope your memory returns soon. Look after yourself, dear. It's been nice knowing you.' She leaned over the bed and kissed Diana on the cheek. 'I'll miss you, you know. Not for your conversation but for your companionship. Take care!'

With that final comment, she picked up her suitcase and left the room to disappear out of Diana's life forever. It was a bitter blow to be left alone. Now she had only Ahmed to assist her although he was pretty useless except when he entered her dreams.

* * * * *

The next day, the nurse entered the room with a wheelchair followed by the hospital doctor who had been treating her.

'We're going to complete your treatment today,' he told her candidly.

'What sort of treatment?' asked Diana fearfully.

'We're going to fill the ridge in your skull with bone-paste,' he told her bluntly. 'You can' go round with a hole in your head for months waiting for the bone to heal across it. We'll be very careful not to touch your brain. The end result is that the bone-paste will harden, protecting you from any infection when the bandages are removed.'

It seemed a simple procedure but Diana felt that she had to ask the question. 'Is it absolutely necessary?'

'I think it is,' returned the doctor. 'You'll be able to have the bandages removed with absolute safety.'

'Why wasn't this done earlier?'

'We're in Agadir, Mrs. Templeton, not London. We don't have all the necessary equipment or supplies. They have to be ordered and flown in. Now… let's get you to the operating theatre.'

The nurse assisted Diana into the wheelchair and swept her out of the room into the corridor on her way to the operating theatre. The operation was quite swift and practically painless, taking less than twenty minutes. Diana soon found herself back in her room again where a visitor was standing at the foot of the bed.

'Who are you?' asked Diana somewhat bewildered after the minor operation.

'I'm Laura, your sister. I've come all the way form South Burbank, Los Angeles, to see you.'

'My sister?' Confusion reigned in Diana's mind.

'I'm your younger sister, Laura. Charles rang me to tell me what happened and I've come to see you.'

'Charles?'

'Your husband. Robbie and Karen will make their way here soon. You'll be delighted to see them.'

'I don't know a Robbie and Karen,' bleated Diana tearfully, bereft at the idea of names being put forward to her.

'They're your son and daughter,' came the response. 'My… you do have it bad!'

Diana sat on the bed with tears running down her face as Laura went to her, hugging her tightly.

'Come on, Diana. Don't fret so. Your memory will return to you soon. You can count on it.'

'I've just had bone-paste to fill the hole in my skull.,' cried the patient tearfully. 'I can't remember a thing!'

'Give it time,' commented Laura hardly knowing what to say as she held her sister closer.

Suddenly a vision appeared in Diana's mind of two children playing on a beach making sand-castles. It flashed through her brain just for a second but it was there.'

'Did we once play on a beach?' she enquired moving away from her sister. 'When we were about eight or nine years old.'

'I recall that,' replied Laura casually. 'It was on Pengelly Beach in Cornwall. We went there with Mum and Dad for a week.'

'Mum and Dad!' repeated Diana dolefully. 'Why aren't they here to see me?'

Laura went to the end of the bed pausing before she replied with sadness welling up inside her. 'They were both killed in a car crash in the South of France over ten years ago.'

Diana's face looked extremely sad as she absorbed the facts of her parents' demise. 'I can't remember anything,' she blurted out with frustration. 'Not even that!'

'Time's a great healer, Diana,' related her sister. 'Let me remind you of something about our lives together. It may help. But first I'll tell you about my life in America. I married Jim MacIlroy from California. And we have two children… Rusty and Chuck. They're sixteen and fifteen years old.'

She prattled on for some time as Diana climbed into her bed and stared at the blank white wall opposite. The words uttered by her sister sailed over her head for she was unable to connect anything that was said and a wave of despair enveloped her. Her sister had come all the way from the United States and she couldn't even recognise her. How bad was that? What a dilemma to be in! Worse still, her parents had died in a car crash over ten years ago and she could remember nothing about it. She was simply a shell of a woman without a mind… a vegetable living in an abyss of discontent.

'I have an idea,' suggested Laura eventually. 'Why don't you come and stay with us in Los Angeles for a while… until you get better? I've discussed it with Charles and he agreed. He said that the climate will do you good.'

'Go to America with you?' She tried to focus her mind on making such a hard decision but found herself drifting away.

It was then that the nurse intervened turning to Laura.

'I think your sister's too tired to think straight. She's had a very stressful morning in the operating theatre. She's still suffering badly from the shock of the attack.

Laura stared at her sister and nodded. 'I've booked into a hotel in Agadir,' she told Diana, taking her hand and squeezing it gently. 'I'll come and see you again tomorrow.'

She left feeling miserable about her sister's plight, devastated that she was unable to do anything to help her.

After she had gone, Diana left the bed and stared out of the window at the courtyard watching her sister leave. The sun was shining brightly and it was clearly hot outside but the room in the

hospital was cool with a fan spinning in the ceiling dispensing cool air. She felt as though she was in a different world; one that was light years away from reality.

CHAPTER FOUR

Diana went to Dr. Mahmoud's office twice within the next two days. He gave her some tablets to swallow each time, telling her that it would a few days before the elements in them were properly absorbed into her body.

'The green tablet is from the Beotag plant. The red one is from another exotic plant which is so rare it has no name at the moment. Beotag has a strange effect, it is possible that all your hair might fall out but it will grow again much stronger. The effect of the other tablet is unknown and it would be appreciated if you would tell me of any side-effects as soon as they occur.'

'What kind of side-effects are we talking about,' asked Diana with interest.

'Anything from dizziness, vomiting, stomach pains, toothache… you name it.'

'I'll definitely do that,' she told him, swallowing both tablets with the help of a glass of water. She sat back afterwards inhaling deeply. There… the deed was done! She had started on the experiment but she had no idea where it would take her. She was definitely under Dr. Mahmoud's care now. It mattered to her if her hair should fall out but she could always use a wig to hide the baldness. The important thing was to recover her memory.

Mahmoud stared at her with a slight smile on his face. 'You are deeply concerned about your memory, aren't you?'

'Wouldn't you be?' she retorted rudely. 'You have no idea what it's like for your mind to be completely blank.'

'Do you know you're more concerned about your condition, which is hardly dangerous to your health, than most cancer patients when they learn they have the disease?'

'I can't help that,' she countered curtly. 'I think that before the attack I was an independent person relying on my mind. And then there were the dreams.'

His eyebrows shot up at the comment. 'Dreams?' he repeated. 'What sort of dreams?'

Diana wondered for a moment how she had thought about her nightly adventures. Subsequently, she became quite reticent at having to reveal anything about her inner thoughts. Mahmoud recognised this instantly and urged her to come clean.

'Come on!' he encouraged. 'Don't be shy. You must regard me as a priest who will not divulge anything you tell me to another soul.'

Her resolve weakened and she found herself telling him the truth. 'I've only dreamt this a few times since the attack,' she revealed to the scientist. 'I dream of a sexual incident with Ahmed… the man employed by my husband to report my progress back to him. But each time we're on the edge of making passionate love, the dream ends.'

Mahmoud pursed his lips and stroked his goatee beard. 'Hm,' he muttered. 'In my opinion, you're starved of sex and the frustration builds up inside you. It comes out in your dreams. There's nothing wrong with that. In fact it's quite common among many women.'

'But it's over before anything happens,' she complained bitterly. 'Just as we're about to make love the dream ends.'

'It's your conscience telling you that it's wrong,' he explained.

'You want to experience having sex but you realise you are married and you know it's wrong to do so with another person. That's why your dream ends so suddenly.'

'That's just it,' she remonstrated. 'I don't know that I'm married. I've no recollection of it. My alleged husband is a stranger to me. So why should I have a conscience when dreaming?'

Mahmoud found himself unable to answer the question and Diana was soon ushered from his office with an appointment for the next morning.

An hour before she went to see him on the following day, Ahmed came into her room at the hospital. On this occasion, she became very dispassionate deciding to tell him about her dreams.

'I've been dreaming that I'm in a Bedouin tent on the edge of the Sahara Desert making love to you,' she blurted out breezily.

He looked surprised for a moment. 'I'm flattered,' he managed to say. 'No one has ever revealed their intimate feelings about me before. Go on… tell me more.'

'There isn't any more to tell. The dreams end suddenly. I don't know whether the love is reciprocated or not.'

'Are you saying that you think you're in love with me?' he asked quietly with a smile touching his lips at the thought of it.

'No I'm not!' she returned adamantly. 'I'm just telling you my dream. After all, with my memory gone, you're practically the only person I can relate to. It's not surprising that my mind turns to love when I think of you but don't make anything of it.'

'I really don't know how to respond to that,' he countered amiably, pausing to think how he could continue the conversation. 'I don't think you really mean what you say. It's your state of mind… your condition… that makes you think that way. One never knows what will show up in a person's imagination in their sleep. Of course, none of it is real.' He paused again for a few moments waiting for her to respond but she failed to do so. 'After all,' he went on, 'as you say, I'm probably the only person you know here in which case such ideas are bound to happen.'

'You were definitely the only person in my dreams,' she persisted. 'Unfortunately they end so abruptly before…' she tailed off stopping short of what she was about to tell him.

He appeared a little embarrassed at the trend of the conversation and stepped away from the bed. 'You seem a little better today,' he commented swiftly changing the subject. 'You'll be seeing Dr. Mahmoud shortly I understand.'

'I'm going to see the Wizard of Agadir. That's what I'm calling him. I doubt that he'll find the right formula for curing me though.'

'He has a remarkable reputation for being successful in his field,' Ahmed continued solemnly.

'For diseases such as cancer, hepatitis and other things maybe but not for someone with a loss of memory.'

'We shall see,' retorted the young Arab. 'In the meantime, I'll report back to your husband telling him that you're much better in spirit.'

'Is that what you think I am?' she countered smartly. 'Better in spirit. You don't know how much I would give to get out of here.'

'There's a Chinese proverb which goes "cursed is the man who achieves his ambition!" Be very careful what you wish for, Diana.'

Deciding that his duty had been done, he turned and went to the door. 'I'll visit you again in two days' time. We'll talk again then.'

Without further ado, he departed leaving her to face the blank walls of the room. Indeed, she was feeling so much better believing it was the effect of the tablets given to her by Dr. Mahmoud. Ostensibly, the void hung over her like a dark cloud and she still could not remember anything of the past. She lay back in the bed wondering what her life had been like before the attack. What had been her relationship with her husband? Did she love him or merely tolerate him? Was he henpecked? Did they make love together either regularly or sporadically… or not at all? What was the attitude of her children towards her? Was she possessive, domineering or very loving? Did they live at home or had they flown the nest? Did she interfere in their lives? Was she employed at work? If so, what kind of work was it? Did it have anything to do with brainpower, clerical or manual work? What had been her spare time interests? Did she go to aerobics, play bridge, enjoy gardening, write poems, go jogging or do something else? Did she have any close friends? And what about her sister who lived in Los Angeles. How close was their relationship? Her mind had become active once more and questions began to bombard her brain. She tried hard to commit her memory, pushing firmly inside her cranium. However, her efforts were futile. Nothing came… nothing happened. She now understood that she was passing through a long dark tunnel knowing that there was likely to be light at the end of it, although she was unable to see it. It gave her hope of recovery at some time in the future but she could not predict when it might happen. In her heart, she pleaded with her mind to take wings and speed up the process. It was a very mean hope to consider.

The meeting with Dr. Mahmoud that day was quite brief. He passed two tablets across the desk which she swallowed asking whether she had experienced any side-effects after their previous meeting. It was too soon really for him to pose such a question but she realised that he intended to be kept informed at all times and be completely satisfied with her condition.

'I feel much better today,' she told him. 'Do you think it has anything to do with the tablets?'

'I don't know,' he admitted frankly. 'I don't think it has anything to do with the Beotag essence. It takes a little time for it to manifest itself in the body. I do not know about the other essence which I've named ferradil-x in my classifications. It's an unknown factor.'

'Well I don't mind being a guinea pig if it helps me,' she remarked, staring at the scientist's face, but he showed no sign of anger or surprise. 'I just hope it kicks in fast.'

'We shall see,' he told her hopefully. 'You're the only person to whom I've given ferradil-x so you're unique in that way… if it's any help to you. But you must report any side-effects to me immediately they occur. It's extremely important that you do. Is that understood?'

She nodded her assent. 'I promise to tell you immediately. You have no worries about that.'

'I'll give you this phial of tablets,' he went on, passing two small canisters of pills to her. 'Take one of each in the morning and the same at night. I'll see you in seven days' time.'

She took the pills, staring at the labels. Dr. Mahmoud had entered his telephone number on each canister leaving no doubt of the importance of contacting him if anything untoward occurred.

'What could happen?' she asked herself. 'Headache, depression, vomiting, malaise, palpitations… perhaps she would grow another head or more fingers.' Now she was becoming whimsical and stupid although she was prepared to lose all her hair if it brought back her memory. At least she was alert, feeling as though she was starting a new life.

When she returned to her room, she found her sister waiting for her.

'Laura,' she began brightly. 'I'm glad you're here. There's something I've been meaning to ask you. What was our relationship like in the past? I can't for the life of me remember. Were we close or distant?'

Her sister pulled a face at having to answer the question truthfully. 'To tell you the truth,, it wasn't good.' There was silence in the room until she continued. 'We haven't spoken to each other for nine years.'

Diana stared at her dolefully. 'We haven't? For nine years? Why not? What went wrong?'

Laura paused to reflect the sad tale. 'Our parents died in a car crash in the South of France. They left a Will which involved a house valued at two hundred thousand pounds and cash and securities worth a hundred thousand. You were married to a rising Civil Servant and had accumulated a house, two cars, and a fair amount of money. I married Mac in the United States. He was only a car mechanic and we were having serious financial

problems. Mum and Dad knew the score so they wrote a Will giving me the house and you the money.

'Which meant that you had twice as much as I did,' bleated Diana weakly.

'Yes... that was the problem. But you didn't need any money at all. Well the proceeds of the sale of the house was the lifeline that Mac and I needed. We went on from there. Bought ourselves a house, paid all the debts and had money in the bank. It changed our lives completely whereas it mattered little to you whether you received fifty thousand or a hundred thousand.'

There was a long pause as Diana asked the obvious questions. 'Did I contest the Will?' The words sounded hollow and she prayed that she hadn't done so.

'Yes you did,' came the stark reply, causing Diana to feel an empty pain in her stomach. 'You delayed the whole thing for over nine months causing Mac and I great anguish. In the end, the Court refused to overturn Mum and Dad's Will but we never spoke to each other again after that... not until now.'

'After all that, why did you come to Agadir to see me? I'd have thought you would have hated me for the rest of your life.'

'Charles telephoned me and said that you had part of your skull blown away in the attack and had lost your memory. He was very concerned that you might die. Blood's thicker than water and you are my sister. I thought if you were dying, I'd stay with you until the end.'

Diana sat up in bed to make contact with her sister clutching the hand of the other woman. 'You really are a true sister and I'm sorry if I offended you. Will you forgive me?'

'It's all in the past now, Diana. I would have been satisfied with a hundred grand but you were so toffee-nosed about it, fighting me every inch of the way. I had no option but to challenge you in Court.'

'Forgive me, Laura. I really am sorry,' she pleaded. 'I don't know what could have got into me. I must have been a real bitch.'

'Don't knock yourself out about it.' The look on Laura's face and the fact that they were holding hands meant that no further words were needed. The two sisters, after a span of nine years, were united… they were together again!

'Why don't you stay with us in Los Angeles?' invited Laura, warmed by the reunion with her loving sister. 'You'd like it there.'

'I would dearly love to, Laura, but I'm under Dr. Mahmoud

for treatment. I call him the Wizard of Agadir. But when I recover fully, if I ever do, I'll take you up on your offer. Thanks for the invitation.'

They continued to look at each other in a new light and Diana felt that her life was picking up at last.

* * * * *

That night she fell asleep and began to dream. However this time it was anything but pleasant. Contrary to those that she normally imagined, it turned out to be an awful nightmare. For the first time in her life she envisaged darkened clouds overhead and found herself up to her chest in deep water. A large vessel, similar to a Spanish galleon, sailed towards her and the height of the waves increased as it came close so that the water moved up to her neck. She feared that she was going to drown until the ship slowly drifted away into the distance behind her but the water failed to recede threatening to reach higher than her neck. The situation worsened in her sleep and she kept twisting and turning vigorously, trying to escape from the dilemma until an enormous figure suddenly appeared on the skyline. It was the Devil himself and he had arrived to haunt her. He was dressed in black and carried a trident in one hand with which he teased her by pointing it at her head and she could see forked lightning flashing with jagged spears from the dark sky. After that came the sound of terrifyingly loud thunder which almost frightened her to death. She awoke abruptly at that point and sat up screaming at the top of her voice causing the nurse to rush into the room to find out what was wrong with her patient. It soon became apparent that it had been a particularly cold night and the nurse had placed a blanket over the sheet on her bed. This had ridden up to her neck which was the reason she had felt so discomforted in her sleep.

'It was terrible!' she told the nurse with a doleful expression on her face. 'Absolutely terrible! I don't want to think about it let alone talk about it!' She shuddered as a shiver ran down her spine.

The nurse smiled and straightened the blanket. 'It's best that you try to go to sleep again. The doctor will want to speak with you later.'

'That sounds serious,' commented Diana with an element of concern sounding in her voice. 'What does he want to speak to me about?'

The nurse shook her head. 'He'll tell you later. Go to sleep!'

Diana settled down again but she was wide awake. What on earth did the doctor want? Dr. Mahmoud would have discussed with him all the relevant facts regarding any complications. Well there was nothing she could do about it . She would have to wait and see.

Sleep refused to come again, not that she wanted it to. A haunting nightmare was enough for one night. She lay in bed staring at the ceiling thinking of nothing for a full two hours before the doctor arrived. He checked her pulse and removed the bandages from her head, examining the wound.

'Good!' he uttered thoughtfully. 'The bone-paste has hardened and the wound looks as though it's pretty well healed now. I think it's time for you to leave us, Mrs. Templeton. There's nothing more that we can do for you.'

'Leave you!' she stared at him with dismay. It was the last thing she thought he would say. 'Has the money for my treatment run out... the money they pay for me to stay here?'

'It's not that,' he explained sharply. 'It has nothing to do with that. The problem is that we're a very small hospital. We need your bed to treat a patient who was admitted last night. So if you would care to make other arrangements, we shall part company shortly.'

'But where would I go?' she bleated desperately. The horror of her situation never seemed to bottom out. There were always worse problems to resolve. 'If you want more money, I'm sure it can be arranged.'

'It's not a matter of money,' he went on. 'If the hospital board learned that I was turning away Moroccan patients for treatment in favour of tourists I would be in serious trouble. You can understand where I'm coming from, can't you?'

Diana pulled a face and nodded her head slowly. She had the invitation from her sister to go to Los Angeles but that would take her away from her wizard scientist. 'What does Dr. Mahmoud say?'

'He agrees that you can be treated as an out-patient. It's only a matter of renewing your supply of pills and undergoing a brief interview every two weeks. You are quite free to leave the hospital immediately.'

'So even though I can't remember anything, you still want me to go.'

'That's exactly the position, Mrs. Templeton.' replied the doctor. 'We do need this bed urgently. If you contact your husband…'

'My husband!' she reacted sharply. 'Not only do I not know him but I can't remember what he looks like. He hasn't been here to see me except for that very first day. What use is it for me to contact him?'

The doctor shrugged his shoulders aimlessly without wishing to become involved. At that moment, Ahmed appeared in the doorway.

'Hi!' he greeted with a slight smile touching his lips. 'How are we today?'

'We are terrible!' retorted Diana sharply. 'We've had an awful nightmare… the first I've ever had in my life. It was awful!'

'I take it that you didn't dream about me then,' he said with an element of amusement.

'What are you doing here today? I thought that you weren't coming for two days.'

'You're right… that's so, but I was informed that they needed your bed so I came along with an offer.' He moved past the doctor to the edge of the bed and took her hand which he kissed gently.

She stared at him with a smile touching her lips. 'You're a real charmer. Did you know that?'

'We are what we are in life, Diana,' he told her philosophically using her first name freely.

'Very well, Ahmed. 'What do you have to offer?'

'I want you to come and live at my house. It'll only be a temporary arrangement until you can sort out where you intend to go.'

'From my knowledge of the local houses in Agadir,' she uttered critically, 'it'll be exceedingly small with few rooms and your family who live with you.'

'You're very perceptive,' he remarked hoping that she would accept his offer. He paused to reflect for a moment. 'You're right of course. It's a small dwelling and we have only two bedrooms for myself, my mother and my three brothers and sisters. We always manage somehow. I mean this is a state of emergency for you. They want this bed in the next hour.' An hour! Panic began to race through her mind. There was hardly any time to make a decision. 'I don't think you have a choice,' he went on. 'I'll leave you to get dressed.'

The doctor took his cue from the lawyer and they both left the room. Diana opened the cupboard at the side of her bed and removed her clothes which had been folded neatly and placed there. She dressed fairly quickly, examining her hair in a hand mirror, fluffing it slightly, before going to the door. She had no additional luggage which had been taken to England by her alleged husband with the exception of her handbag and it few contents. She took a final glance around the room. It had been her prison but now she regretted that she had to leave.

Outside, Ahmed waited for her in his car. He climbed out as she came through the hospital gates and opened the door for her on the passenger's side to allow her to get in. Then he drove half a mile away to his house on the outskirts of the town.

If ever Diana was to receive a culture shock this was it. The house was very small and she entered the tiny passageway to the stench of curry and other cooking smells. The rooms were extremely dingy with little furniture and there was Ahmed's family of himself, his mother, and three children. The walls of the main room had once been white but now they were discoloured with black marks in various places where young hands had been pressed against them. The furniture was ancient, well-worn and torn or damaged in a number of places… the settee exposing a flush of ugly foam. A dirty old carpet with one end turning upwards stretched across the floor. Nothing was clean. Except for the mother, the children were crowded together in the tiny room watching the screen of a large television set.

'Mother's in the kitchen,' said Ahmed noticing the unhappy expression on Diana's face.

She shuddered to think about the state of the kitchen as her nose twitched with the stench. She could visualise its filth with cockroaches scurrying about in every corner. Night time was going to be horrendous. There were only two bedrooms to accommodate her and five members of his family. She had no idea where she was supposed to sleep.

The attention of the children moved away from the television screen as their eyes stared directly at the stranger. They were clearly unhappy that a foreigner was going to stay with them… in their already overcrowded house.

Ahmed provided an old chair for her to sit on and she sat down to face him. He waved his hand to dismiss the children who left the room to play in the street.

'Tell me about your work,' ventured Diana trying to make the most of the situation.

'I'm a lawyer… a solicitor in Agadir. I'm the senior partner in a firm which is the reason why I have so much time to spare.'

'You don't seem to have much work. Don't you have any clients?'

'Sharia law is very specific,' he explained. 'It's not as laborious as British law. If a thief is caught, his hand is chopped off as punishment. In England, the lawyers and barristers would take months to bring the case to Court. Here it's over in a very short time without repercussions. Our law is different but precise. It's far easier that way.'

'Where do you usually sleep?' Her question was precocious but she felt she had to ask it.

'I sleep on this settee,' he told her, pointing to the old piece of furniture with foam sticking out. 'This allows my mother privacy in one bedroom and for the children to sleep in the other bedroom from head to toe.'

She nodded as the children started to argue loudly outside. They all spoke in Arabic; only Ahmed was capable of speaking English so she had no idea what they were saying. For a moment, she became paranoid and imagined that they were talking about her. However, Ahmed explained the true nature of their debate which related solely to the game they were playing. She realised that the change in accommodation was going to be a harrying experience and she regretted not to have agreed with Laura to return to America with her. The urgent requirement of the hospital bed at such short notice had thrown her life into disarray.

'Would you like something to drink? Some coffee perhaps,' he suggested in an attempt to show her some hospitality.

The children ran into the room, turning on the television set which blared out music in high volume. All of them stared at her as though she had come from another planet. It was very doubtful whether they had been in the presence of an English woman before... certainly not with one staying with them at their house.

'Yes... I'd like a drink, thank you,' replied Diana feeling most uncomfortable.

He left the room and returned shortly with two cups of coffee on a tray. She sipped it and screwed up her face at the taste.

'Ugh! This is disgusting!' she complained bitterly.

'Living here will mean that you'll need to condition yourself

to our ways,' he told her curtly. 'Our culture and customs are far different to those in your country.'

Diana remained silent thereafter wondering why she had ever chosen Morocco as a holiday venue. Very little changed that day with the exception of meeting Ahmed's mother who showed her little courtesy. Clearly, the woman resented the intrusion of a foreigner in her home and wanted to have nothing to do with her.

Later that evening, at quite an early hour, everyone went to bed. The children continued to show a great deal of resentment towards her and they muttered their discontent when Ahmed told them that he was going to sleep on the floor in their bedroom. Animosity towards their guest reigned supreme.

'I'm going to give you the privilege of sleeping on the settee here,' he informed her whimsically. 'It's my bed usually but you can have it for the time being. I hope you sleep well and wish you good night.'

He disappeared leaving her to her own devices holding an ugly brown stained blanket. She didn't have any nightclothes. In any case, she would be certain not to undress for fear that someone might come into the main room either later in the night or early in the morning. She lay on the old settee in discomfort wondering how she was going to escape from her dilemma. The stench of the stale curry permeated through the room so much that she was forced to keep her head under the blanket provided for her. Not that such action helped because the blanket itself smelled disgusting. Not surprisingly, sleep did not come easily that night and she remained awake for what seemed to be an eternity. Then, at about four o'clock in the morning, she dozed off in a light slumber, twisting and turning as the uneven state of the settee forced her to keep changing positions.

Although she was still half asleep, she came to a definite decision about her immediate future. Come hell or high water, she would not stay in this hovel for one minute longer than she had to. That was for certain!

CHAPTER FIVE

At the break of day on the following morning, the sound of the children stirring in the next room awoke her. She didn't need to dress as she had slept in her clothes and she crept out of the house

before anyone could know of her absence. The sun was shining brightly in a beautiful blue sky and it was clear that the day was going to be hot. Diana paused for a few moments as she closed the front door quietly, looking both ways to determine how she could get back to the hospital. There was only one thought in her mind... to find Laura and get her to book a room in a hotel. Ahmed would be furious when he discovered that she had flown the coop and, no doubt, he would be searching for her very shortly. However she had no alternative but to leave and find a more suitable place to stay. There was also the problem of her clothes. She couldn't continue to wear the same apparel day in day out in this temperature. She feared that she had already begun to perspire which meant that she need to take a shower to give off a much more pleasant aroma.

She decided on a particular direction and stepped off at a relatively fast pace. The last thing she wanted was for Ahmed to chase after her and take her back to his hovel. She never wanted to return to that place again. The further she walked, the more she began to perspire which made her feel very uncomfortable. The hospital wasn't very far away yet, in her haste to get there, it seemed to be exceedingly distant. At last she came to a signpost which indicated that it was close and she picked up her pace until she reached her destination. Panting with the effort, she held on to the iron gate at the entrance pausing for a break. Laying for a long time in hospital had not improved her fitness. She glanced at her wristwatch which indicated that it was seven-thirty and, at that moment, the sound of a muezzin could be heard from a nearby minaret crying out for people to come to prayers which resounded throughout the area. It was obviously a recorded prayer similar to the bells rung in English churches but it made no difference to her as the sound reverberated over the southern part of the town. This was a country where most people believed in daily prayer and they were driven by it.

She had no idea what time Laura would come to the hospital. There was no alternative but to wait for her to arrive. She had no choice in the matter. As the muezzin's voice faded away into infinity, a large house flashed into her mind.

It was a Georgian built property with a grand façade sporting a tall fountain and a wishing-well in the front garden. She noted its features well for a few seconds as it registered in her mind. Where was that place? Was it her home in England? Her hopes rose as she realised that she had seen something from the past. Her memory was starting to recover albeit very slowly. She tried to recall the same image again but nothing happened. Half an hour later, someone emerged from the hospital to unlock the iron gate and then open it. As she stared at the man, a further memory came into her head. She could hear the voice of the cabbie who had picked up her and her husband from the airport when they had first arrived in Agadir.

'On February the twenty-ninth 1960,' came the voice, 'we suffered a great earthquake killing many people. Fifteen thousand people died in fifteen seconds. There were so many bodies for us to handle so we buried them at the end of town covering an enormous grave with cement. Money poured in to help us from all over the world and we used it to make Agadir a beautiful place. Over there you can visit the Purple Mountains; here you can see the beautiful blue sea.'

She stood quite still for a moment polarised by the discovery that something was happening in her mind... it had to be all to the good. Cheered by the sudden recall, her head went up and she began to look at her life in a different way. If it continued, she would soon recover. It was quite plain that her attacker had not only taken her memory but he had ruined her life.

The hours passed and Laura still did not come. At noon, a bus stopped nearby, the passengers alighted, and they all knelt down facing the East to pray. Then, after a short while, they climbed back on the bus and continued on their journey. It was true... the people here were driven by religious belief.

Diana waited as people entered and left the hospital during the morning, her mind remaining blank, and it was almost two-thirty when Laura appeared. It was a highly emotional moment for Diana who threw her arms around her sister and hugged her tightly.

'Hey, hey, hey!' exclaimed Laura, noticing her sister's distress.

'What's going on? Why are you waiting for me outside the hospital?'

Tears ran down Diana's face as she held tightly on to her sister. She took her hand and they moved away from the hospital gates walking in silence for a short while as they proceeded down the road.

'They threw me out!' sobbed Diana eventually as the tears continued to roll down her cheeks. 'They needed the bed so I had to go.'

'When was this?' asked Laura with concern in her voice.

'Yesterday.' Diana's chest heaved up and down uncontrollably. 'They needed the bed and Ahmed, the man employed by my alleged husband to report back to him of my progress, took me to his home.'

'That was nice of him.'

'Oh… it was a dreadful place. The stench was awful. Five of them in the family. Two tiny bedrooms and everyone resented me… especially his mother. I left there early this morning. I had to sleep on an old settee in these clothes. I haven't anything else to wear.'

'I don't suppose you've eaten anything either,' uttered her sister miserably. Diana shook her head slowly. 'Come on… let's get you to a restaurant. Then you can come and stay with me at my hotel.'

'I don't want to put you out,' bleated Diana not wishing to impose on her sister. 'Maybe it would be a good idea to book in to the Hotel Sahara where I'm supposed to have stayed with my alleged husband. Maybe I can even get the same room. It might help restore my memory.'

'I've booked in to the Hotel Sahara myself,' returned her sister. 'The first thing is to buy you some new clothes. That'll make you feel better. Then you can have a shower in my room. Shopping for clothes in Agadir. I like the sound of it.'

Diana nodded again. She could hardly believe that the two of them had not spoken for nine years because of an idiotic dispute over their parents' Will. But Laura had turned up trumps as a true sister in her desperate hour of need. Diana wouldn't have known what she would have done without her.

After enjoying a light lunch at a nearby restaurant, they went on their shopping spree buying two dresses and some lingerie. When they returned to the Hotel Sahara, Diana took a shower and sat on the bed thoughtfully. All the bedrooms in the hotel were the same and, to her dismay, nothing triggered in her mind. She moved out to the balcony looking down at the point where she had been attacked but still there was no memory.

'They told me at the hospital that I was attacked down there outside this balcony,' she said casually in a wistful manner. 'What a thing to happen! The attacker hanged himself in prison. He actually ended his life after he was caught. And what for? They told me that I had no money on me.'

'The laws in these countries are very strict with regard to crime,' stated Laura bluntly. 'They chop off one of your hands if you're caught stealing.'

'But he didn't steal anything from me because I didn't have any money. He gave up his life for nothing.'

'You were his victim, Diana. He deserved to be punished for what he did. An eye for an eye. That's what it's all about.'

‘Have you spoken to my alleged husband since you’ve been here?’

Laura shook her head. ‘No… there was only one single phone call when he contacted me about you. Why do you ask?’

‘Well,’ continued Diana sadly, ‘for a man who’s supposed to be a loving husband, he’s not been in touch or visited me. I haven’t seen him at all. Why hasn’t he been here to see me?’

Her sister pursed her lips and stared at her dismally. ‘Charles was always a workaholic. We all recognised that. The main thing in his life is his work. I’m afraid you’ve always had to take second place.’

Diana remained silent for a few moments. ‘There we have it!’ she muttered uneasily. ‘I’m a workaholic widow with an alleged husband who couldn’t care less whether I lived or died.’

‘All I can say is that if I was in your position, Mac wouldn’t have left my side for a moment. But then we choose men on a whim of love and have to take the consequences.’

Diana moved away from the balcony and brushed out the creases in her dress even though it was a pointless task. After combing her hair, Laura suggested that they get some fresh air and look around the other shops in the town. They went to a local bazaar, examining the goods exhibited for sale. There were clothes suitable for the Western woman including kaftans dyed in different colours and Diana managed to find some nightclothes of a daring nature. Afterwards she felt much better as they returned to the hotel together. The night in the hovel was starting to become a distant memory; the love and company of her sister had replaced it.

That evening, with Diana wearing her newly-purchased clothing, the two sisters went on the town. They found themselves in a marquee which advertised the entertainment of a Moroccan evening, and they enjoyed themselves immensely. They danced with the natives, ate crusty bread, gorged on lamb cutlets and cous-cous, and drank plenty of the local wine. As the evening wore on, the tempo of the music became faster and faster. The two sisters threw themselves into the party spirit and Diana forgot all the problems she had endured during her stay in the country, assisted by the volume of wine which she had imbibed. By the end of the evening, they were relatively inebriated and they staggered back to the Hotel Sahara giggling all the way. When they arrived there, they managed to get to their room and lay on the beds still giggling.

‘I’m not going back to that hovel,’ declared Diana drunkenly.

‘No you’re not. You’re staying here with me.’

They giggled for a while longer discussing some of the main features they had enjoyed that evening before they both fell asleep. It was an evening of great enjoyment and for the first time in many weeks Diana felt happy.

They were awakened early the following day by someone knocking loudly on the door. Diana opened her eyes as a pain shot through her head. It was not the agony relating to her injury but a terrible hangover.

'We don't want anything yet!' she shouted closing her eyes tightly to shut out the light.

There was a loud muttering outside the door and then a further long knocking. She looked to Laura who was fast asleep so she lifted herself up and went to the door unsteadily to open it. Ahmed stood there with an angry expression on his face.

'Is it your custom to treat people badly when they try to help you?' he remonstrated irately.

'What?' she managed to say, her mind being completely befuddled.

'I took you into my home and you leave without saying a word. What kind of a person are you?'

'I'm sorry she managed to say.' trying to focus her mind on his problem. 'You'd better come in.'

He entered the room and sat down angrily on a chair sulking like a schoolboy, staring at Laura who was still asleep. 'I had to explain to my mother why you had left. It made me lose face. But, as you're a foreigner, I think she understood.'

'I'm really sorry,' apologised Diana meaningfully. 'It was all so strange to me. The smallness of the room… the smell of the curry… the language I didn't understand. I couldn't handle it. I had to get out.'

He calmed significantly at her explanation. 'Maybe the change in culture was too much of a shock for you,' he reasoned, screwing up his face. 'But you can see how it looked from my point of view. You left without warning.'

'It was wrong of me,' admitted Diana as Laura began to come to life. 'I should have spoken to your first.'

'Well you're staying here now,' he went on as his anger began to diminish. 'Do you know how hard it was to track you down? I've been all over Agadir looking for you.'

Laura shook her head to bring herself back into the real world. 'You've found her,' she snapped, 'so what's the problem?'

'I'll tell you what the problem is, lady,' he retaliated becoming irate again. 'She offended me and my family. She agreed to stay with me and we made arrangements for her to do so and then she walked out without saying a word. I offered her hospitality and she threw it back in my face!'

'Oh, for Heaven's sake, man, get off your high horse!' she snapped back at him with annoyance. 'Can't you see she's in pain. She can't remember anything and then she's thrown out of hospital. What do you want from her?'

'In my country…' he began before he was sharply interrupted.

'In your country, a gunman blew a hole in my sister's head. Does that satisfy your insult… or is the victim yet a victim again!'

He drew in his horns at her reasoning and held his hands in front of him. 'Okay, I understand but we all have to live in the same world whatever our situation.'

'You're in contact with my allege husband every few days, aren't you?' ventured Diana with a plan in mind. Ahmed nodded slowly. 'Well I want you to stop doing it.'

'But he's paying me to do so,' bleated the lawyer meekly.

'I'll pay you more… although it'll come from the same source… presuming I have my own money.'

'Why would you want to do that?' asked Laura puzzled at her sister's demand.

'I'm going to teach him a lesson… one that he won't forget.

He may be a workaholic but I'm not going to take second place any more.' She turned to the young lawyer seriously. 'Will you work for me instead of him?'

'If that's what you want,' he replied concerned at the change in orders. 'He will soon contact me when nothing is received.'

'When he does,' continued Diana, with the bit between her teeth, 'tell him to come over and visit me whatever work he has on hand. Tell him that I'm the priority. Is that understood?'

Ahmed shrugged his shoulders aimlessly. 'Okay… I'll tell him.'

'Good for you!' congratulated Laura. 'If I read you correctly, that man's in for a hiding.'

'You bet your life he is!' declared her sister smartly. 'I'm going to make him realise that family always comes first… far more important than work.' She went over to the balcony with satisfaction showing on her face. 'I've got a new life ahead of me and he's going to have one as well or it's all over.' She burst into laughter and her sister joined in although the lawyer failed to be amused, shaking his head slowly in disbelief. The last thing he wanted was to become embroiled in a domestic row between a husband and wife.

* * * * *

Laura stayed with her sister for one further night just to make sure that she was settled after the trauma she had suffered at Ahmed's house. However, Diana's joy at the change from hovel to hotel was short-lived. When she rose from her bed on the following morning, she stood in front of the full-length mirror preening herself as she had done so often in the past but she soon checked and moved nearer to examine herself more closely. It was then that she received the shock of her life. To her dismay, her body was covered in little red spots from head to toe.

'Oh my God!' she cried loudly, waking her sister. 'Look at me! Just look at me!'

Laura rose and went over to stare at the red spots shaking her head slowly. 'You'd better see a doctor right away. I think you've got chicken pox.'

'Nonsense!' retorted Diana. 'People of my age don't get chicken pox!' She paused for a moment. 'How old am I?'

'You're forty-three.'

Diana looked away from the mirror momentarily. 'Forty-three and I've no memory of anything that happened in the past. That's terrible!'

Laura's eyes moved across to her sister's bed and her body stiffened. 'I think that some of your hair's on the pillow.'

Diana turned to her bed, screwed up her face, and nodded. 'Dr. Mahmoud told me it might fall out. It's the Beotag that causes it to happen.'

'The what?' asked her sister perplexedly.

'Don't worry about it. But he did say it might happen.'

Her sister stared at her with a concerned expression on her face. 'Who's this Dr. Mahmoud? Are you sure he knows what he's doing?'

'He's renowned in these parts. I call him the Wizard of Agadir. I had a friend at the hospital who had cancer and he cured her completely after all the English doctors gave up on her.'

'Well I'm really concerned,' stated Laura bluntly. 'He's making quite a mess of you.'

'To be fair, he did ask me to report any side-effects from the treatment. He said there might be some.'

Laura was extremely critical. 'Side-effects! Is that what he calls it? Losing your hair… covered in spots…' she paused for a moment to look at her sister closely. '… and I think you've got bloodshot eyes. What next?'

Diana turned to stare into the mirror miserably, moving her head from side to side, although she was not particularly concerned about her condition. 'It's not very nice but it's only a side-effect. It'll go away soon.'

'I think it's diabolical!' savaged Laura intensely.

Twenty minutes later, Diana made her way to Dr. Mahmoud's office with her sister.

'I hope you know what you're doing!' accused Laura pointing to her sister's face. 'Have you seen the state of my sister? The spots are all over her body, her hair is falling out and she has bloodshot eyes. What are you doing to her?'

Mahmoud appeared unmoved by the onslaught. 'Sit down,' he said calmly to Diana 'Let me have a look at you.' He rubbed his hand lightly over her cheeks and then applied the necessary application to check her blood pressure. After that, he examined her hair, pointed a torch into her mouth to look at the back of her throat, and then examined her eyes. 'Your eyes are bloodshot,' he pronounced eventually, 'and you have rubella... German measles. Your hair has thinned a little but you're not likely to lose more. Your immune system has been affected by the ferradil-x but all is well. After a few days, the spots will disappear. I'll take a blood test but you seem to be all right generally. I think you may have lost six pounds in weight.'

'The weight loss has probably nothing to do with the treatment,' cut in Laura informatively. 'She's had a hell of a time over the past two days after being thrown out of the hospital. It was enough to make anyone lose weight.'

The scientist disregarded the comment looking at Diana's hands. 'There's also a discolouration of your fingernails,' he went on. 'I'd like you to continue with the treatment for a little longer. I

find that once patients get over the first hurdle, however bad it seems to have been, they get the full benefits of the treatment.'

'Are you saying that you expect these things to happen?' asked Laura trying to unravel the logic of the scientist's thinking

'Of course,' he replied assertively. 'If we scientists backed out of every project each time it appeared to go wrong at the start, no advances would be made. I have great faith in the essences I procure for my patients.'

Laura pulled a wry face as she felt uncertain about the scientist's procedure. 'Okay... we'll see what happens from now on.'

'Just keep taking the tablets,' advised Mahmoud strongly. 'I'll supply more before you run out.'

'Don't you have any suggestions for this... rubella?' asked Diana curiously.

'Go back to your hotel and stay in bed for two days. You'll find that you are cured after that,' he said finally, ignoring both women by picking up a random file and looking at the notes.

Laura took her sister's arm and led her from the office. 'I'm impressed with him,' she said encouragingly. 'I'm not sure that he will help you find your memory but he seems to know what he's doing. Listen to his advice for the moment and be patient. Let's get you back to the hotel.'

As they left the building, Laura hailed a taxi and they returned to the Hotel Sahara quickly. Once there, Diana climbed into bed as her sister ordered coffee to be sent up to the room. It was going to be a long two days but there was nothing more to do than rest.

'What does my house look like in England?' she asked reflecting the flash of the building she had experienced when standing outside the hospital gates waiting for her sister.

Laura shrugged her shoulders. 'I don't know. I've been in the States for over nine years. Charles sold the apartment you used to live in and he bought a house in the country but I've never seen it.'

'So you don't know if there's a tall fountain and a wishing-well in the front garden.'

'Not a clue,' came the response. 'I've never been there.'

Diana lay back in the bed. It was going to be a long two days in bed before the red spots started to disappear but there was no option but to wait patiently until it happened.

* * * * *

Laura decided to go out for some entertainment that night leaving Diana on her own. There was nothing for her to fear. Any food or drink she desired could be obtained by a single telephone call to the reception desk. However one thing that no one could cater for was the images that passed through Diana's mind. That night, she fell into a deep sleep and began to dream. It was much more pleasant this time, not against the background of the Sahara Desert but oddly enough in the Arctic near to the North Pole. She was dressed in thick brown furs with a bearskin hat that came down over her ears, and large leather gloves. Behind her was a tent that had been pitched into the ice. The atmosphere was cold… icy cold… with snow drifting down from a black sky. In real life, she snuggled under the sheets trying to keep her body warm clasping her arms around her. In the dream, she began to sing a popular tune and, as she did so, a man, also dressed in furs, wearing a snow-visor, came towards her on skis. He crashed lightly into her in order to stop, laughing as he did so. Then he placed one gloved hand inside her coat feeling her breasts in a token of intimacy.

'Naughty, naughty!' she chided with a smile on her face. 'Let's go inside!'

He followed her into the tent and removed his skis without delay. Then he took off his coat and the sun-visor. She stared at his face in disbelief. It was Ahmed… in the Arctic! He eased her coat off her shoulders and started to undress her slowly. It was still cold but suddenly warmth began to permeate her body. She felt a thrill as he touched her and they fell on to the mattress that lay on the ice, giggling as they landed.

'I love you,' he told her amorously, staring deeply into her eyes before placing his hand gently on her nipples. 'I need you… I want you!'

Her body stiffened slightly as he lay on top of her and her legs began to open widely in anticipation. His hands moved slowly over her bosom and then down to her legs. He started a series of kisses all over her arms, her breasts, her stomach and her pelvis. The feelings that surged up inside her made her feel like bursting. This was the moment of extreme desire… of the highest emotion… of wonderful fantastic penetrating love… and she was the woman being seduced by the greatest lover in the world. However, although the dream did not end with the same fate as

those she had experienced previously, it suddenly began to fade into a thick mist in the middle distance. Ahmed seemed to disappear from her grasp and she found herself sailing through the air back to Morocco. Within a few seconds, she woke up feeling extremely frustrated at having lost the essence of the dream.

'Damn!' she shouted angrily, striking the bed with her hand forcibly. 'Damn! Just a couple of minutes more and…' She tailed off huffing and puffing irately but she knew in her heart that she would go through to the end in the course of time. The strange element was Ahmed. Why did he always turn up in her dream? He was about fifteen years younger and she didn't particularly care for him… certainly not as a lover! Not at all! He was just a young handsome man and she didn't want him as a toy-boy. Yet he was the one who always turned up in her slumbers.

* * * * *

Diana fell into a deep sleep and awoke late on the following morning. She took some time to bring herself back to reality and rose to examine herself in the mirror. The little red spots were still there. It was difficult to tell whether any of them had started to recede. Laura had left a note on the dressing-table to say that she had gone out early for a morning jog so Diana ordered breakfast from the reception desk and enjoyed the meal after it arrived. She was about to pour herself a second cup of coffee when she heard a key turn in the lock in the door. She looked up in trepidation as a young man holding a bouquet of flowers peered into the room.

'Surprise, surprise!' he exclaimed brightly as he entered. He stared at Diana's face and halted in his tracks. 'What in Heaven's name happened to you?'

She stared at him blankly in shock at his sudden entry. 'Who are you?' she cried with concern. 'How did you get in here?'

He paused to reflect for a moment and sat heavily in a chair. 'I'm your son, Robbie,' he announced sad at having to explain himself. He placed the flowers in front of her on the bed. 'Robbie!'

Tears ran down Diana's face as she looked at him. He was a strapping young man, quite handsome, but she was unable to recognise him. 'My son!' she managed to say.

He recovered his poise and smiled at her. 'Don't worry about it, Mom. Dad told me that you'd lost your memory. It'll come back eventually. You won't mind if I don't kiss you. What is it… chicken pox?'

'It's rubella… German measles.'

'Karen will be coming shortly. She's been held up with her work.

'Karen?' Diana's mind went into a spin. Who was Karen?

'Your daughter… my sister,' he told her, realising that his mother's situation was far worse than he had imagined.

'Do I live in a house with a tall fountain and a wishing-well in the front garden,?' she asked.

'Of course you do,' he replied easily. 'Grantham Hall… that's where you live.'

She offered up an inwards prayer thanking God for restoring a tiny piece of her memory. It was beginning to return… very very slowly. 'I had a flash of it but I don't remember your father or you.'

'All in good time,' he told her philosophically. 'I understand you're having some kind of strange treatment.'

'Yes,' she responded wondering how she had given birth to such an intelligent handsome man. 'I'm under a scientist by the name of Dr. Mahmoud… the Wizard of Agadir. He's prescribed Beotag and ferrdil-x tablets. Unfortunately they produce side-effects, one of which you can see for yourself. Apparently it tests the immune system to its fullest extent but it will correct itself in due course.'

'What the hell is ferradil-x?' he demanded sharply.

'It's the extract of a plant with no name that grows in North Borneo. Dr. Mahmoud's a very capable scientist. He cured a cancer patient at the hospital… a woman who was given only three months to live by English doctors.'

'How good is he on memory?' The question was fired like a bullet from a gun.

'That's the sixty-four thousand dollar question. We'll find out eventually. But some things have already started to trigger in my mind. A couple of days ago I remembered a conversation with the cabbie who brought us here from the airport. It's coming.'

He looked around the room impressed by its excellence. 'Well at least you've a decent place to stay in the meantime. Dad told me you were in hospital so I went straight there only to learn that you'd been discharged.

'Discharged!' she echoed. 'They threw me out saying they needed the bed urgently. What did you do next?'

'Dad told me that he'd employed a local lawyer to look in on

you regularly and report back to him so that he could know how you were progressing. I looked him up and he said you were here. I told reception that I was your son and they gave me a pass key to get in. I wanted to surprise you but it's turned out to be a damp squib.'

She put out her hand to touch his arm. 'You're wrong. You certainly did surprise me. Anyhow the important thing is that you found me,' she said warmly staring at his face with a love that only a mother could express when looking at her child. This was her son! This handsome good-looking young man was actually her son! She came back to reality very quickly and pressed him for information. 'I know it's a bore but tell me about yourself.'

He seemed put out to have to explain his life story to his mother but after swallowing hard he began to relate the tale briefly. 'I'm twenty-one, my birthday was two days' ago. I work on a major newspaper… the sports column. I own a small apartment in in Wapping, London, which I share with Stella who I intend to marry soon. You'll really like her. That's about it in a nutshell.'

'I'm proud of you,' she managed to say. 'Even if you seem to be a stranger to me.'

He smiled weakly and then stood up. 'I think I'll share some coffee with you.' He went to the telephone and rang the reception desk. No sooner had he replaced the receiver when Laura pushed the door open and ran flushed into the room.

'Phew!' she muttered. 'It's getting too hot out there to run.' She stared at Robbie quizzically. 'What's going on here?'

'This is Robbie… my son!' boasted Diana proudly.

'Gee!' exclaimed Laura in surprise raising her arm to waist level. 'He was only that high when I last saw him.'

'I was almost twelve years old when you went to America, Aunt Laura.' he told her with a smile on his face. He went over to her and kissed her lightly on the cheek. 'It's lovely to see you again. We've got a lot of catching up to do.'

'You can say that again,' she laughed holding him at arm's length 'Let me look at you!' She scanned his face and body nodding her head vigorously. 'You've turned out to be a real handsome man,' she told him warmly. 'Yes indeedee. You take after your mother.'

He seemed embarrassed by the attention and pointed to the chair so that she could sit down. 'Karen will be here in the next one or two days. She's grown up to be a beautiful woman since you last saw her.'

'Well I'm damned! Fancy seeing you here in Agadir,' expressed Laura unable to get over his presence there. 'To tell you the truth, I never thought I'd ever see you again..'

'We're a pretty close family,' Robbie told her. 'In England that is.' He regretted saying that words after he had uttered them wishing he could have bitten his tongue. 'I thought that you and Mom didn't speak to each other.'

'That's all in the past, Robbie,' concurred his aunt freely. 'We've finally made it up.'

'I'm glad ' he said precociously. 'It's good that you've both buried the hatchet. Any chance of a free holiday out there?'

'You're always welcome, Robbie,' conceded Laura easily. 'Any time.'

The young man turned his attention to his mother. 'Dad asked me to make arrangements for you to come home.'

Diana stared at him wondering what her home looked like from the inside and she became fearful at having to live with a man who called himself her husband. She resented the suggestion so much that she was determined to put it off. Yet at the back of her mind she realised that she could not stay indefinitely in a hotel in Agadir. However she could put off the move for a while at least. 'I'm Dr. Mahmoud's patient,' she explained lamely, 'and this is a critical period for my treatment. Look at me now! I can't go back to England looking like this. No one will sit next to me on the plane!' No… I can't leave Agadir at the moment.'

Robbie shrugged his shoulders aimlessly. 'Dad'll be very disappointed,' he remarked unhappily.

'It would have been nice had he come to visit me in hospital here,' riposted his mother curtly. 'I notice that he's not beating a path to my door.'

Robbie shrugged his shoulders again. 'You know what Dad's like,' he muttered sagely. 'His work comes first. It always has.'

'I'm beginning to learn all about him over again,' complained Diana with disappointment sounding in her voice.

'Your eyes are less bloodshot today,' intervened Laura changing the subject quickly, 'but your fingernails are blacker.'

Diana stared at her hands in despair. Her fingernails were as black as the ace of spades. 'What do you know?' she gasped, clenching her fingers so that they were hidden from sight. 'I'm going to let the treatment run its course as Dr. Mahmoud suggested. It's the only way I can find out whether or not it will cure me.'

'Seeing that you're in such good spirits today, sister,' ventured Laura laughingly. 'I'm going to take a quick shower and then show my nephew around the town centre and treat him to lunch. We'll come back to see you later on.'

She went into the bathroom and emerged ten minutes later.. Then she and Robbie left. The coffee ordered by her son arrived and Diana poured herself a cup sipping it slowly. She mused that her son had travelled all the way to Morocco to see her. A son she had completely forgotten. And there would be more excitement to come when her daughter arrived. She could hardly wait to see what she was like. However there was still no sign of her delinquent alleged husband. Perhaps if Ahmed kept his word and refused to report back to him, he might be able to see sense and visit her. How could he actually allow work to come before his wife? It was inconceivable! She continued to sip her coffee with random thoughts crossing her mind. She would wait and see if anything happened!

* * * * *

Ahmed soon got over his indignation. He was not the kind of person to bear a grudge and he forgave her for leaving his home without warning. He turned up at her room in the hotel during the afternoon accompanied by another Arab who was poorly dressed.

'This is Mohammed,' he explained. 'I've brought him along because like Joseph in your Bible he can interpret dreams.

Diana instinctively flinched at the man's presence. She did not want anyone to interpret her dreams and she considered that the young Arab lawyer was far too presumptuous to have brought the man into her room at the hotel. 'I don't need his interpretations,' she snapped angrily.

‘Please,’ pleaded Ahmed. ‘Don’t take umbrage. It may be a means by which you recover your memory… in the same way as a hypnotist works.’

‘It’s totally unnecessary,’ she went on miffed at the idea. ‘I can interpret my own dreams. I don’t need someone else to do it for me!’

‘Please!’ begged the young lawyer. Try him… just try him!’

‘I am an expert at dreams,’ muttered Mohammed in clipped English. ‘I tell you the truth of your mind and imagination.’

He seemed very confident and she inhaled deeply about the dream she had experienced so recently. ‘Very well,’ she conceded

intending to make a fool of the man. ‘I’m in the Arctic wearing a fur coat, hat and leather gloves. It’s snowing and very cold. A man wearing a sun-visor and a bear skin coat skis towards me. We go into a tent together and he undresses me. He removes his sun-visor and undresses himself before he starts making love to me. Before anything interesting happens everything gets very misty and I find myself flying through the sky towards the Sahara Desert in Morocco. That’s just about it.’

‘Do you recognise the man after he removes his sun-visor?’

‘No!’ she countered angry at herself for having to lie but she refused to reveal that it had been Ahmed while he was standing in front of her.

‘I think you do,’ declared the visionary adamantly. ‘You know his face well… very well.’

Diana quickly tired of the game and decided to come clean. ‘Okay… okay!’ she admitted. ‘If you must know… it was Ahmed, the man beside you.’

Mohammed nodded his head slowly and clenched his hands in front of him at waist level. The room fell silent for a long time. Then his head shot up, he unclenched his hands, and stared directly into Diana’s eyes. ‘It is not a difficult dream to unfold,’ he told her point-blank. ‘Everything runs in the proper order and there is no puzzling mystery. I presume you’ve been married for many years.’

‘That much is obvious,’ she snarled, beginning to think that she was wasting her time with a fake ‘I’m wearing a wedding ring.’ She turned angrily to Ahmed. ‘Does he think he’s going to be paid for this service?’

‘I’ll take care of him,’ stated Ahmed swiftly. ‘You don’t have to worry, Diana. This is on me. I must help you to get better one way or the other.’

‘I wish my alleged husband was as enthusiastic about my welfare,’ she uttered with rancour. ‘I haven’t heard or seen him since I’ve been here!’

‘You do not love your husband,’ pronounced Mohammed staring above her head at the picture of a camel on the wall. ‘You’ve never loved him in all your years of marriage. He does not show you affection and you often feel alone.’

'Well if I had to rely on him I would be,' she ranted.

'There has been no sexual relationship between the two of you for a long time and you are extremely frustrated for love.' he

continued in his judgement. 'As such, you have been denied some of the great pleasures of life. Now you have fallen in love with Ahmed even though he is much younger than you in years. In your dreams you want him to ease your frustration and accept his love readily. But…'

'There always has to be a 'but', doesn't there?' she interrupted rudely.

'… but you do not have the confidence to let your inner feelings go free. You dwell on the vows you gave your husband on your wedding day... and they inhibit the satisfaction you so desire.'

Diana felt that her life was being unrolled out before her like a carpet in a very indelicate way. 'So you're saying that I love Ahmed. Well let me tell you that it's as far from the truth as we are from the moon. If I loved him, I would go for him, but that's not the situation.' She turned up her nose in disdain as she gave the visionary some advice. 'Do me a favour, Mohammed, get a life. What you've told me I could get from any agony aunt in one of the major newspapers.'

'You can fight the truth but I tell you it's true,' he insisted disregarding her disinterest. 'I am a teller of tales and I can say that this is the truth.'

'You're a teller of tales all right,' she told him disrespectfully turning to Ahmed. 'You've wasted your money here, my dear. What he's saying is a load of nonsense. He's told me nothing I don't know myself. And the only reason you're in my dreams is that you the only person I know.'

Mohammed shrugged his shoulders. 'What more can I say?'

'At least Joseph had a forecast when he spoke to Pharoah,' she spat harshly. 'He predicted seven good years and seven bad ones. You tell me nothing.'

'Not yet,' replied the visionary, 'but if you'll hear me out I shall tell you.' Diana remained silent and waited for his prediction. 'You will eventually overcome your lack of confidence. It may take time but you will make love with Ahmed provided he wants to partake in the exercise. I can see you leaving your husband to live with him.'

'Not in that hovel where he lives!' she reacted sharply resenting the observation. 'No… I don't think so! In any case, he's so much younger than me. I'm not interested in a toy-boy! All I can say on that one is 'don't hold your breath!''

'It will be the happiest time of your life,' expressed Mohammed ignoring her comments.

'Get him out of here, Ahmed,' she ordered with an edge of anger in her voice. 'He's getting on my nerves!''

'He's trying to help you,' the lawyer told her forcibly. 'Take heed, it may jog your memory somehow.'

'I don't think so,' prattled Diana. 'He's just robbing you of your money for something anyone could have told me.'

'Have you had any other dreams?' asked the visionary trying to recover the situation.

'Not that you need to know about,' retorted Diana irately. 'Not unless you can interpret nightmares. But I'm not getting into that one.' Mohammed continued for a while but Diana was saved by the return of Laura and Robbie.

'What's going on?' asked her sister when she saw the two men in the room. 'What do they want?'

'There's no problem. They were just leaving,' stated Diana finally. 'Goodbye and thank you for your thoughts. Believe me they're appreciated. I wish to thank you for your consideration.' The two men left without saying another word and Diana turned to her sister shaking her head. 'You don't want to know about it.' Nonetheless, the presence of Mohamed disturbed her.

Later that evening, Laura took Robbie for a night on the town. Diana sat up in bed, fluffing the pillow behind her to make herself more comfortable and she thought about the visionary's predictions. He said that she had never loved her husband. How true was that? If that was the case, why did she marry him in the first place? She tried to think it through but her memory failed her. She couldn't even remember what her alleged husband looked like. And what about all that guff concerning Ahmed. How could she fall in love with a man so much younger than herself? It was not impossible of course but very much improbable. No… it was inconceivable! The visionary told her that she would leave her husband to live with Ahmed. Well she knew nothing about the first part but to live with the young Arab in his hovel was the last thing she wanted to do. The recollection of the smell of stale curry, the confrontation with his mother, the three children, the awful furniture, the sleeping arrangements… the idea sent a shudder through her body. And what did he mean when he said it would be the happiest time of her life? Wasn't she happy before the attack? Was she yet another of the mass of women living out their lives unhappily with a husband they no longer loved… or one they had never loved before? It was a horrifying thought that began to

haunt her and she despised Ahmed for bringing Mohammed to her room in the hotel.

CHAPTER SIX

Three days later, the spots had vanished, her bloodshot eyes were normal and her fingernails looked white and bright again. Although her appointment with Dr. Mahmoud was not imminent, she decided to take the bull by the horns and go to see him. Her presence seemed to knock him off his routine and he appeared to be irritated from the start as she sat down in the chair opposite him without an appointment.

'Do you realise I have a full list of activities I need to pursue this morning?' he reproached irately. 'You'll remember I took you on only because your condition needed little assistance and would not take up my time. Now you break into my routine without notice. It's not good enough, Mrs. Templeton!'

She paused to reflect her name. Mrs. Templeton! It sounded rather grand. 'Do you know you're the only one who mentions my name.'

He slammed the cover of the file in front of him and gave her his full attention. 'What do you want?' he demanded with a sharp tone to the edge of his voice.

'I came to tell you that all the side-effects have disappeared. I'm over the first hurdle. What do you say to that?' She appeared very smug at the result but the scientist seemed to be less than impressed.

'It's expected,' he riposted,' but now you're over the first hurdle I want you to double the amount of the ferradil-x tablets.'

She leaned back in the chair for a moment concerned at the suggestion. 'Isn't that a rather forward step to take? I mean you told me that ferrdil-x was relatively unknown to you... only experimental you said. Doubling the dose might mean that I will suffer worse side-effects than before.'

'I don't think so,' he responded hoping to overcome her resistance. 'You've passed the first hurdle. The side-effects have run their course. In my opinion, they will not manifest themselves again.'

'But it's all experimental. What if they do?' It was as though he deliberately intended to turn her world upside down. The

effects of a double dose of the extract was uncharted in medical history. Her mind went into a spin when she realised that anything could happen.

He began to show extreme anger at her question and slammed his fist down hard on the desk. 'Who is the doctor here... you or me?' he shouted at the top of his voice, causing her to ride back in the chair.

'No offence,' she apologised lamely. 'I'm sorry to have taken up your time but it seems that you're taking me to extremes.'

'That's exactly what scientists do, Mrs. Templeton,' he retorted curtly. 'We take new discoveries to extremes. But I would not do such a thing if I wasn't sure it was safe. I do not experiment on people and use them as guinea pigs. Everything is tried and tested over a period of years including ferradil-x although you're the first human-being to use it.'

She relaxed a little, breathing a sigh of relief. 'Well it's good to know that your patients are important to you, doctor,' she muttered. 'It's good to know.'

He leaned back in his chair more calmly now that the tension between them had subsided and he moved his hand down to the bottom drawer of the desk to remove a canister of tablets. He passed them over to her and she took them readily. 'Take two ferradil-x tablets every morning and evening together with on Beotag. Are you clear on that?'

She nodded briefly and placed the canister in her handbag. Lord knows what the end result would be she thought to herself. Was Dr. Mahmoud as good as everyone made him out to be or was he simply an experimental scientist hoping for a break through? At that moment, the vision of her house with the tall fountain and the wishing-well in the front garden came to mind.

'My memory's starting to come back,' she told the scientist. 'It's patchy and doesn't come often but it's happening.'

'I'm pleased to hear it,' he returned offering a revelation which she didn't expect. 'You do realise that neither Beotag nor ferradil-x

will help restore your memory.'

Her facial expression indicated the way she felt about his comment. 'What do you mean?' she demanded. 'That's the sole reason I came to you!'

'You were too good a subject to lose,' he explained. 'The tablets you take are indeed experimental with regard to human-beings but you will benefit tremendously when I tell you of the long-term effect they'll have on you.'

'Go on.' she urged. She was becoming extremely angry with the scientist for duping her and her first reaction was to report him to the authorities for malpractice.

'I've tested both Beotag and ferradil-x on animals for some years. Together they make a cocktail which had a resounding effect on them.'

His prevarication was too much for Diana to bear and she interrupted him at the end of the sentence. 'Will you kindly get to the point!'

'It appears that the cocktail seems to prevent ageing,' he revealed to her astonishment. 'The animals have remained exactly the same over the years never getting older... very healthy... and they look the same as they did when

I started the experiment. Some of them had a life expectancy of only two years yet ten years later they're still alive and well.'

'But you haven't yet tested it on humans, have you?' she forwarded rhetorically. It then dawned on her that she was the only human-being used in the experiment. 'I see.' She inhaled deeply to take in the situation. 'I'm the first one.'

'I want you to take two ferradil-x tablets morning and evening,' he repeated. 'You see, I did that with the animals after they recovered from the side-effects and they thrived. The treatment will be exactly the same for you. Don't you want to live as a young healthy woman for say two hundred years looking exactly as you do today?'

The revelation took her breath away. Suddenly, everything in her life had changed. In her present situation, without a memory, she really had nothing to lose. If Mahmoud was correct, she could be the first woman to look young even in old age. 'If it works,' she asked almost holding her breath for the answer, 'will I really look the same as I do today… even when I'm a hundred?' The question was posed in very quiet tones.

'The animal seemed to do so. I can't see why it shouldn't work with you.'

She exhaled deeply astonished at the prospect. 'When do you want to see me again?' Her mind was in a whirl as it tried to absorb all that he had told her and she hardly knew what she was saying.

'I only need to see your every six months now,' he told her solemnly. 'You can go back to England and fly back here twice a year. I will continue to send the tablets to your home address.

However there is one thing you need to do. You have to keep the experiment a secret. No one else needs to know otherwise I will be inundated with requests from millions of women demanding the tablets. Can you imagine what they would do to kept their looks to a very old age and live longer? It must be our secret. Once you tell one person, the whole world will know. Can I have your promise on that?'

She nodded her head slowly. 'You have my promise. I won't tell a soul.' She paused to reflect the situation and another question entered her mind. 'Will the tablets affect any other functions of my body… sexual or otherwise?'

'Not to my knowledge,' he replied. 'The animals in the experiment carried on with their lives in a normal way. Some even had cubs.'

Diana left the office in a daze. Would the experiment really be successful? Only time would tell. She now had two options. Firstly, to ignore the scientist's advice and not take the tablets at all. Secondly, she could take them and hope for the best. However one thing was certain… she would never tell her secret to anyone. It was her second secret; the first one being the content of her salacious dreams although Ahmed and Mohammed now knew of them. Other than that, her life was becoming filled with clandestine secrets.

CHAPTER SEVEN

Diana was in a state of confusion when she returned to her room at the hotel. Her stay in Morocco was coming to a swift end and she placed the few items of clothing she had purchased on the bed in readiness for her departure. Laura had gone for a jog and Diana realised that she needed a holdall as there was insufficient clothing to fill a suitcase. She had asked Robbie to make arrangements for her to fly back to England… the word seared through her like a dagger. As far as she was concerned, Agadir was pleasant, warm and comfortable and she could spend time there on her own without interference from anyone. England was something quite different. Her position was almost untenable in that she knew no one there. In time her memory would return and she could deal with the matter in a casual fashion on her own but returning to her own country now meant that her life would be invaded by strangers… especially her alleged husband. She would not be allowed to get back to normality without pressure. Places would be blank in her mind; people who regarded themselves as her friends in the past would now be strangers because she could not remember their faces or the relationship she had with them. It would be an uphill struggle for quite some time. Not only was she fearful about facing reality but she was scared of embarrassing herself… and this was likely to happen often. It was an ordeal she was forced to undergo mainly because she could not stay in Morocco any longer now that Dr. Mahmoud wanted to see her only every six months. She no longer had any excuse to stay there.

Laura came back shortly, perspiring in the heat and she flopped down tiredly on the chair.

'I've got some news,' she told her sister, 'and it fits in with my plans perfectly. 'My flight to Los Angeles takes off in six hours… long after yours to England. I need to get to the airport to get the flight ticket. I've got plenty of time to pack.' She rose and went over to Diana to take her hands. 'It's been fantastic to see you again,' she advanced staring directly into her sister's eyes. 'Don't forget about the invitation to South Burbank. You're always welcome there. Mac, Rusty and Chuck'll be delighted when I get back. I'm sad about your loss of memory but it brought us back together again if nothing else.'

'Where did you get the names Rusty and Chuck from?' laughed Diana easily.

'Mac chose them. It was okay by me. They're fine boys. Chuck'll be a motor mechanic when he's older. He's a whiz with cars and engines. He takes after Mac. Rusty's more academic. Maybe he'll be a lawyer.'

'Can you go to town and buy me a holdall?' asked Diana. 'I'll need one for all this.'

'Consider it done. I'll be back in half an hour.'

As she left, Robbie arrived smiling at his mother. 'I just passed Aunt Laura in the corridor,' he told her. 'She said you're leaving today. That's great news. Have you made the flight arrangements?'

'I thought I asked you to do it,' bleated his mother fearfully.

'No you didn't, Mom. You probably thought you did. Don't worry. I'll contact the airport and get flight tickets for both of us. I'm not letting you travel back to England on your own. You'll have to bear up with me as company. I don't suppose you'll remember where you live.'

'You're a good son,' she said thankfully, hugging him with all the love she could muster. 'Thank you so much, Robbie I really appreciate it.'

'Hey!' he laughed, extricating himself from her grip but still holding her arms, staring into her eyes. 'Why shouldn't I do it. You're my mother!'

She smiled at him warmly wonder what she had done to deserve such a caring loving son.

The flight back to Britain was scheduled at seven thirty that evening. Laura came to the airport to see them off, waving her arms vigorously as they boarded the plane. Diana waved back although she could not see her sister but she knew that she was there. The arrival of Laura in Morocco had been a real bonus re-establishing the relationship between them. They were speaking to each other after a long period of time which was a beneficial feature to say the least. Secondly, she could travel to Los Angeles any time she wished to live with her sister's family. Yes… it was indeed a bonus!

She sat next to Robbie as the aircraft took off. Leaving one world to enter another frightened her although she dared not convey her inner thoughts to her son. The nightmare she had experienced had come back but this time it was real. She felt that she was on a hiding to nothing.

After they landed in Britain, Robbie led his mother to his car which he had left in the car park.

'It's an hour's drive,' he informed her. 'Do you want something to eat at the airport before you leave?' She declined his offer deciding that postponement was not the best strategy. It was a better plan to proceed to the hell she expected to face. 'I rang Dad from Agadir,' he told her. 'He'll probably be waiting for us when we get home.'

'Probably?' she questioned in her mind. She turned to her son with a harshly critical comment. 'I wonder if his work will allow him to do so. Maybe he won't be there. In truth, I hope that he isn't. I don't really like the man I saw when I was in hospital and his lack of action has done nothing to make me change my mind.'

He screwed up his face at her remarks. 'You'll soon get used to everything once I get you home. It'll all fall back into place.'

In due course, they arrived at her country house. In the darkness she could barely see the tall fountain and the wishing-well which had flashed as a vision in her mind in Agadir. She

stared at the façade of the house. This was the place she had seen which proved that her memory was beginning to return. However to her surprise there was only one light on in the hallway as Robbie led her to the front door.

'Are you all right with this?' he asked slowly opening the front door which was unlocked.

His mother nodded and they went inside. She looked around furtively but nothing registered in her mind Charles was not at home as she had expected... he was tied up with his work. He had left a note on the mantelshelf in the lounge to apologise for his absence saying that he was unavoidably detained and would return in the morning. Things would certainly have to change in this household if she was ever going to experience any happiness in their marriage. The prediction of the visionary Mohammed came swiftly to mind and his words rang out in her ears.

'You will eventually overcome your lack of confidence,' he had told her. 'It may take time but you will make love with Ahmed provided he will want to partner you in the exercise. It will not be just once but many times. I can even see you leaving your husband and living with him.'

She considered his prediction very carefully. He may have been right after all about leaving her husband. Her first task, however, was to recover her memory. After that, anything might happen.

'Sorry that Dad's not here to meet you,' muttered Robbie with disappointment in his voice. 'Something important is holding him up.'

'Yes,' countered Diana acidly. 'Like the world's coming to an end... or the ozone layer's collapsing... or aliens have arrived from outer space!'

He shrugged aimlessly almost not knowing how to respond. 'I'll stay the night with you,' he offered sympathetically, 'just so you can familiarise yourself with the place. I'll ring Stella and tell her what's going on.'

He left her in the lounge and she stared at the décor. None of it registered in her mind. It was a beautiful room with elegant curtains, paintings on the walls, bright regency wallpaper, excellent furniture but she recalled absolutely nothing about it. Was this the place where she had lived in the past? Was this how she really lived… in relative comfort… in a house filled with affluence? She sat down gingerly on a settee and stared at the

decorous paintings on the walls. No doubt each one of them would fetch a high price in an auctioneer's room. In addition, the bric-a-brac which littered the room was exquisite. An exceptionally large globe of the world identifying the continents and major cities… a pair of large ceramic hunting dogs in the hearth… a beautiful standard lamp in the corner with a wonderful multi-coloured shade… as well as many other expensive items all assisted in the embellishment of the room.

Robbie soon returned with two cups of coffee on a tray and some cakes and biscuits on a plate. 'Here,' he told her. 'This'll warm you up.' He sat down opposite her. 'Is anything familiar to you yet?'

She took one of the cups of coffee shaking her head slowly. 'No,' she bleated miserably. 'Nothing. Nothing at all.'

'Well at least you're home now,' he stated. 'That's one thing which ought to please you. There's no place like home.'

Diana wished that she could confirm that comment but it was far from the truth. At that moment, she was displeased to have left Agadir. Worse still, she deplored the fact that she would come face-to-face with the man who called himself her husband the next day.

* * * * *

Sleep didn't come easily to her that night. The surroundings were strange to her even though she had once lived in the house for many years in comfort. The trauma was never going to end until her memory came back and there was the matter of the experiment being carried out by Dr. Mahmoud. The import of his studies were beginning to worry her now that she was such a long distance away from him. What if he was wrong in his assumptions? The experiment may have worked on animals but it was unproven on human-beings. It was possible that the tablets would have no effect on her in the long run. She would have simply been wasting her time taking them and suffering the side-effects. If that happened, she would just grow old like everyone else It might be that the Wizard of Agadir was but another lunatic scientist hoping to make his mark on the world. And then she remembered Betty Naylor, the woman whom he had cured of pancreatic cancer when everyone else had given up on her. Fate or fortune… which one was it?

Diana rose from her bed in the middle of the night to stare at herself in a full-length mirror. Her skin was smooth... very smooth. She had no lines on her forehead or bags under her eyes and she appeared to be very young... about fifteen years younger than her actual age. By taking the tablets, would she still look that way in ten or twenty years time? In the confines of her elegant bedroom, doubt crossed her mind. Surely Dr. Mahmoud was off-beat in thinking that he could stave off old age and lengthen life! Methuselah was purported in the Bible to have live for over nine hundred and fifty years but that figure was highly debatable. Someone surely had made a huge mistake in their calculations. After all, no one knew of ferradil-x in ancient times... or did they? Was it possible for a human-being to live for two hundred years as the scientist had predicted? It was a mind-shattering concept for a person who might be expected to live that long. Furthermore, if the experiment happened to be successful, how could she retain the secret? People would begin to notice that she never aged and they would want to talk to her about it. What could she say... how could she explain what was going on? It was quite clear that she was in a catch twenty-two position whichever way she looked at it.

As she stood in front of the mirror, a fleeting flash crossed her mind of three other women sitting at a green-baized table. She didn't recognise any of them but they were playing cards... a game of bridge. As the vision ended she felt a degree of pleasure in the knowledge that her memory did have a life of its own after all. It was coming back! However, the night was going to be quite memorable for her because half an hour later, as she slept, her body began to twitch and then entered a phase of unusual contraction. She shuddered violently, her arms trembling, her body shaking, her legs moving involuntarily, as though she was experiencing an epileptic fit. Not only that but vicious pains shot through her body until she could stand it no longer. Perspiration ran down her face as well as all over her body and she was forced to scream at the top of her voice as a result of the pain. Within a couple of minutes, she stopped shaking and took a deep breath in relief as the pain passed away. What was going on? Dr. Mahmoud had told her that she would have no more side-effects yet this one had been riveting and extremely painful. Shortly, the door opened and Robbie entered, staring at her before hurrying to the bed.

'Are you all right, Mom?' he called out, trying to get her attention. 'What's wrong?'

The agony she had suffered showed in her face but she shook her head not wishing to worry him. 'It's nothing, Robbie,' she managed to say. 'Just a bad nightmare. Go back to bed. I'm sorry I woke you.'

He stayed with her for a while offering to bring her a cup of tea but she shook her head refusing it. After a while, he left the room, satisfied that she was all right although he had noticed the excess perspiration on her face.

Diana lay back and tears began to run down her cheeks. Nothing was going right. Now her body had started contractions … the whole of her body! Something was definitely wrong. Should she continue to take two tablets of ferradil-x morning and evening every day? Why not give them up and lead a normal life without them? But then she was the subject of a serious experiment that might eventually change the lives of every person on the planet if it proved to be successful. It was a problem of an ethical nature which haunted her right into the start of the day.

It was pointless to expect her husband to come early. In fact Charles arrived at twelve-thirty in the afternoon. During the morning, Diana wandered her way through the house going from room to room, hoping that something would spark in her brain but there was no impression of the past at all until she came to the kitchen. Even though nothing registered, she seemed to know where everything had been placed or stacked… the cupboards with the crockery, the drawers with the cutlery, the odd items that only a housewife would know where to find them. She even knew how to operate the washing-machine recalling that one of the switches always got stuck. Into her mind came the comments of a radio interviewer who once said that however old a person is, if they had driven a car in their lifetime, they would always remember how to drive even if they lost their memory. Perhaps it was instinctive for her to recognise where everything was in the kitchen or maybe it was something more.

Robbie left at eleven o'clock and she settled down in the lounge reading a magazine as she waited for her alleged husband to arrive. Eventually the door opened and Charles entered moving towards his wife with the intention of kissing her. However she deliberately drew away preventing him from doing so. This was the man she still didn't recognise and to whom she had taken a particular dislike. How could she have married such a pompous person… someone who obviously cared so little about her?

'I should imagine you're annoyed with me because I didn't come to see you in Agadir,' he began without any kind of remorse.

'You can say that again!' she retorted tartly. 'It's quite obvious that your work comes a long way before me.'

He paused to reflect her words as he poured himself a drink from the cocktail cabinet. 'How's your memory? Has any of it come back yet?'

'Nice of you to ask after all this time,' she responded sarcastically.

'I was informed of your situation by the lawyer I hired in Agadir,' he countered sharply. 'He sent me regular reports.'

'I thought we were a married couple,' she muttered angrily.

'Of course,' he returned with surprise in his voice. 'We are married, with two children... Robbie and Karen.'

'Then where was the other half of this marriage when I lay in stress in hospital? Where were you?' She was going to say 'Where were you, Charles?' but she couldn't bring herself to speak his name.

He sipped his drink slowly before replying. 'I had very urgent business to deal with, Diana. The Deputy Prime Minister...'

'Deputy Prime Minister!' she spat irately. 'I'm your wife! The person to whom you should show love and respect... and tenderness. I'm not interested in the Deputy Prime Minister! What was so important that you couldn't catch a plane and fly to Agadir for a day or two to spend a few hours with me in hospital? No... that was too much to expect! I mean you would have to miss meetings and that would be the end of the world. My God, if it wasn't for Laura and Robbie, I'd have been in a terrible state. You have no idea what I went through in Agadir.'

He seemed to be somewhat embarrassed by the tirade. 'I'm afraid I don't,' he uttered almost under his breath. 'What did happen?'

'I was thrown out of the hospital and had to live in a hovel where your lawyer lived. I had nowhere else to go. It was necessary for me to leave the place because of the awful conditions there.' She felt tears welling up inside her but she was determined to finish the sentence. 'And if it hadn't been for Laura, I'd have been out on the street all alone in a foreign country!'

'I'm sorry,' he apologised although it was quite clear that he didn't mean it. 'I had no idea. Admittedly, I should have come to

see you but you know how busy...' He tailed off at the sight of her caustic glance.

'I don't recognise you... I don't know you... and I don't like you,' she told him angrily. 'Everyone knows you're a workaholic and if that doesn't stop and you continue to neglect me I'm afraid we're going to have to do something about it. We'll have to part company. I don't think I can stay with you on those conditions.' She could hardly believe the words that came out of her mouth. It had to be the influence of the visionary Mohammed who had forced the position with his prediction.

'Easy on, Diana,' cautioned Templeton stunned by the attack. The last thing he wanted was an incursion into his workload. At the same time he did not wish to alienate his wife... not to the extent to which she had suggested.

No one in his family had ever divorced and he was not going to be the first one to do so. 'I think you're bitter about being attacked in Morocco and you're frustrated that you can't remember anything. I'll go along with that It will change in time. We had a good relationship in the past. We can go on from here in the future.'

'Not if you don't change your attitude to work,' she retorted curtly. 'You took me for granted in the past and it's obvious I saw nothing. Well let me tell you it's going to be different from now on.' She paused to reflect what she had just said. How did she know that she had said nothing in the past? Was this the sign that her memory was starting to improve?

Templeton placed the empty wine glass on the coffee table and turned to her again. 'I only came to see how you were,' he explained briefly. 'I have two meetings to attend this afternoon so I must be off. How about dinner this evening? We can go to Liberty's if you so wish.'

'Liberty's?' Diana's expression showed that she was confused.

'It's a high-class restaurant in town. We used to go there on special occasions.'

She huffed and puffed for a few moments and then nodded. 'Very well. What time will you be back?'

'Say seven-thirty. I'll pick you up then.' He thought about kissing her and actually started to advance towards her but he had second thoughts and turned walking to the door, realising that such an action was likely to offend her in the light of what she had told him.

Despite her onslaught, Diana was still a workaholic widow with only half a mind. Then a flash went through her head and she could see herself standing in the church on their wedding day. Templeton looked really handsome in a tuxedo and she was wearing a beautiful white wedding dress. Life appeared to be so wonderful then but he had changed over the years. The effort he had put into his work had altered him. The image lasted for only a few seconds but it brought back a precious moment in her life.

CHAPTER EIGHT

Following her retreat from Morocco, Diana considered that her hair was in a terrible mess. It had thickened as Dr. Mahmoud told her it would and she couldn't do anything with it. If she was going to dine out with her alleged husband that evening in a high-class restaurant, it was essential that she looked her best. She picked up a telephone directory to choose a hairdresser and, not having the confidence to drive her own car, she took a taxi to get there. As she entered the salon, the owner look at her and smiled.

'I haven't made an appointment,' began Diana apologetically.'

'I hope you can fit me in.

'Of course, Mrs. Templeton,' welcomed the hairdresser warmly. 'You're a regular customer. We can always fit you in.'

Diana stepped back to look at the woman but nothing registered in her mind. She was a complete stranger to her.

'Are you all right?' asked the hairdresser noticing the vacant expression on the customer's face.

'Yes... of course,' replied Diana slowly, trying to get her mind into gear. She had chosen a hairdressing salon at random yet she was known here as a customer.

The hairdresser looked at her rather strangely as she picked up a clean apron and opened it out. 'You always call me by my first name,' she continued 'Sandra! Here come and sit down in this chair!'

Diana obeyed and sat staring at herself in the mirror. She had to pull herself together and realise that everyone and everything would remain strange to her for a while. She needed to put on an act and pretend to know people. After all, she didn't need

to know their names or what they did in the past in order to pull it off.

The woman in the next chair with her hair sprouting with curlers looked across at her. 'Glory be! It's Diana Templeton! You're back at last. We thought we'd lost you.'

Diana stared at her bleakly as she pulled herself together. 'Hi!' she muttered weakly. 'It's good to see you again.' That was more like it. The secret was to bluff it out.

'I heard you were attacked in Morocco,' continued the woman with interest. 'Tell me about it.'

Sandra began to comb through Diana's hair with a puzzled expression on her face. 'Your hair has got really thick. Are you washing it with something I don't know about?'

Diana shrugged her shoulders and continued with her dialogue. 'I was mugged by a man who fired a gun at me. He blew off the back of my skull.'

'I can see that,' commented Sandra curtly. 'The hair won't grow back on it for a long time.'

'The worst of it was that I lost my memory and had to stay in the local hospital for quite some time.'

'We wondered what happened to you,' continued the woman. 'Well blow me down! You just don't know what's going to happen, do you? I said to myself, "Gloria, it's just as well you don't go to these strange places abroad. You never know what's going to happen there." And I'll tell you another thing. The laws in those countries protect those who live there... not the tourists.'

'They treated me very well,' Diana went on as Sandra continued to comb her hair.

'When are we going to meet up again for a bridge session?' asked Gloria bluntly.

Diana winced for a moment as she realised that the woman had been a close friend in the past although she could not recognise her. 'Shortly,' she uttered in a low voice. 'Very shortly. I only arrived back from Agadir last night. I need to get over the jet-lag.'

Gloria nodded. 'It must have been a great ordeal. I'm glad you're better.'

Sandra washed Diana's hair and cut and blow-dried it. By the time she had completed the task, Gloria had gone and the salon was empty. As Diana opened her purse to pay for the hairdo Sandra touched her arm gently, lowering her voice to a whisper.

'Look, Mrs. Templeton, don't take this the wrong way. I don't know what you've been eating or drinking or whether it's something to do with your hormones but your hair and your head's in an awful state. I think you should go and see your doctor. You have massive dandruff which you never had before and your hair has a strange thickness about it... twice as thick'

'It's the tablets I'm taking,' stated her customer deciding not to bluff it out. 'I take them but they don't seem to help my memory. I don't remember you or Gloria. It was a coincidence that I'm here today. I looked you up in the telephone directory.'

'That's terrible!' cried the hairdresser showing sympathy. 'You should have told me when you first came in.'

‘I’ll be okay in due course. That’s what everyone tells me,’ returned Diana mournfully.

‘The sooner the better,’ retorted Sandra quickly taking the money and putting it in the cash register.

Diana left the salon looking better than when she first got there but she was concerned at Sandra’s comments and could only conclude that the ferradil-x tablets were causing further repercussions. Now the side-effects were beginning to affect her hair and her head. She wondered whether to report the change to Dr. Mahmoud but then decided against it. She would soldier on for six months until her next appointment with him. In the meantime, it would appear that she had to suffer the slings and arrows of outrageous fortune.

* * * * *

Just before seven-thirty that evening, Karen came to the house to see her. As she entered the lounge where Diana was sipping coffee, a vision came to her mother’s mind taking her back into the past. She could see a young girl of fourteen years of age in her school uniform holding a satchel as she waved goodbye to her. It was an image which truly represented something she remembered from way back. Diana quickly returned to the present as her daughter moved towards her.

‘Karen!’ she greeted even though she wasn’t certain if it was her daughter. ‘How lovely to see you!’

The young woman leaned over to kiss her mother on the cheek and then sat down beside her to hug her warmly. ‘It’s good to see you back, Mom,’ she said with an edge of excitement in her voice. ‘How’s the memory?’

‘That’s what I’d like to know,’ joked her mother calmly. ‘It’s gone and I’m trying to get it back without much success. I had a flash of the front garden in Agadir but I didn’t know where it was. I just had a vision of you as a schoolgirl with your satchel and beret. It’s all so sketchy and remote.’

‘Don’t worry, Mom,’ returned her daughter easily. ‘Just give it a chance.’

‘Never mind me,’ cut in Diana. ‘How are you getting along?’

Karen held her chin up high as if she had good news to report before pouring herself a cup of coffee. ‘I’m now the head nurse at the hospital… the youngest ever. How about that?’ she boasted immodestly.

‘Good for you!’ exclaimed her mother proudly. ‘I’ve done very well with you and Robbie, haven’t I? I couldn’t have two nicer intelligent children.’

‘We’re not children any more, Mom,’ chided her daughter casually with a smile on her face. ‘Tell me all about Morocco.’

'Oh, it's all so boring,' related Diana sadly. 'The mugger pointed a gun at the back of my head and pulled the trigger. He blew a piece of my skull exposing a very small part of my brain and the shock caused my memory to disappear. Just like that!' She snapped her fingers to make an impact. 'I was in hospital and they patched up my skull with a compound called bone-paste, would you believe. Then I learned about a scientist who worked in an annex of the hospital. He gave me special tablets to help me but my memory's still lost in the mist.' She felt like telling her daughter the secret relayed to her by Dr. Mahmoud but stopped herself in time. There was little doubt that had she revealed it, her daughter would have scoffed at the idea and ridiculed it.

'That's awful.' Karen was appalled at the story. 'It must have been very painful.

'The pain might have been eased had your father come to visit me occasionally,' criticised Diana mournfully. 'As it happened, Laura came to see me all the way from Los Angeles and Robbie came.'

'You mean Aunt Laura spoke to you? There was surprise in the young woman's voice.

'We made it up,' informed her mother happily. 'We made it up at last. She was kindness in itself. I couldn't have done without her. I don't know why we never spoke to each other. She said it was for nine years.'

'I'm pleased for the both of you,' retorted Karen with delight. She paused to reflect for a moment. 'Does this mean we can go to the United States for free holidays?'

Diana burst into laughter and shook her head. 'You and Robbie are the most devious pair of children I've ever known. That was the first thing to go through his mind.' She exhaled deeply with an air of mock despair. 'I really don't know what this world's coming to these days!'

Both mother and daughter laughed at the comment and they hugged each other again. Diana looked at her wristwatch and screwed up her face with concern. 'You're father's coming to take me out to dinner but he's late.'

'Oh Dad and his work!' muttered Karen miserably. 'Work, work, work! That's all he knows.'

'I met a mystic in Morocco... well a man who said he could interpret dreams.' She paused for a moment wondering whether to continue but she decided that now she had started she would reveal the details to her daughter. 'He predicted that one day your father and I would split up mainly because he's a workaholic and neglects me. He was quite definite about it and I think he may be right. I spoke to your father about our future earlier today but he obviously hasn't listened.'

Karen thought deeply about the remark. 'Well Robbie and I are both adults now. If you make that decision we'll stand by you. Naturally we love you both but things change for older people as life goes on and we have to recognise it.

Diana placed her hand on Karen's arm. 'That's very wise of you, darling,' she said, marvelling at the sagacity of her daughter. 'Indeed... I'm a workaholic widow.'

Karen placed her hand over that of her mother in sympathy. 'I know. You don't have to tell me.'

Diana waited a further three-quarters of an hour but her husband did not show up. Karen stayed with her until the telephone rang and Templeton muttered a pointless apology. He had been held up at an important meeting and he would be further delayed at the House of Commons so he suggested that she should go to the restaurant to eat on her own. Diana was devastated to have been stood up so neglectfully and fury raged inside her. At the same time, Karen was distinctly unhappy at her father's careless attitude and she offered to take his place and dine with her mother. It wasn't at Liberty's though. They went to a local modest restaurant and ordered a meal but Diana was less than hungry as a result of the situation. She felt that she was being used and it was already beginning to become the nightmare she had expected. Everyone around her was kind and loving with the exception of her alleged husband. He was the proverbial fly in the ointment!

* * * * *

The following morning, Templeton returned to the house to tell his wife that he would take her for dinner. He began quite boldly to say that it was necessary for them to discuss their relationship and, even though she resented at having to dine with him, she capitulated. They took a taxi to Liberty's and entered the fine restaurant to be shown to a table at the far end of the room. They settled into their chairs and were passed menus by the waiter who hovered in the near distance hoping to be called forward for their orders.

'What did you want to talk about?' she asked impatiently.

He took time to straighten his cuffs before replying. 'Let me begin by saying that it's not my intention to part from you. We spent many years together and have two excellent offspring. Dammit, we're a family and I don't wish that to end!'

'Come to the point!' she told him savagely still not wishing to call him by his first name. She resented the man very strongly but there was little in her power to make him simply go away. As far as she was concerned, life would never be marital with him again… not ever!

He inhaled before telling her what was in his mind. 'You call me a workaholic and you're probably right. I'm not alone in this. Many men become alcoholics, reckless gamblers, or they chase women until their old age. I'm simply one of them… a workaholic. It's not a choice I made but a decision to further my career many years ago. Promotion doesn't come by sitting laid back and doing nothing. One has to work for it. Now I'm finally on the cusp of breaking through. I've been offered the post of Deputy to the Minister of Health. All my hard work has finally paid off.'

'That's as maybe,' she countered sharply, 'but it's all been at the cost of your family. What about all those school sports day and parents' evenings when the children were at school? You were always too busy to attend them. There were so many other times that you weren't there. We all made excuses for you. Have you ever thought of what you put us through? You've gone way off the chart. You've forgotten how to lead a normal life.'

'It isn't easy in government,' he tried to explain. 'I'm in my element in my office or in the House. I wake up each morning dying to get there to start work. It's like a drug.'

'It certainly is,' she rattled on. 'You're absent from my life… not that I particularly care at present. 'I don't like you… I don't like the look of you! I can't understand what I ever saw in you!'

He looked startled at her frankness as the wine waiter came

forward to their table. Templeton ordered an expensive bottle of wine and the waiter went away after taking their wine menus. The Civil Servant stared at his wife bleakly as a volley of thoughts passed through his mind.

I don't really want a separation but it seems to be the only solution,' he ventured seriously, reverting to his autocratic attitude. 'To sum up the facts…'

She interrupted him rudely. 'We're not at one of your meetings now, Charles!' she reproached irately in a loud voice which caused other diners to turn their heads towards them. Diana almost bit her tongue at calling him by his first name. She had been determined not to use it but now it had been done.

'I'm serious,' he went on solemnly. 'To sum up the facts, you're a lady of leisure. I've always insisted on that. You like being at home, playing bridge with your friends, and occasionally shopping. I like being in the office, at the House of Commons, and furthering my ambitions. We live in worlds apart. I'm away for most of the time and we rarely see each other. Love and affection are things that we left behind many years ago. Our aim was to bring children into the world. We did that and they've grown up and gone their own way. There's really nothing left between us. If we continue together we shall only make each other more miserable and angry. We need to separate.'

'It suits me,' she told him calmly as though the decision had been made a long time ago.

'It does?' he echoed in surprise. He had expected a long harangue with voices raised but she reconciled the situation without hesitation.

'Your absence in Agadir was just about the last straw. It's obvious that we fell out of love years ago. It took a mugger in Morocco to make us both realise that we had nothing in common any more. It's the shadow of a relationship held together by something that we promised each other in church many years ago. I agree that we need to separate but I'm not going to move from the house.'

'That's all right,' he continued thoughtfully. 'You can live in there. I have my apartment in London which suits me fine. I'll pay you a sum of money each month and all the bills on the house. How does that suit you?'

'I think you're getting off lightly,' she countered.

'You may think so,' he returned with rancour in his voice, 'but such a settlement really suits both of us. We can continue our lives in any way we want.'

She considered the offer for a few moments. It was very much in her favour. She would be able to continue living in the house for which all the bills would be paid by him and have a monthly allowance of her own.

'Can we run this through a solicitor and arrange for it to be a legal separation,' she asked tentatively.

'I don't see why not,' he concurred. 'I think it should be a legal separation. What do you say?'

She added her acceptance without reluctance although the expression on her face indicated another issue which entered her head. 'I think we should be together when we tell Robbie and Karen.'

He sat still for a few moments as the idea passed through his brain. 'We're not getting divorced so I don't see why we have to tell them anything,' he retorted, rejecting her suggestion without hesitation. 'Why can't this be our little secret? In that way they'll never know.'

He was quite right. The children would never become upset or concerned about the situation because they need never know. She pursed her lips in thought reflecting on the other secrets she had to keep. This was yet another to add to the burden... keeping the news of their legal separation from their children. She wasn't certain that she would always do it but after some hesitation she finally agreed. Her whole life had started to become filled even more with secrets!

* * * * *

The arrangement she had made with her husband proved to be very fitting. As Deputy to the Minister of Health he would earn a small fortune each year in salary so his financial situation was extremely satisfactory. Within a short period of time, a solicitor drew up the necessary papers and all the items promised by her husband were detailed, signed, witnessed and sealed. Her husband provided her with a generous monthly allowance which was far greater than her needs. However, from her point of view, she never had to see him, speak to him or make contact with him at any time in the future. Her dislike of the man had become so intense that even the thought of him having any physical contact with her made her shudder. On his side, he had an apartment in London, a handsome salary, a major appointment in the Government and, best of all, he could work all the hours of the day and night with no one to hassle him or reproach him for not being there. Both of them were free to do as they wished without the shackles and fetters of their marriage which locked them together. In truth, they never needed to see each other again. Templeton was in his glory, applying himself wholeheartedly to his work while Diana welcomed her privacy and freedom albeit she was not able to function fully because of her failed memory. But that was no longer his problem. The parting was sweet, without argument or rancour, and they both revelled in the agreement.

CHAPTER NINE

It was two months later when Gloria telephoned Diana with regard to playing bridge.

'I haven't seen you at Sandra's salon having your hair done lately,' she began lightly. 'When are you going to resume your place at the bridge table?'

'Yes... bridge!' returned Diana thoughtfully. 'I'd like to play again. Where are you meeting next and where?'

'At my place as usual,' stated Gloria which was no help to Diana because she didn't have the faintest idea of the location.

'Samantha and Jane were asking about you, so come to forty-four tomorrow evening if it fits in with your plans.'

'Yes I'm free,' declared Diana worryingly. 'Forty-four...'

'Westley Gardens,' cut in the other woman suddenly recalling that her friend had lost her memory. 'Make it seven o'clock.'

Diana sighed with relief at the information. Without it she would have been completely lost. After replacing the receiver, she went through a number of drawers in the furniture in the lounge and her bedroom. There had to be a diary of events or a record of the names and telephone numbers of her friends somewhere. However despite her desperate efforts to locate it, she was eventually forced to give up.

The four women met the following evening and after being handed a glass of sherry they made themselves comfortable at the green-baized table in the centre of the room. Diana remembered having a vision of the four of them playing cards there some time ago but it was only momentary.

'How are you now?' asked Samantha earnestly. 'Has your memory come back?'

'I wish!' retorted Diana curtly. 'Everything's still pretty foggy. I get occasional flashes of the past but it's impossible to marry them up with anything.'

'What a terrible thing to happen,' intervened Jane sympathetically. 'Did you see your attacker? Do you know what he looked like?'

'I know I did but as I have amnesia I can't remember anything at all. In fact I'm scared that I'll go to sleep one night and wake up recalling it. I've no idea what my reaction would be.'

'Those Arabs are horrible people,' cut in Gloria acrimoniously.

‘Isn’t that a little xenophobic,’ reproached Samantha. ‘Not all people are the same.’

‘They’re horrible!’ repeated her host sharply. ‘Horrible! Dressed in rags… looking like gypsies. Sleeping in tents in the desert or in awful hovels built on sand. And you can’t trust any of them!’

‘I met a lawyer… an Arab lawyer… who studied at Oxford.’ stated Diana firmly although she realised she would never influence her host to reality. ‘He was a fine young man dressed in Western clothing.’

‘Was?’ challenged Jane. ‘What happened to him?

‘I didn’t mean to use the past tense. He’s still alive. My husband employed him to check on me every few days and report back to him.’

‘Well if he went to Oxford,’ added Samantha firmly, ‘he must be civil to say the least.’

‘Now that you mention it, Diana, we haven’t seen anything of your husband for quite some time. How is he?’

There was a long pause before Diana replied. ‘My husband and I have separated,’ she admitted openly. It was the first time she had revealed the secret to anyone but it hardly mattered now as she considered that the other women were her friends. There was no point in hiding the fact from them as they would certainly learn the truth at some time or another. She looked at the pack of playing cards on the table eager to get on with the game. ‘We split up and that’s it! Okay… let’s play cards!’

The room went dreadfully silent as Gloria shuffled the pack and dealt them. None of the women knew what to say about Diana’s revelation and they declined to respond to it.

‘One club,’ offered Samantha loudly as though her partner would not be able to hear her even at such close proximity.

‘Double!’ countered Jane confidently.

‘Two clubs,’ uttered Diana, unhappy with the cards she held in her hand but insistent on making a contribution.

‘Double!’ Gloria almost shouted the words in the hope that her partner would respond.

‘Three clubs,’ ventured Samantha intent on playing the first hand herself.

‘Three hearts!’ Jane was determined to play the hand and bid accordingly.

Everyone passed and after the first card was laid down by Diana and the dummy went down. As it did so, play became halted as Jane’s inquisitiveness overcame her.

‘I can’t believe you and your husband have split up,’ she blurted, folding the cards. ‘You made such a handsome couple. Why did it happen?’

‘Especially as you’d lost your memory,’ cut in Samantha, taking an interest in the conversation. ‘What was the reason?’

‘He was totally into his work… I couldn’t even remember who he was. It’s quite clear that we fell out of love a long time ago so we discussed the problem civilly and came to the conclusion that our lives ran on different tracks. Thereafter, we decided to call it a day. It was the most sensible thing to do.’

‘But you’re not getting divorced, are you?’ pressed Gloria trying to carve out every detail.

‘No, we’re not. It’s a legal separation which has worked out very well for me,’ Diana told them frankly. ‘I have the house, a generous monthly income, all the bills are paid and best of all, I don’t have to see him. He has his work which he dotes on and an apartment in London. There’s no other woman in his life, if that’s what you’re thinking… just work. The good news for him is that he’s been appointed Deputy to the Minister of Health.’

‘That sounds a very good arrangement for you,’ reflected Samantha wishing to get on with the game. ‘Shall we continue?’

They were about to restart when Diana closed her eyes to welcome a vision from the past. She saw herself playing out a hand in three no trumps with the same three women. She played one round of hearts but on the second ply Gloria threw the three of clubs indicating that she had no hearts. Diana played a third round of hearts and Gloria produced the queen of hearts. In the vision, Diana stared at the woman in disbelief and her face puckered into anger rebounding on her.

‘You revoked!’ she gasped in annoyance. ‘You played the three of clubs on my heart and when I continued you threw the queen of hearts. That’s a revoke and you lose a trick… you lose a trick… you lose a trick.’ She opened her eyes to find the three women staring at her bleakly.

‘My dear,’ began Gloria sympathetically. ‘What’s wrong?’

‘You revoked with the queen of hearts!’

‘That was ages ago,’ explained the host surprised at the late allegation. ‘It was a year ago.’

‘A year ago?’ repeated Diana blankly, then her chest heaved and tears welled-up in her eyes. ‘I could have sworn it just happened. My memory… … … ‘ she tailed off sobbing.

It was the end of the game… the end of the evening for the four women. Gloria eventually rang for a taxi and Diana left still sobbing with embarrassment. Her memory was coming back but it was so fragmented that she was unable to put the pieces together in the right order. It was like a haphazard jigsaw. What a fool she had made of herself! It would be some time before she could find the courage to go back at that card table again with the same players.

She was so upset that her hands shook and her eyes were blurred from weeping. As a result, she made an error with her tablets that night. Instead of taking two ferradil-x pills she accidentally swallowed three of them. Her mind was still trying to cope with the embarrassment at Gloria's house and she mishandled the tablets. After swallowing them, she realised what she had done but considered that it made little difference whether she took two or three of them. However that inference was far from correct as she was about to learn. She lay between the luxurious sheets in bed but the incident in the card table refused to expunge itself from her mind. Sleep would not come.

At about two o'clock in the morning, her body suddenly became racked with pain. She became agonised from heat to toe, with reactions in every organ, every limb, every muscle and every tissue without recourse. She screamed out at the top of her voice but no one could hear her and she was forced to endure the agony for about ten minutes during which period she was certain that she was about to die. The change in her body structure was clearly another of the side-effects from the tablets and the intensity was so great that she could hardly stand it. When the pain subsided, she rose very slowly from the bed, finding that her movements were excessively slow and difficult. A great rage of fatigue ran through her body as she switched on the light to look at herself in the full-length mirror. As she did so, she screamed at the top of her voice and threw her arms across her face. Her brain cried out inside her skull at the awful sight before her. After a few moments, she moved them to confirm the change that had taken place, receiving the shock of her life. She was no longer the youngish beautiful woman of whom she was so proud but an ancient-looking old hag. Her face was heavily wrinkled, with great puffs under her eyes and thick lines creeping across her forehead. Her hair had turned white and the skin under her chin hung down like a huge crop. She lifted her nightdress to observe her body which had equally aged exposing a mass of hanging flesh. She was a woman well over a hundred years old and it went through her mind that her life was over. How could this have happened so quickly? It was a nightmare and she pinched herself to check whether or not it was real. There was no doubt that she could never show herself in public… not in this way. She cried out again in anguish and turned her eyes away from the mirror in despair, reaching out with one arm to steady herself to the bed. It was a bitter end to her life and she would have no answer when people wanted to know how she had aged so fast.

She turned again towards the mirror, hoping that the image would disappear but it failed to do so. It was real; she was a very old woman! After looking at herself for the best part of two minutes, with her brain seizing up on the fear of dying, she returned to the bed and sobbed heartily as a result of her adverse condition. It wasn't long before she fell asleep. When she awoke in the morning, she hurried to the mirror again with fear striking in her heart. To her amazement, her face and body had restored themselves and her hair had turned black again. She was normal… once more a forty-three year old woman who looked as though she was only twenty-eight. She was very aware how it had happened and she was determined not to make the same mistake again. She would never take three ferradil-x tablets instead of the two either morning or night. It would never happen again! She peered deeply into the mirror touching her face with the tips of her fingers, delighted that her body had also returned to normality. It was an experience she hoped would never occur again at any time in the future.

CHAPTER TEN

Diana was having lunch in the dining room watching the television a month later when the doorbell rang. She answered it to face a short stubby middle-aged man wearing a smart grey-striped suit. His podgy face exhibited thick flabby lips and his black hair was parted neatly in the middle. He held a large bouquet of beautiful flowers in his hand which he held before him.

'Hello!' he greeted warmly with a smile touching his flabby lips. 'You may remember me. I'm Alan Greenfield. I've been here three times at your parties.' He offered her the flowers but she refused to take them staring at him without recognition. As far as she was concerned, he was a complete stranger to her. 'I have something important to discuss.'

'I don't remember you,' Mr. Greenfield,' she returned, biting her bottom lip for failing to recall any incident with the man.

'I know all about your amnesia,' he went on. 'I spoke to Charles the other day and he told me about your condition.'

She riled at the thought that she was being discussed with other people by her husband. 'You know my husband?' The last thing she expected was a friend of her husband to call on her.

'Yes… you might say that we work together.' He paused as though to pick up courage offering her the bouquet again but she ignored his action. 'May I come in? I'd like to talk to you. It is important.'

She hesitated for a moment and then opened the door widely to let the man enter, leading him into the lounge. 'Pour yourself a drink if you must,' she invited negatively.

He placed the bouquet of flowers on the coffee-table before moving behind the cocktail cabinet to stare at the bottles. 'Do you want one?'

'It's a little early for me but I will have a martini.' She watched the man like a cat ready to pounce on a bird.

He poured out two drinks handing one to her before sitting down. 'Lechaim!' he toasted cheerfully, holding up his glass towards her. 'It's all right,' he explained, 'I'm Jewish and that's a Jewish toast.'

'What did you want to talk to me about, Mr. Greenfield?' Her voice was cold and sharp.

'I spoke to Charles and he told me that you'd separated,' he said slowly, moving into dangerous territory. 'Allow me to express my regrets. It must have hit you badly.' He was pretending to be suave but it wasn't working for him.

'Why do you say that?' she demanded waiting to hear the reason for his presence at her home.

He seemed somewhat embarrassed by her question. 'Well... two people who've been married for a long time with two grown up children. Separation is a big step from a marriage.'

'That's just the point,' she countered curtly. 'With separation there is no marriage!'

He sipped his drink slowly. 'Indeed, Diana. I hope you don't mind me calling your by your first name.'

She began to tire of the game and demanded an explanation. 'Why are you here? What's so important that you want to discuss?'

He hesitated for a few moments to get his mind into gear and took a large sip of his drink for Dutch courage. 'I hope you don't think I'm too precocious,' he began nervously, his flabby lips moving up and down, 'but at your parties here I became besotted by you. I couldn't help but see you in an amorous light.'

She was stunned by his overture. 'Would you kindly clarify that remark please,' she insisted.

He inhaled deeply before replying. 'You're a very beautiful lady,' he told her awkwardly knowing that his delivery was all wrong. 'You look so young and attractive. I have to admit I couldn't take my eyes off you and I went home dreaming about you. I've come here today, knowing that you've separated from your husband, to see whether you'll allow me to take up the reins.'

'Take up the reins!' she repeated in astonishment. She was shocked by his unsolicited advances and stared at him angrily. 'You're a middle-aged man, Mr Greenfield. I'm sure that you're married and have children. To be crude, you have your own wife to make love to.'

'Love!' he echoed. 'There's an old saying that Jewish foreplay is twenty minutes of begging. My wife doesn't understand me. We haven't made love with each other for years. She's not the one I desire.'

Diana was affronted by the proposition and she stood up indignantly.' Get out!' she shouted. 'Get out of this house right away, you horrible man! You think you can have an affair with me? When hell freezes over! Get that into your mind!'

'Is it because I'm Jewish?' he asked lamely.

'It has nothing to do with religion!' she snapped harshly.

'But every woman has needs. Sexual needs. Just because you lost your memory doesn't mean you've become a vegetable. You need love in your life and I'm the one willing to give it to you.'

Diana started to lose her temper at his prevarication. 'I said get out! Don't you understand English?' she shouted vehemently.

Greenfield placed his wine glass on the coffee-table and moved towards the door. 'Does this mean you're not interested?' he continued with sincerity. 'Only some women say no when they mean yes. It's a common feature between men and women.'

'Out… you horrible little weasel!' There was no mercy in her tone of voice. She picked up the bouquet of flowers and followed him to the front door. She opened it and thrust the flowers into his hands. He placed one hand into his pocket and produced a calling card. 'If you happen to change your mind…'

The expression on her face emulated that of Medusa in Greek mythology and he scurried out of the house quickly without looking back leaving the flowers in the hallway. If there was one thing she disliked it was Greeks bearing gifts.

She returned to the lounge and picked up the two glasses. What an outrage! The colleague of her husband having the nerve to try to proposition her when he discovered that she had separated from her husband. She was extremely indignant although she should have been flattered. What did he think she was… … a courtesan playing the field? Well she soon sent him packing! For certain she had no time in her life for men at present… certainly not one with a wife and family at home. Her only aim was to recover her memory. That was the priority. Nothing else mattered!

* * * * *

Six months soon passed by and Diana made arrangements to visit Dr. Mahmoud in Morocco. The time had gone very quickly and she clenched her diary in which she had recorded every detail of the side-effects she had suffered over the past half year. He was sitting at his desk as she waltzed into his office and sat in the chair opposite him confidently. He looked up from the notes he had been reading and a slight smile touched his lips as he recognised her.

'Mrs. Templeton! How is my experimental patient?' he asked with a twinkle in his eye for in his opinion she looked exceedingly well.

'I'm fine, thank you,' she returned brightly, passing her diary over the desk.

He stared at it, picking it up, and turned the cover to read the first page. 'Very interesting,' he muttered as his eyes gazed at the text. 'So that's what's been happening to you.' He paused to look up at her. 'I presume you've been taking the tablets every day as I prescribed.'

'Of course. I never miss a day. But the side-effects still continue. You told me they would go away but they haven't... not completely.'

'It's all very experimental,' he explained easily. 'We're reaching the boundaries of science and overtaking it. No one knows what reactions will occur. That's probably the most exciting thing about it. We extend the boundaries and go on from there.'

'It's not so exciting when you're the one who has to suffer the side-effects,' she complained as she thought of some of the episodes that had frightened her.

'When you know they're going to happen you should be prepared for them,' came the response.

Her mind went back to the night when she had become a very old woman and a chill ran down her spine at the thought of it.

'Unfortunately there are some that we cannot be prepared for,' she volleyed fiercely. 'I think you'll find one of them on page eight in the diary.' There was silence for a few moments and then she ventured a question which had been on her mind for some time. 'How would I cope if anything happened to you?' Her heart beat a little faster at the fearful idea. 'I would run out of tablets and no one would be able to provide them for me.'

His face broke into a broad grin. 'My dear Mrs. Templeton,' he laughed. 'I take ferradil-x tablets every day as well. You don't think I'd let you gain all the benefits of this experiment and not get anything out of it myself. As you go forward into immortality, I shall do the same. You never need to concern yourself about the supply of tablets.'

Immortality! She might be able to cope with the knowledge that her features might not age and that she might live to the grand old age of two hundred but now the doctor was talking of immortality... living forever! Surely the scientist had to be somewhat over-ambitious in his research. It was an accepted fact that everyone who lived had to die at some time. The idea of continuing life forever was very daunting... much more than any human-being could handle.

'You talk of immortality,' she forwarded casually. 'You can't be serious.'

'Maybe and maybe not,' he retorted. 'Experiments take time and science progresses in small stages with regard to the human body. In time, it may be possible. We shall be like machines with organ transplants produced by other methods, which will be used when different parts of our bodies malfunction. As for us, at the present, we simply have to wait until it happens.' He turned over the pages of her diary and read some more. 'Tell me about the time when you body grew old.'

She explained the pain and anguish she had suffered that night to tell him of her mistake by taking three ferradil-x tablets instead of two.

'Is your memory improving?' he asked.

'Not very much,' she replied bluntly with sadness in her voice. 'Sometimes I have visions related to the past but they're fragmented. I can't seem to marry them up with anything.

He shrugged his shoulders with a slight smile touching his lips and he pulled on his goatee beard. 'We can't expect miracles in everything we do,' he rambled on. 'Only occasionally.'

Diana left the office with a two large boxes of tablets feeling highly delighted that the scientist was using ferradil-x himself. It gave her far more confidence to continue with the experiment. There were two of them now involved in the research. However, a visit to Dr. Mahmoud was not the only reason she had flown to Agadir. She was determined to see Ahmed in order to keep in touch with him. There was no obvious reason or intent for the action, simply an instinct to see him again now that she was in the country. She took a taxi to his office and found him poring over some legal documents.

'You may not wish to see me again but I've come anyway,' she began as he looked up to see her.

He rose to his feet with a surprised expression on his face and thrust out his hand. 'Mrs. Templeton... Diana!' he gasped joyfully, shaking her hand vigorously. 'I'm so pleased to see you!' He raced around the desk to bring forward a chair so that she could sit down. He returned to his seat to face her. 'How marvellous! I must say you're looking much better.'

'I hope I'm not interfering with your work,' she said frowning slightly.

'Not al all... not at all!' he beamed. 'It's all rather boring stuff anyway. Tell me what happened to you in the last six months. Has your memory returned?'

'Not really,' she confessed. 'I've separated from my husband and I'm leading the life of a lady.' She felt like biting her tongue for having blurted out the information. He didn't need to know. There was a brief silence before she continued. 'How's your family?' She recalled the hovel in which she had lived in briefly and momentarily shuddered.

'As families are,' he retorted staring at her seriously. 'So you've left your husband. I have to say he showed very little interest in you at your time of need. Tell me... do you still dream about me?'

She burst into laughter delighted that she had come to see him. 'Don't get above yourself,' she guffawed. 'I haven't had a dream in months.'

There was an awkward silence for a few moments and then he posed a direct question. 'Why have you come to see me? I mean we don't really know each other.'

She seemed put out by his directness and sought to find an answer. 'I came to Agadir to see Dr. Mahmoud so I thought I'd visit you as well.'

'Is this fate... or destiny... or something else?' he asked casually. She failed to reply so he rose and went towards the door. 'I'll fetch you some coffee. I'll back in two shakes of a lamb's tail.' He left the room and she stared at the law books on the shelves and the files stacked up on the floor.

'Espresso if you have it,' she shouted. 'Not that awful black stuff in those tiny little cups!'

His laughter could be heard from the other room and Diana searched in her mind for the reason why she had come to see him. When she had set out from England, the only thing in her mind was the appointment with Dr. Mahmoud. Suddenly she found herself sitting in Ahmed's office. There was no logic in her being drawn to him.

He returned shortly with two cups of coffee and handed one to her. 'So you don't dream about me anymore,' he said with an amused tone in his voice. 'I'm sorry to hear that... not that it affects me at all.' He sat down behind the desk to face her.

'Truth is I don't dream at all,' she admitted candidly. 'I'm sure I used to enjoy it.'

'What did Dr. Mahmoud have to say to you?'

'He was quite satisfied with my progress.'

'But your memory is still not good. I don't need to have the gift of Mohammed to realise that you're still suffering.'

'You're very perceptive,' she retorted with surprise.

'I'm not only a lawyer,' he boasted easily. 'I have other talents. When are you going back to England?'

'Maybe tonight. It all depends.' She sipped her coffee and found it to be reasonable.

'Depends on what?'

'Whether I decide to stay on or not,' she replied, placing the cup down on the desk.

He drummed his fingers on the desk not knowing how to continue the conversation. 'Does your decision have anything to do with me?'

She burst out laughing again. 'I don't think so, Ahmed,' she returned curtly. ‘It all depends on whether I can get a flight. My visit here was just to see you… an old friend.’

He seemed to relax with relief at her response having been concerned that she wanted more of him than he wished to give. In his opinion, she was a very lovely lady, now separated from her husband but she was so much older than him. Added to that she was British and knew nothing about the Arab culture.

‘I don’t think you really know why you’ve come here,’ he ventured bluntly, not caring whether he offended her.

She paused to think for a short while. ‘Do you know, you’re absolutely right. I don’t know. I mean there’s no intent in my mind with anything regarding you. I don’t wish to be crass but all I can say is that you’re a very pleasant man with whom I’m not in love. I don’t think you’ve anything to offer me. In fact I’d say it wouldn’t matter if we never saw each other again.’

They stared at each other with strange expressions on their faces and Diana wondered why she had made such a critical comment.

‘Yet you’re sitting here in my office,’ he rationalised clenching his hands in front of him. ‘Age is not always important between a man and a woman,’ he went on calmly. ‘But think on this… when I am your age, you’ll be over sixty years old. It’s all very well to dream about me but in real life there’s a wide chasm between us.’

She felt embarrassed at his gentle tirade and stood up to leave.

‘I knew I was wrong to come,’ she declared sadly, ‘but you’re one of the few people I’ve got to know since the attack. You don’t realise how much that means to me.’

He shrugged his shoulders intending to apologise for his remarks but he was too late because she left the office causing him

to feel guilty.

‘Of course,’ he thought to himself. ‘She has amnesia and I’m one of the few people she considers to be her friend in Agadir.’ Nonetheless, he knew in his heart that, as far as anything else was concerned, that the bridge between them on a number of points was too far to span. She was Christian; he was a Moslem. She was forty-three; he was so much younger. She lived in England; he was in Morocco. The bridge was much too far to span!

* * * * *

After she returned to England, Diana felt listless. The main thing she wanted when separating from her husband was freedom. But now it had been attained, it was a total bore. In truth, she had so much time on her hands life had become extremely dull. She was on her own for most of the time as she failed to recognise anyone in particular as her friend. Ultimately, she began to rue the life that she was leading. Then, one day, she rose early as a new idea came into her mind. The house boasted a large loft that she and her husband had once considered turning into two bedrooms. However when that prospect died a death, they began to store lots of bric-a-brac and family treasures up there. Throughout the years, they had placed many items there which had grown to a considerable amount. If she sorted through the items, she might find something that would trigger thoughts of the past in her mind and help to dispel the amnesia. She went to the upper hallway and pulled down the metal ladder, climbing the steps steadily to enter the loft. There were numerous wooden chests and some cardboard boxes located there. She looked into one of the boxes to find toys and dolls once so beloved by Robbie and Karen. She stared at some of the other objects… the pushchair for Karen as a young child, the football kicked by Robbie, the long cane which her husband once used, the broad-rimmed hat she had worn once on a holiday abroad. She stared at a large blond-haired teddy bear momentarily recalling that her son used to go to bed holding it. Her heart began to beat faster as she realised that there was light at the end of the tunnel. She was able to remember some odd items. Her search continued and, in another box, she discovered an enormous large magnet. Her husband had once run all over the house waving it at items, attracting all kinds of metal objects to its magnetic tips, laughing loudly as he did so. She remembered having called him a fool but it was one of those magical moments that creates fun within a marriage for, as soon as he stopped playing with the magnet, they had hugged each other fiercely. Then they kissed and went up to the bedroom together to make passionate love. That was the day Robbie was conceived. Yes… some of it was starting to come back to her now although there were good days and bad days. She rummaged through a chest to find the beautiful dress she had worn at her wedding. It looked rather faded now, having turned slightly yellow from the original shining white, and then she came across a colourful fan she had purchased when they visited Brighton. It had been the centrepiece of the shop window and it had taken her fancy. Her husband paid a pretty price for her to own it. Those were the days when they were young and in love! She found a pair of red shoes

That she had worn at a friend's party. My goodness, she thought, that was twenty-five years ago! She sat on the edge of a chest looking at them lovingly. She was so beautiful that night; everybody had told her so. But it was the red shoes which had made her look so wonderful. Then she found the dress she had worn on the same evening. It was red to match the shoes and quite low-cut. She had met her husband there that evening and they immediately fell in love. He was very handsome, dressed in a tuxedo with a large black bow tie. He showed her so much love and tenderness, paying attention to her the whole evening and for years afterwards. How time and situations changed people as they continued with their lives! Yes… it started to come back to her although the visions catered for only a small window of the past.

She continued to rummage more items, surprised at what she found, but nothing more registered in her memory. She took a number of treasures down the ladder when she left and laid them on the table in the dining room. What connection did she have with an old Bush electric radio? Was it the first one that she and her husband bought? Did they listen to it every evening? And what about the empty bottle of Moet & Chandon champagne? There had to be a special reason for it to be stored in the loft so many years ago. She looked hard at a tome entitled 'The Book Of Dreams' recalling that she hadn't dreamt for a long time. One pundit talking on television had said that everyone had to dream or they would go mad. Well perhaps she was mad… perhaps she was after all. Having only half a mind was pretty much there anyway. A book of dreams! That was something to interest her over the next few days. She recalled Mohammed, the visionary in Agadir, and wondered what he would make of the contents of it. He said he was an interpreter of dreams although he tended to dwell on the obvious. Maybe this tome would have enlightened him except that he would never have the chance.

She handled each of the items brought down with great care, struggling to recall why they had been kept. She was delighted to have remembered about the large teddy bear which belonged to her son. However she considered that she had failed in the effort, with the exception of the bear, her red dress and the shoes, because she realised she could not remember anything about all the other items.

After a while, she gave up trying to think about the past and placed the items in a corner of the room hoping to return to them another day and try again. If fortune favoured her, the memories of the reason why they had meant so much to her would come to the fore. She could only hope, that in the course of time, something would figure in her mind to retrieve some wonderful old memories.

CHAPTER ELEVEN

As the months passed by, Diana contacted Gloria in the hope that the group would still want to play bridge with her again. The woman was delighted to receive the telephone call making no bones about welcoming her back to the fold. When she arrived at the apartment, the host clutched Diana's hand firmly in friendship.

'We really missed you,' she told her with a smile on her face. 'While you were away we had to put up with my neighbour for a fourth who can't play for toffee. I'm delighted you're back and ready to play.'

The four women sat down at the green-baize table making themselves comfortable ready to start playing. However Jane felt obliged to ask whether there had been any progress in Diana's health.

'I don't suppose you've had any joy with your memory,' she uttered, almost as though the subject was clandestine.

'Don't keep on at her!' reproached Gloria sharply. 'She'll tell you all about it in the tea break.'

Diana smiled at them warmly. 'Don't concern yourself on my behalf. I'm all right in health and in spirit. Let's play cards. That's what we're here for.'

'I think you're handling your problem very well,' Gloria ventured shuffling the cards. 'But there is something I must say. My friend recently went to a therapist and she was helped tremendously.'

'I don't think a therapist would be of any use to me,' retorted Diana firmly. 'It's a matter of time before my memory returns.'

'You never know what a therapist might turn up,' uttered Jane trying to help her friend.

'Tessa Wainwright went to see one. She caught her foot on the edge of a paving stone and fell over suffering awful problems with her head for weeks,' continued Gloria still shuffling the cards. 'The doctor wasn't able to cure her and sent her for a scan which showed nothing. Then she went for five sessions to this therapist and came out a new woman. There's no harm in trying.'

'I wouldn't know where to look for one,' admitted Diana, more interested in getting on with the game than chatting aimlessly about her condition.

'That's easy,' joined in Samantha brightly. 'Just go to your doctor. He'll recommend one.'

'I can't see how it will help me,' insisted Diana adamantly, becoming impatient at have to wait for the cards to be dealt. 'Can we play now? I feel lucky this evening.'

Gloria shrugged her shoulders and dealt out the cards with a final caustic remark. 'There's none so deaf as those who won't hear.' she muttered almost under her breath although everyone at the table could hear her.

When she returned home that evening, Diana sat in the lounge sipping a dry martini thinking about the conversation with her three friends. They were right. There was no harm in seeking the help of a therapist. After all, if the first session proved to be negative she didn't have to go again. But what did a therapist actually do? She looked up the word in the dictionary which referred her to 'psychotherapy' and she read the description out aloud. "Psychotherapy is the treatment of emotional and psychometric disorders based on the application of psychological knowledge, rather than exclusively on the use of drugs, surgery or other physical treatment." She pulled a face after reading the description three times trying to absorb the meaning but it made no sense to her. Still, if there were no drugs involved and no surgery or other physical treatment she would definitely come to no harm... but what use would it do? Nonetheless, maybe a visit to a therapist was the answer. After all, nothing would be lost.

Her local doctor was less than enthusiastic about her decision. He failed to understand how a therapist would be successful in getting her memory back. At her insistence, however, he picked up the telephone receiver and dialled a number contacting Vivien Williams who he knew was well-known in his field and he made an appointment for her.

When the day arrived, she sat in the waiting room and stayed there for ten minutes before her name was called. She was shown into a room to meet the expert. He was a short tubby man with a bald head and an unusually large nose which was red at the tip, indicating that he over-enjoyed imbibing wine or spirits. His clothing was strange in that he wore a black garment which covered his ordinary clothes, similar to a priest's cassock, with a large gold disc at his chest which hung from a slender chain around his neck. As she entered the room, his head moved forward and backward similar to a parrot in a cage and he moved in his chair as if to try to make himself look taller.

'Mrs. Templeton.' he began, placing his hands in front of him on the desk. 'Please take a seat.'

'I thought I was seeing a female therapist,' she complained. 'Vivian Williams.' She sat down in a comfortable executive chair opposite the therapist.

'Vivien's a name used by both men and women,' he returned with a slight smile on his fat face. 'En for a man; An for a woman. I understand you've been suffering from loss of memory.'

He was not slow in cutting to the chase. No good morning... how are you... tell me a little about yourself. He went straight to the point.

'I was attacked by a gunman who blew off part of my skull but the shock caused me to lose my memory,' she explained briefly. She sighed becoming very tired at having to tell the same story over and over again.

He stood up and walked around the desk to stand behind her. 'Let me have a look.' He rummaged gently through her hair at the back of her head before moving it one way and then the other. 'Hm,' he muttered afterwards, 'you have a nasty scar there.' He retreated to his chair and placed his hands in front of him clenching them together this time before looking directly into her eyes. 'As you're no doubt aware, memories are experiences from the past. Three processes are required: registration, in which the experience is received in the mind; retention, in which a permanent memory trace or engram is preserved in the brain; and, thirdly, recall in which a particular memory is brought back into the consciousness. It's the third one that's causing you problems. The part of the brain which harbours the memory is the hippocampus... either of two ridges along each lateral ventrical of the brain that form part of the limbic system.'

Diana stared at the man as though he had just arrived from another planet speaking a strange language that she didn't understand. It was clear that he knew his subject but how was a patient expected to translate all that gobbledegook? The man had lost the art of plain speaking and Diana wondered how his other patients felt about the situation. There was a long pause as his hand moved to the large gold disc hanging from his neck and he manipulated it slowly from side to side. 'Have you been sleeping well lately?' he asked innocuously in a deep tone of voice. 'Only you appear to be tired. Very tired. Very very tired. You really want to go to sleep. You need sleep. Lots of sleep.'

Diana stared at the golden disc bleakly and then shook her head slowly. 'I'm sorry, Mr. Williams,' she said, stopping him in his tracks., 'but you won't be able to hypnotise me. It's been tried before but, apparently, I have a strong resistance which means it doesn't work on me.'

His face was unmoved by her declaration and he stopped playing with the golden disc. 'Very well,' he went on undaunted. 'Let me say that loss of memory in some cases is entirely false. The reason for it is psychosomatic whereby the brain is affected by various reason of stress or guilt causing the defect. It might be totally involuntary.'

'I assure you that in my case the memory loss is real,' she countered. 'The reason I'm here today is because I'm desperate to recover it.'

He nodded slowly and moved his hands away from the desk. 'Then let's go to the next stage,' he uttered confidently. 'Most people find it easier to remember by word association. By this means, links are forged in your mind between new impressions and those you experienced before. One thing reminds you of another and a chain of thought is created which lays down the new impression to be stored and reproduced when required.'

'What are these word associations?' asked Diana with an element of interest sparking in her mind, hoping that the therapist was a genius and not a charlatan.

'Let's focus on your childhood,' continued Williams. 'Can you remember anything about it at all?'

His patient shook her head. 'Not a thing!'

'Focus your mind on prams, rattles, nappies, school, parents, night lights, buses...'

'Buses?' she interrupted rudely. 'What association can I have with buses in terms of my childhood?'

'The mind plays unusual tricks on memory,' he informed her sagely. 'One never knows what will help it to kick in. I'll repeat them again... prams, rattles, nappies, school, parents, night lights, buses. Do any of those items trigger anything in your mind? Think hard!' Diana thought for a moment and shook her head again. 'How about colours? Red, green, blue, brown, violet, orange, purple, gold, silver, the monarchy.

Is this man for real, she thought to herself. How could the monarchy be included in colours? What was he trying to prove?

'No,' she replied, beginning to think that her visit here was a complete waste of time.

'Clubs, diamonds, hearts, spades and forks,' he went on unaffected by her negativity.

'There you have me,' returned Diana smartly. 'I play bridge with three women every week. They were the ones who suggested I come to see you.'

'Go back in your mind with bridge,' he persisted, thinking he might have found a way to resolve her problem. 'Close your eyes, go back, and think hard.'

She obeyed his command and closed her eyes tightly. Then the vision came. She was playing in three no trumps and Gloria revoked in hearts. Diana was reliving the moment again only this time the vision continued. As it played out in her mind, Gloria apologised for the error and the game continued to the next hand in which Samantha played in five diamonds. Diana opened her eyes as the vision ended and stared at the therapist. 'I did go back to a hand played a year ago,' she told him.

'Excellent!' he exclaimed jubilantly. 'Now... the important thing is to marry up the memory with something that occurred recently.'

'That's simple enough. I play cards with the people in that vision regularly.'

'Right... let's focus on that for the time being. One memory at a time.' He continued his game of word association for the best part of half an hour and then suggested that Diana booked a series of further appointments. 'There is another alternative,' he told her finally. We could always resort to electroshock treatment. I believe that could be the way forward for you. With that treatment, contacts are applied to your head and then a series of electrical charges are passed through your brain. The end result might be the restoration of your memory. It may be the best way ahead.'

She cringed at the idea and it helped her to expedite her departure. It was the catalyst that drove her away from him for ever. Electroshock treatment with electric charges through her brain... he had to be out of his mind! She regretted having gone to the man in the first place. Nothing had been gained in the session. Nothing of any importance emerged in the time she spent with him but her head was spinning form all that he had told her. What the heck was an engram? She had never heard of it before let alone consider that she might have one. But the point that really irritated her was the fact that he tried to hypnotise her without her permission. She wasn't sure whether he was breaking the law by doing that but clearly he had used the operation on his other patients. What kind of therapist was he not to inform his patient about it first? As far as she was concerned, Vivien Williams, with an En, was a very clever man but her problem was out of his reach. Shock treatment? She had trouble trying to expunge the thought from her mind... it was so horrific. No drugs, no surgery no physical treatment... yet he had suggested electroshock treatment! She was certain never to darken the door of his surgery again.

CHAPTER TWELVE

Following their session in Morocco, Laura kept closely in touch with her sister and she telephoned her late one afternoon to press her on the invitation.

'Months have gone by since we last saw each other,' she began in earnest.

'I know, ' agreed Diana sadly. 'Time seems to whiz by. One minute it's one week and then the end of the next week seems to come like a tornado.'

'When we were in Agadir I invited you to come and stay with us. Well Mac and I were talking about it last evening and he's dying to meet you. So how about it? When are you going to come over here and stay? I'm not taking no for an answer.'

Diana was not surprised at the invitation but it peeved her to have to make an instant decision. She had mulled over her sister's offer in Morocco but eventually dismissed the idea. Los Angeles was a long way off and she didn't feel comfortable about imposing on her sister's family even though Laura would have scoffed at any imposition.

'Come on!' urged her sister adamantly. 'Give yourself a break. We have a room waiting for you. The weather's brilliant. Sunshine every day… except when there's the smog from the motor cars.' Her voice trickled into laughter.

Diana weighed up the idea in her mind. Why not? There was no reason for her to stay in England… and it would be only for a couple of weeks anyway. It sounded ideal and, as a lady of leisure, she had the opportunity to take advantage of the offer. The die was cast! 'Okay,' she uttered eventually. 'I'll come on condition that you let me pay my own way. I don't want you to spend your money on me.'

'Will you just get on that plane and come here!' savaged Laura with mock anger in her voice. 'We already have a room for you. The food you eat will be negligible. Get on that plane, sister, and get here as fast as you can. I won't ask you again!'

'Very well,' responded Diana warmly. 'I'll see you when the plane lands at Los Angeles airport.'

'I'll be there waiting for you,' exclaimed Laura with delight at having influenced her sister. 'Don't let us down. We're all dying to meet you. I'll check when the next flight gets into LA and ring you back with the details. The rest is up to you.'

Diana hardly had time to delay the trip because the line went dead. Clearly when Laura got an idea into her head it was difficult to shift it. Everything was happening so fast but that was the way that destiny worked its wonder on people. Some of them won large sums on the lottery, others were lucky with bingo, while investor made or lost their fortunes on the Stock Market. Destiny worked quickly and effectively in many mysterious ways. Going to America was a fantastic opportunity for Diana that wasn't to be missed. She would see new sights in a welcoming country and be with the rest of her family. It was definitely good fortune knocking on her door. Without hesitation and not bothering to wait for her sister to ring back, she contacted the airport and booked a flight later that day for Los Angeles. Excitement began to well up inside her as she put some clothing into a suitcase and found her passport again. She was on her way to see her sister again… on her way to the United States!

When she landed at LAX (Los Angeles Airport), there was a serious problem because she did not have the necessary visa to enter the country. It was extremely fortunate that Laura was there at the immigration barrier waiting to welcome her. She explained to the official that Diana was her sister who was having medical treatment in England and, after a great deal of discussion, they were taken into an interview room where they were able to explain the situation in detail. The fact that Laura, an American citizen, was her sister and that she was had asked her to live with them for only two weeks, and because Diana's husband was an eminent person in the House of Commons, it swung it for her. However, the official interviewing them was less than pleased with the lack of documentation. After it was over, Laura directed her sister to her motor vehicle and drove to her home in South Burbank, north of Los Angeles. It was a large timber building with an outstanding façade, highlighted by a long balcony which ran the length of the house. The location was absolutely beautiful set in the foreground of a wood which was outlined by hills at the rear.

'What a wonderful house!' exclaimed Diana when the car stopped in the driveway.

'It's what Mum and Dad's money bought. As you can see, we didn't squander it.' They climbed out of the car as Mac and the two children came on to the balcony. 'Meet the family!' she said proudly. 'This is Mac and this is Rusty and Chuck.' She looked towards them lovingly. 'This is my sister Diana.'

Diana hesitated then she climbed the steps to the balcony and held out her hand to Laura's husband shaking hands with him vigorously.

'Glad to meet you, Di!' greeted Mac with a broad grin on his face. 'Glad you came over the pond.' He had never met his sister-in-law before and he was surprised at her beauty. She had been a distant person who lived in another country, on another continent, and because the two women fell out as a result of their parents' Will, they hadn't spoken to each other for over nine years. The truth was that he had never even seen a photograph of her. 'Come inside!'

They all entered the house and sat in a very large room filled with furniture. Everything had a material value in terms of comfort. There were two settees, three armchairs, a table, a dresser, exquisite curtains, and lovely carpets. No paintings adorned the walls. Instead fixed there were spears, lances, the horns of a cow, a moosehead and the proverbial hunting rifle over a gigantic hearth. Drinks were poured for everyone, the boys being restricted to cola and orange juice, as Diana acquainted herself with the rest of her family asking Rusty and Chuck about their school, the subjects they studied and their plans regarding employment when they left school. Mac was employed as a motor mechanic but he was negotiating the purchase of his own garage not far away. He talked long and hard about it and it was clear he was extremely enthusiastic about the project.

'Mac's fantastic with cars,' boasted Laura, over the moon that her sister had come across the Atlantic Ocean to stay with her.

'I always knew that Laura had an elder sister from the Court case,' subjected Mac calmly when the boys had left the room to play elsewhere. 'She just didn't tell me how attractive you are.'

'Steady, Mac!' warned Laura with mock irritation. 'This is my sister you're talking about!'

'I didn't mean it that way,' he chided. 'I'm tellin' the truth. She's a beautiful woman.' He turned his attention towards Diana. 'Laura tells me you've separated from your husband. How're you makin' out without him?'

'Not too badly actually,' came the reply. 'It's a relief in a way not to have to face him. You have to understand that I didn't recognise him after I lost my memory. In fact I didn't like the look of him at all when I woke up in hospital.'

'He's a senior Civil Servant,' explained Laura. 'He's a workaholic. Always busy with his work and no time for his family. It's no wonder they separated.'

'I was in hospital in Agadir for quite some time. He never came to visit me. Always too busy with his work in England,' bleated Diana. 'He employed a local lawyer to come in every few days to report to him on my progress.'

'That was Ahmed, wasn't it?' intervened her sister.

Diana regretted having been so bold as to criticise her husband but she could not stop herself from continuing. 'I visited him when I went to see Dr. Mahmoud… the scientist who's treating me.'

‘A scientist in Morocco!’ retorted Mac in surprise. The words seemed to stand out in the room as large as the moose’s head hanging on the wall.

‘It was just a visit, ‘ returned Diana constantly reminding herself of the bridge that separated her from her Arab friend.

‘Well to change the subject, you have a partner for dinner,’ announced Laura proudly. ‘Just a partner, mind you. Nothing more… especially when you find out more about him. His name’s Greg and he’s an old friend.’

Diana shrugged her shoulders aimlessly. ‘You didn’t have to pair me up with someone.’

‘That’s just it,’ her sister went on. ‘We didn’t. It was a coincidence. We hadn’t see him for the best part of a year and then he turned up on the doorstep so I invited him to dinner. I knew that you were coming and that you wouldn’t mind. You’ll like him. He’s a movie producer.’

‘Interesting,’ echoed Diana who was always keen on watching films on television. ‘What has he made? Anything I might have heard of?’

Laura rattled off the names of three films which her sister had seen in England. They were not masterpieces but it was evident that the coming guest was renowned in his profession. ‘I must warn you though. He’s very handsome and he likes pretty women.’

‘Hey!’ laughed Mac pausing after drinkin beer from a can. ‘Who’s steppin’ across the line now?’

When Greg arrived for dinner, Diana stared at him with her eyes wide open. He was certainly handsome… as good as any male film star who wooed the crowds. He was six feet tall, with hair slightly greying long before its time, blue eyes, a masterful face, an athletic figure and he wore a light blue suit that fitted him perfectly. As he entered the room, his eyes fixed on Diana as he scanned her face and figure.

‘Who’s the good-lookin’ dame,’ he asked Laura excitedly clearly impressed with the new visitor.

‘Diana’s my sister,’ declared Laura. ‘She’s come from England to stay with us for a while. And she’s not a dame… she’s a lady.’

Greg smiled briefly before approaching Diana, taking her hand gently and kissing her fingers tenderly. ‘Hi, Diana!’ His voice was smooth and in a low tone. ‘Nice to meet you, honey!’

His hand moved to her chin which he turned slightly one way and then the other staring at her face with his eyes slightly narrowing. ‘I’d like you to take a screen test. I think you might be photogenic enough to be in my movie.’

Diana froze on the spot, surprised that she hadn’t reacted to his actions. She would have been affronted had anyone else taken such a liberty.

‘Do you really think so,’ ventured Laura, excited at the prospect that her sister might be able to take on a role in a movie picture.

‘Look at those features,’ added the film producer. ‘You should have told me you had a younger sister.’

Laura appeared to be insulted by the comment. ‘Just hold it there for a second, Greg,’ she snapped in mock anger. ‘She’s two years older than me I’ll have you know!’

Greg raised his eyebrows. ‘She doesn’t look more than about twenty-eight,’ he said without taking his eyes off Diana’s face.

‘Then I’m twenty-six… I wish,’ laughed Laura teasing him.

Diana was riveted by the man. He had amazing charm which surrounded him like an aura. He had a remarkably easy attitude that was refreshing… overwhelming. However her enthusiasm about him was soon dented.

‘How’s your wife, Greg?’ asked Mac, handing his friend a can of beer.

‘My first, second or third?’ enquired the guest.

Diana’s mouth opened widely in astonishment at Greg’s reply.

‘You’ll need to watch him, I warn you,’ related Laura hurriedly. ‘He’s deadly where women are concerned. He meets them at parties, likes the look of them, charms them, marries them and then divorces them. He’s really a little devil.’

‘Don’t listen to anything she says,’ snorted Greg in mock annoyance, his blue eyes staring directly at Diana. ‘She hates me!

She was extremely sad to learn of the film producer’s weakness with the female sex. He was the kind of man who excited her and she wouldn’t mind becoming involved with him romantically. However his track record with women removed him from the equation. She decided to admire him at arm’s length and take everything that he said with a pinch of salt. It was the best way… it was the only way! A serious romantic relationship with him would almost certainly leave her heartbroken in the end.

They sat down to dinner that evening and Mac carved a giant turkey.

‘I’m serious about that screen test,’ began Greg staring directly into Diana’s eye across the table. Despite her rejection to any advances he might make, she still felt her legs go weak as their eyes met. ‘Come with me to Universal Studios tomorrow. I could arrange for the take then.’

‘I’m not sure I want to be a film star,’ she laughed somewhat embarrassed by the offer. Although she was keen on watching films on television she was completely ignorant with regard to how they were made.

‘You English!’ he chided gently. ‘You’re so sensitive about showing yourselves in the public domain. I’m offering you something that most people would give their right arm for. Come with me tomorrow!’

'Why not?' intervened Laura encouragingly. 'At worst it's a trip around Universal Studios.'

'Go for it!' added Mac. 'You'll never get another chance like it.'

The banter went on through the dinner and, afterwards, the four adults sat drinking in the lounge sitting in comfortable chairs.

'I think I'll take you up on that screen test, Greg,' accepted Diana suddenly. It was an impulsive gesture but life was full of adventure if one let it happen and it compensated for her condition. 'But,' she added. 'I don't know if I could ever remember my lines.'

'If the test is successful,' returned Greg, 'you'll be a waitress in the movie which is called 'Sweet Fountain of Youth' and you'll have only one line to say. It's "Have you decided what you want to order?" That's all. If you can do it in an American accent all the better. What do you think about that?'

'Take a shot at it,' urged Laura quickly. 'As Mac said, you'll never get another chance like this.'

Diana nodded her head meaningfully. Yes... it would be a new adventure. Destiny was beckoning to her again. Her mind ventured into fantasy. Who knew where it all might end if she passed the screen test and took a role in the film. Hundreds of actors and actresses had made their mark that way, starting with a very small part. However at the back of her mind she didn't expect it to go any further. She was forty-three years old. It was far too late for a woman to start an acting career!

Greg left after a while. As he departed, he leaned towards Diana, put his arms around her and kissed her firmly on the lips long and hard. She felt a wave of emotion rush through her body and the warmth of sexual sensation as he did so, and adrenalin passed through her body causing her legs to start to wilt.

'I'll pick you up at ten in the morning,' he informed her briefly after releasing her. He took his hat, waved an arm towards Laura and Mac, and then left.

'I told you to watch yourself,' warned Laura as she closed the front door behind him. 'He's a ladies' man, full of charm, and I don't think he has a conscience.'

Diana went to bed later that night staring at her new surroundings. Everything was strange... the wallpaper, the small chandelier, the paintings on the walls, the four-poster bed, the thick patterned carpets. At this point in time she challenged her decision to come to the United States. Everything was happening so fast, her mind could not keep up with it. The fact that she wanted to meet the rest of her family had caused her to be caught up in the tentacles of fate. And then there was Greg! She thought about the kiss… that warm, sensuous, emotional moment that had thrilled her so much. She hadn't felt that way for a very long time. Regrettably there was no hope of continuing the relationship with a man who couldn't keep his hands off women. It was always going to be a short-term intimacy to say the least. She snuggled into bed between the sheets, fatigued from the flight, and as soon as her head touched the pillow she fell fast asleep. Everything in her life was suddenly becoming important but, by necessity, it would all have to wait until the next day.

* * * * *

Greg arrived at ten o'clock the following morning. He came in a white stretch limousine obviously intending to impress her. She was ready for him dressed appropriately in a short black outfit which came down just above her knees and she climbed rather nervously into the vehicle. The time had come for her to start on her new venture and she wasn't sure that she was ready for it. Greg was a perfect gentleman, opening the door for her and closing it behind her. He then drove directly to Universal Studios where they avoided joining the tourists on the trolley cars. She stared at the lake with a dummy man in a row boat and the shark's fin moving towards it. The dummy fish demolished the vessel and went on to terrify the people in one of the trolley cars, stopping short before it could do any damage.

'That's for the tourists,' informed the film producer. 'As you know, it was a scene to represent the movie 'Jaws',' He pointed to a house which was on fire. 'That's been used in many movies. And over there are the pebbles where they filmed 'Spartacus' starring Kirk Douglas. We go this way. ' He led her to one of the large nissen huts on the site and they entered.

She saw that it was a film studio in itself split into three parts. A small film crew stood at the far end of the hut working to establish a background. One of them waved to her and handed her a microphone.

'Say something… anything,' he ordered. 'We need to test your voice and speech.'

She hesitated for a moment and then recalled the dialogue Greg had mentioned the night before. With the best American accent that she could muster she uttered: "Have you decided what to order?"

Greg was ecstatic. 'You remembered the words I told you!' he said gleefully. 'And the accent wasn't too bad. We'll have to work on it a little.'

A make-up artist came forward to work on her face and then a white apron was placed around her waist and someone handed her a pen and pad.

Greg examined the set and prepared to shoot the scene. 'Remember you'e a waitress… not Greta Garbo. Just take it easy.'

After the screen test, which seemed to please the film producer, Diana did not know whether to laugh or cry. The last thing she wanted to do was to portray herself in a film but she had put her head in a noose and now it had been drawn tight. There was no way she would be able to refuse to take part… not after al the trouble Greg had taken to arrange the screen test. In addition, her sister wouldn't allow her to return to England until she had acted in the film.

She returned to the house and told Laura the good news. 'Greg was very impressed. He wants me to take the part of the actress in the film he's making.'

'You're going to be a film star!' echoed Laura absolutely delighted at the news. 'My sister… a film star!'

'It's only a tiny part,' returned Diana quietly. She had enjoyed the morning, especially being with Greg but she knew that she had to keep her distance. Becoming embroiled with a ladies' man was unnecessary even though the moments that she spent with him would be exceptional. In the long run, however, it simply wasn't worth it.

Greg returned two hours later with a disc of the screen test. 'You can show it to whoever you want to,' he said with a grin all over his face. 'We continue filming that scene in two days' time. You can do your part then.' He took her hand gently. 'Now… how about having dinner with me tonight.'

'What about your third wife?' rattled Diana perniciously.

'She's dining with someone else,' he replied casually as though it didn't matter. 'We're getting a divorce soon so there's no point in us being together.'

'Am I the target for your fourth wife?' she challenged, closing her eyes momentarily for having uttered the words. What a stupid remark to have made. Why didn't she think before she allowed her tongue to go into action?

'Hey!' he laughed loudly, 'aren't you getting a little ahead of yourself? I only invited you to dinner.'

'That's good!' she retorted blandly. 'Only I'm not in love with you. You're too much of a flibbertygibbet for my liking.'

'What's a fliberty… thing do?' he asked jokingly. He was clearly teasing her, possibly lining her up as his next prey.

'Never mind!' she said with a tinge of mock anger in her voice. She had dug a hole for herself and was slowly sliding into it. 'I'll come to dinner with you but that's it… no hankey-pankey! Is that understood?'

He raised his arms as if in defeat. 'I'm a very understanding fella,' he conceded. 'You'll find that out eventually.'

He took her to a fine restaurant on the outskirts of Los Angeles that evening and they faced each other across the table.

'I've known Mac since my schooldays,' he explained, running briefly through his life history. 'He was always a motor mechanic ever since he was a kid. I had my eye on better things. I drifted into the movie industry when someone fell ill at Columbia Studios. Until then, I was a shirt and tie salesman. All that was a long time ago. You see, America's a land of opportunity but, when the time comes, you've got to grasp it with both hands. Otherwise you'll end up like Mac workin' for someone else all your life. The movie industry's alive and you're young enough to may it pay for you.'

'You don't really know how old I am, do you?' She challenged with a smile touching her lips.

'To me you look about twenty-seven or twenty-eight,' he told her smartly believing it to be near the truth.

'I'm almost forty-four,' she revealed although she didn't know why she was being so candid with the man.

'Wow!' he exclaimed shaking his head. 'You really are a stunner. Do you know that? A real stunner. If I'd met you instead of my first wife I reckon we'd still be together. But that's how the cookie crumbles.'

'But you wouldn't have enjoyed yourself so much with your second and third wives,' she fired back at him.

He burst into laughter and shook his head. 'What makes you think I enjoyed myself with them? I was a fool… a complete fool! A pretty face and I fell for it. Do you know why women suck up to me? It's because they want to get into movies and become stars. That's the only reason. And I was nuts to think they were in love with me.'

'Now there's a tale that Shakespeare would have loved to write about,' she returned, admiring his good looks.

'The difference is you're not one of those dumb blondes I married. You've got poise and style and you're intelligent. I could live my life with you very happily. I know it.'

'Well the invitation was for dinner… nothing more.'

He burst into laughter again. 'Gee, you play hardball, Diana,' he told her jokingly, 'and you have humour as well. I like that. You have everything a man could want.' His hands moved across the table to take hold of her hands. 'And whatsmore, you're beautiful… really beautiful.'

It was evident that he was ecstatic about her but it was a one-way street. She couldn't possibly fall in love with a man who had married and divorced two women and was about to do the same to his third wife… whatever the reason. It was inconceivable! For a while she dwelt on the idea of having a brief romantic affair with him but there was a serious problem which could emerge to cause her great difficulty. Lawyers had already been employed to undertake his current divorce. If she became involved with him, she might be quoted as a correspondent in the case. He was a well-known figure in the film industry. As soon as the facts were revealed, she might well be quoted in the litigation as a woman committing adultery with Greg by a detective employed by his third wife. It was too dangerous to become seriously involved regardless of what the man had to offer her. She could well do without the hassle. She would act in his film but, despite his worldly charm, his good looks, and the way she really felt about him, that would be the end of it.

* * * * *

Diana stayed on in America with her sister for a further two months, travelling to San Diego, the ghost town of Calico, the Grand Canyon and, Hoover Dam before spending three days in Las Vegas. The trip to the United States had proved to be exciting in every way. In addition, she was staying with the rest of her family and they had been very kind to her. The main concerns about imposing on her sister were very wide of the mark but there was always a right time to leave and Diana decided that it had finally arrived. She would let her sister, Mac and their children enjoy their own space and the peace of their home by themselves. During the period of her stay, she went out with Greg a number of times. He tried his utmost to create a relationship with her but Diana would have nothing of it. She actually allowed him to hold her and kiss her many times fully on the lips and he fondled her intimately on a few occasions but, at the back of her mind a little imp danced about vigorously telling her that on no account must she succumb to his whims. Nonetheless, she had to admit that the kissing and fondling, and the gentle touching of her body intimately, was much to her liking, making her feel like a real woman again. On occasion, it was all she could do to prevent herself throwing caution to the winds, to let her inhibitions run wild, and throw herself at him. But it had to come to an end. When she told him of her decision to return to England he appeared to be devastated but she regarded his attitude as a mixture of good acting as well as part of his charm. He begged her to come back to Los Angeles in the near future, promising her a much bigger role in his next film. Not surprisingly she declined the offer for a number of reasons yet she felt an emotion of sadness for him. When all was said and done, he had married three times and would shortly be divorced again which meant that he had to suffer three separate periods of unhappiness and rejection. Such damaging incidents took their toll on people's lives even though they pretended to overcome them in due course. It was emotional baggage they were forced to carry for the rest of their natural lives.

On arrival at Heathrow Airport, she was met by her son, Robbie, who hugged her dearly and kissed her on the cheek.

'You really live the high life, don't you, mother?' he began, relieved that she had arrived back safely. 'You can't fool me. I've been talking to Aunt Laura about your antics.'

'You rang your aunt?' she questioned with surprise as he picked up her suitcase and they walked towards his car.

'She told me you were an up-and-coming film star,' he went on, opening the door on the passenger's side for her.

'Hardly that!' she retorted flatly. 'I was in the film for about ten seconds.'

He drove off with a smile touching his lips. 'My mother a film star,' he rambled on. 'I can't wait to see the disc. I've never thought of you as an actress.'

She laughed at his enthusiasm. 'I hope you're not going to expect much,' she said with humility although in her mind her esteem bgan to rise with the unexpected fame.

'One day,' he predicted with a laugh, 'I'll expect to see your name up there in lights and a star with your name on it outside Mann's Theatre in Hollywood.'

She struck him lightly on his shoulder in mock anger. 'Don't be silly!' she chided.

When they arrived at her house, she waded through a mass of letters laying in the hall. Most of them were confirmation of bills that were paid for by her husband together with junk mail. She herded them all together and placed them on the telephone table in the hall. Then she opened her suitcase, removed the disc of herself in the film, and played it for her son in the lounge. As he watched it, which was only a ten-second clip, he clapped his hands with joy.

'Will that be in the film?' he asked, laughing heartily at the sight of his mother as an actress.

'I've been told that it's the highlight,' she joked, enjoying the expression on his face. 'Everything revolves around that scene. Now I'm sure you've got better things to do while I unpack.'

'I'm going to watch it a few more times and then I've got to go,' he told her. 'Stella's expecting me in half an hour. 'We think she might be pregnant. We're not certain yet. How will it feel to be a grandmother?'

Although she was delighted with the news, she screwed up her face at the idea unsure whether to like the term. A grandmother… it made her sound so old! There was no doubt that she was pleased for Robbie even though he was uncertain whether Stella was pregnant or not. He left shortly afterwards and she went into her bedroom to unpack. She reflected on her visit to America and her sister's family. Suddenly a vision came into her mind of herself and a much younger Laura making-up in front of a mirror in their bedroom. At the time they were seventeen and fifteen years old respectively and both of them were going to separate parties that evening. She viewed the image calmly as they dressed in clothes she had long forgotten they had worn. As they giggled with their efforts, she rearranged Laura's hair in front of the mirror. She didn't know how long the memory lasted but when she returned to normality she mused on the vision hoping that it would be one of many. In some ways her memory was beginning to come back.

She went downstairs to sort out the mail and found one letter with a strange postage stamp. She looked at it more closely to determine that the postmark stated Morocco. She frowned as she opened it, wondering if it had been sent by Dr. Mahmoud but she was mistaken. To her surprise it was from Ahmed. He had written to her pouring out his heart to expunge the guilt he obviously carried on his shoulders.

Dear Diana.

I felt I had to write to you to apologise for my rudeness when you came to see me. I now understand that you came as a friend and I rebuffed you horribly. It was very wrong of me. You are indeed one of my good friends and I shall welcome you most sincerely when you come to Agadir again. Please forgive me for my actions. Keep me for ever in your heart and in your mind.

Sincerely and affectingly,
Ahmed.

She placed the letter down on the table smiling as she did so. It was so touching to receive the apology from him that tears began to form in her eyes, What had caused him to write such a letter? Surely it wasn't simple friendship! It mattered little to her if she never saw him again and had believed that he felt the same way. So what prompted him to write to her? Sincerely and affectionately, he had ended. Affectionately? She was confused. They didn't love each other… she couldn't with all the barriers between them, so why should he write that? Puzzled about his attitude towards her, she went into the lounge and turned on the television set to watch an old film that had just started. The theme was about a scientist who was experimenting on how he could keep people looking younger, setting them on a course for a life of eternity. Diana wondered if Dr. Mahmoud had seen the film because it was exactly his aim. As the film rambled on, Diana fell asleep. When she awoke, she sat looking puzzled. Carol singers were outside singing and the room was quite cold. She went to the door and listened to the carol, placing a few coins in their collection box.

'A merry Christmas,' called out one of the singers as they went on their way.

'Christmas?' muttered Diana in a muffled voice. 'What are you talking about?'

'It's Christmas Eve, ma'am,' came the reply. 'A merry Christmas and a happy new year.'

She went back inside and sat on the settee trying to get her head into gear. Everything was so different. It was Christmas Eve… what had happened to the rest of the year?

If Diana thought that the festival would be a dull run-of-the mill event she was to be very much mistaken. Fate had decided to take a hand and intended to turn her world upside down. The house was decorated very sparsely mainly because it was too large and also because the children had grown up and had left to live elsewhere. However in one corner of the lounge stood a small Christmas tree embellished with many coloured baubles and small bulbs which set it alight. A modicum of other decorations covered the front windows of the house but nothing more. After a while she pulled herself together and decided against watching television sitting back to read a magazine. Shortly the door opened and Robbie entered hold a small box in his hand.

'Hi, Mom!' he greeted cheerfully. 'How are you today?'

'As usual, Robbie. Is all well with you?'

He nodded and poured himself a cup of coffee from the jug on the coffee-table drinking it greedily. Then he handed her the small box with a grin on his face.

'What's this?' she asked with a puzzled expression.

'It's your Christmas present from Stella and me,' he told her. 'I hope you like it. You can open it now if you like. It's not as though you have to wait until Christmas morning.'

She tore off the wrapping and opened the box to stare at a pair of very expensive ear-rings. 'Oh they're lovely… really lovely. Thank you so much.'

He felt into his inside pocket to produce another present. 'I didn't bother to wrap this because it's only a diary,' he told her passing it to her.

She opened it to examine the pages and then burst into laughter. Robbie looked at her totally perplexed.

'They may a real faux-pas here,' she laughed. 'They've put the wrong year in. It's ten years ahead. Now that is a big mistake. I wonder how many diaries they produced incorrectly. Someone should have pointed out the error before they sold them.'

Her son took back the diary to examine it closely. 'No, mother,' he returned. 'It's correct. That's the date for next year.'

'But it can't be,' she said with a worrying thought crossing her mind. 'When I left the hospital in Agadir, I remembered the date most clearly.'

He paused to think how to tell her the truth. 'Mother, you left hospital in Agadir ten years ago.'

'What about my treatment with Dr. Mahmoud?'

'You've been going back to Agadir every six months. Don't you remember?' The room fell silent as her head went into a spin. 'You came to my wedding with Stella eight years ago. Jack was born two years later.'

'Jack?' she echoed dumbly. 'Who's Jack?'

'He's your grandson. You're a grandmother!'

A grandmother! What had happened so that ten years had passed. She didn't remember a moment of it. She had been forty-three years of age… now she was fifty-three! My God, it was a quarter of her life gone in the blink of an eye.

'I think you might have caught me at a bad moment,' she managed to say as she tried to recover.

He took a photograph from his pocket to show her. 'He's a fine lad. I think he has your eyes and chin.' He stood up and went to the door. 'Don't forget. You're having Christmas dinner with us tomorrow. I'll pick you up at noon. I'll see you then.' He closed the door behind him and left the house.

Diana sat in shock for quite a while. Ten years had gone by. How could that have happened? It was impossible. Not only did she have amnesia but it was encroaching on the present day. It had to be either the Beotag or the ferradil-x tablets. There could be no other reason.

She went upstairs into her bedroom to stare at herself in the full-length mirror. She looked exactly the same as she always did. Smooth silk skin like alabaster… not a wrinkle or any sign of ageing apparent… and a beautiful figure that most women would die for. And now she was fifty-three! She recalled nothing of going to Agadir every six months… nothing about Robbie's wedding or the birth of her grandson. She considered that she would enjoy meeting them on Christmas Day. In her own mind it would be the first time she saw Stella and her son Jack. If only she could get her head around the fact that ten years had gone by unnoticed but it was unlikely. The shock of it would remain with her for some time.

CHAPTER THIRTEEN

Diana struggled gamely to come to terms with the loss of ten years of her life as she stood in the kitchen preparing her breakfast the next morning. Then the doorbell rang and she went to answer the call. It was Samantha standing on the doorstep with a worried expression on her face.

'I've been trying to get hold of you for ages,' she began anxiously. 'You seemed to be away for a long time.'

'Tell me about it,' countered Diana ruing the loss of time in her life. 'Come in side and tell me what's going on?' She led her into the lounge and they both sat down.

'It's not good news I'm afraid,' related Samantha starting to become upset. 'Gloria's got cancer and it's pretty much advanced. She knew that she had it but didn't tell anyone. Now she's terminal.'

'I'm so sorry to hear that,' responded Diana with sympathy. 'How has she taken it?'

'Badly I'm afraid. Very much to heart as you can imagine. It was bound to knock her for six.'

Diana shook her head slowly. 'How old is she?'

'About sixty-two I think. She's still relatively young.' Tears began to well up in Samantha's eyes.

'Can anything be done about it?

'They say it's terminal but who knows whether they're right or wrong?'

'They do wonders with chemotherapy and radiation treatment these days,' advanced Diana meaningfully.

Samantha nodded in agreement. 'I heard last week about a man who had a brain tumour. The doctor gave him three months to live and the tumour simply disappeared. They don't know how it happened. It's a complete mystery. So they're not always right.'

'I know a man in Morocco who might be able to help her,' suggested Diana offering a modicum of hope. 'He has a great record when it comes to curing cancer patients.'

The other woman raised her hand pitifully. 'You know what Gloria thinks about people abroad. She xenophobic… hates foreigners. She wouldn't travel there even if she believed that your man might cure her.

'That's stupid. I'm going to visit the same doctor soon. She could travel with me.' Samantha shook her head slowly. 'Can't we visit her and make her see sense?'

'She won't listen to us. You know what she's like.'

Diana considered her own situation. What would Samantha say if she revealed her secret to her? She would obviously think that she was out of her mind… mad… completely mad! For that reason she bit her lower lip and said nothing. It was sad news about Gloria but if the woman refused to place herself in Dr. Mahmoud's hands there was nothing she could do about it. He was so good at healing cancer patients She recalled the situation of Betty Naylor at the hospital who had been cured by him. But then, if Gloria refused to travel abroad, there was really no hope for her. She would simply be left to die. How difficult it was for people who contracted deadly diseases or who were disabled in the world. There was only hardship, pain and suffering for all of them. The quality of their lives was gone!

CHAPTER FOURTEEN

A few months passed by and it was time for Diana to fly back to Morocco to see Dr. Mahmoud again. Her diary was empty so she didn't bother to take it with her. She wondered how the doctor was coping with the experiment after all these years and was eager to hear more about his work. However, the journey was not without incident. The aircraft was flying at thirty-two thousand feet over France when, much to the surprise of the other passengers, she suddenly stood up in the aisle, her body trembling, shouting "Buses!" The image in her mind was a past experience when she and Laura were hurrying to school one day. Carrying their satchels, they had run for a bus, which in those days had a driver and a conductor, and Diana managed to get on to the bus helped by the conductor. Laura who was running behind her stopped watching the bus disappear without her into the distance. Consequently, Laura was late getting there and had to do an hour's detention after school was over.

'Buses!' she yelled again as she stopped trembling before coming back to reality and sitting down in her seat again. Her embarrassment was rife as all the passengers stared in her direction.

Within a few moments a stewardess came to her rather concerned. 'Are you all right, Madam?' she asked pleasantly. 'Is there anything I can get you?'

Diana shook her head and waved her hand in despair to usher her away. 'I'm fine, thank you. I just had a moment,' she managed to say. 'But I'm all right now.' She swallowed hard when she realised what she had done. Buses! Her mind moved to Vivien Williams, the therapist, and his method of word association. Perhaps after all that was the way forward to recovering her memory. Word association! He had told her that the brain functioned in mysterious ways. Maybe she had been wrong to stop seeing the man but it was too late now. Ten years too late! She had cut the proverbial umbilical cord after the first session.

After arriving in Agadir, she entered Dr. Mahmoud's office to find him sleeping at his desk.

'Dr. Mahmoud!' she called out, shaking him gently when he failed to awaken.

He opened his eyes, grunted and stared at her bleakly for a moment.

'Mrs. Templeton,' he muttered gruffly. 'Has six months gone by already? It's like I saw you only a month ago.'

'You don't look so good, if you don't mind me saying so, doctor,' she told him, sitting down opposite the scientist. She noticed the thinness of his face and the way his body seemed to have shrunk. He had lost a lot of weight. He puckered up his face tiredly, staring directly into her eyes. 'I haven't been too well lately,' he muttered softly. 'The side-effects I suffered were totally different to the ones you experienced. With me there was a great deal of vomiting, lack of appetite, lots of shaking, and much sleep. Too much sleep. I find myself awake for only ten hours a day. The ferradil-x tablets are very effective.'

'I'm sorry to hear that,' she told him sadly. 'How do you account for it?'

'It's an experiment,' he replied earnestly, shaking his head slowly. 'Our bodies are made up of chemicals which work in different ways. The effects are not the same for each person. You suffered some strange effects... with me they were different.'

She looked at him perceptively. 'I think that you've swallowed too many ferradil-x tablets in your research and they've taken their toll on your body. You need to take only two each morning and two each night. What you're probably doing is taking three or even four tablets at a time. You're pushing yourself beyond the limit.'

He smiled easily. 'You know, I'm the scientist; you're my patient, yet you have put your finger on the pulse. I shall take your advice. What about yourself?'

Diana shrugged her shoulders. 'As for myself, well I haven't had any more side-effects. The tablets seemed to have settled down.'

'And your memory? What about that?'

She explained that it was returning in fits and starts elaborating on the interview with Vivien Williams.

He nodded his head when she had finished. 'You should have continued with the treatment he offered,' he told her sagely. 'It would do you no harm. It's devoid of drugs or surgical treatment.'

'Except that he suggested electroshock treatment,' she riposted. 'I think he went too far on that one.'

'It might possibly be considered the swiftest answer although I would not recommend it myself. It's brutal to the brain and it could cause you to regress further.'

She had already dismissed the idea so she changed the subject quickly to pose an important question to the scientist. 'How are the animals in the experiment?' she asked point-blank.

'They're all doing fine. None of them appear to be ageing. They're all very well.' He placed a hand under his chin as if he was about to fall asleep again.

'You've lost a lot of weight,' she called out in a loud voice hoping that he could keep his eyes open.

He stared at her blearily. 'That's another of the side-effects but I've started to eat better. The tablets seem to be using up all the fat in my body. If I reduce the dose, I should return to good health in due course.'

She left the office with the renowned scientist fast asleep in his chair. It was a worrying thought that he might fade away with either weight loss or in his sleep. She had never experience side-effects of that nature but, as the scientist had told her, everyone's chemical make-up was different. If he was taking more that two ferradil-x tablets at a time, there was no doubt he would have violent changes in his metabolism.

After leaving, she took a taxi to Ahmed's office, determined to repair the bridge between them. To her dismay he wasn't there. The man in the next office saw her banging on the lawyer's door and he told her that it was a public holiday and the office was closed. Diana was in a dilemma. Should she go to the hovel where he lived or would he be in the public square? She decided on the latter and eventually passed the man in rags playing the flute in front of the swaying cobra in the tall wicker basket to enter. Ahmed was sitting on the same bench seat where he had first met her. He was holding his head in his hands as though thinking deeply and he didn't know that she was there until she sat down beside him and spoke to him.

'It seems that most days are public holidays in Morocco,' she joked.

He looked up and gave a gasp of amazement as an expression of delight appeared on his face. 'Diana!' he exclaimed brightly. 'What are you doing here?' He clasped her hands and moved slightly towards her with joy.

'I came to see Dr. Mahmoud,' she informed him.

He thought for a moment. 'Is there something between you and him?' he asked suspiciously, with a tinge of jealousy sounding in his voice. 'Surely you don't come to Agadir just to see him!' He paused to look at her face. 'Or is it because you come to see me?'

'Just listen to yourself,' she laughed loudly, teasing him in mock anger. 'You're an arrogant pretentious lawyer! Do you really think I travelled all this way just to see you? Well you're truly mistaken!'

This time it was his turn to burst into laughter at her tirade. 'Oh you beautiful lovely lady,' he expressed in the warmest of tones. 'You are humorous. I think I'm in love with you.'

'I bet you say that to all the young women in Agadir,' she riposted smiling at him. 'Do you have a wife or a girlfriend?'

'I don't have much time for women,' he replied with a smile on his face. 'My work takes up most of my time.'

'And pigs have wings!' she guffawed. 'Don't you ever want to get married?'

He became serious for a moment. 'When the right woman comes along.' He paused to clarify the comment. 'In my religion, a man can have four wives if he wants. The problem is financial… one has to pay for their keep. My firm only makes a limited amount of money each year. If I had four wives I would almost be bankrupt.'

'Why don't you start with just one?' she suggested plainly. 'Find one that you love and go on from there.'

'You have wonderful romantic ideas, Diana,' he countered, 'but I'm not in love with anyone… except for you, of course.'

'Of course,' she concurred with amusement although she didn't believe he was being serious.

'How's your memory?' he asked eventually having carefully avoided the subject so far.

'Improving,' she told him tersely. 'I still can't remember much'

'You don't recall how we met and you told me how much you loved me,' he said teasingly.

'You know the one thing I can't stand in life is a person who lies to me,' she told him with a serious expression on her face although she was laughing inside.

'Perhaps if we go back to the Forest of Snakes where you lost your memory something might come back to you.'

She considered his idea for a moment and then decided to follow it through. 'Okay,' she told him bluntly. 'Let's do it but I don't think we'll have much luck.'

'Think positively,' he responded quickly. 'Negativity will get you nowhere.'

He took her hand and they stood up and walked out of the public square, past the ragged flautist playing to the cobra in the basket. They walked up the road which was littered with palm trees on the pavement of both sides. She felt comfortably in his company, holding his hand tightly while he was delighted to be in her presence.

'Had any dreams about me lately? He stared adoringly at her beautiful face.

'Not a thing,' she answered flatly. 'I haven't had any dreams at all. I'm sure I used to enjoy them but they don't come any more.'

They moved on fairly swiftly in the hot sunshine and soon arrived at the

Hotel Sahara which stood opposite the Forest of Snakes. They sat on the same seat as they had done before she was attacked and continued their conversation.

'I left you here sitting on this seat,' he reminded, hoping to achieve a positive result.

She hesitated trying to focus her mind on the past. 'You did and I believe I watched you walk away, although I cannot be certain. At least I might have remembered that.'

'I kissed you on the hand and then left. You watched me go.'

She pressed her mind to try to reveal what had actually happened. 'The man must have come out of the wood and attacked me.'

'What did he look like? What did he say? Was he wearing a black mask? Did you tell him you had no money?'

'Easy... easy!' she countered sharply. 'If I knew the answers to those questions I'd have my memory back.'

'You have to remember something!'

'I must have told him that all my money was in the hotel. I didn't have any on me. But it's all conjecture. It's true though. I didn't have any on me.'

'Then a gun went off. Did you hear the shot?'

'I was once told that you never hear the shot of the bullet that gets you. Look, I appreciate your efforts in trying to help me but this is a waste of time.'

'I'm not a psychologist... I'm a lawyer,' he ventured, 'but I think I have the answer to your problem although it won't be easy to resolve.'

'And what is this fantastic idea that'll resolve all my problems?'

'You need to visit every place where something happened to you in the past. Places where you once lived, houses where you stayed, people you once knew, and so on. As I said, it won't be easy but it's a way for you to bring back all those memories.'

'Oh, Ahmed,' she retorted sadly. 'What about all those people who have gone... the houses that have been demolished, the changes in the places where I used to live. My parents died in a car crash in the South of France. I can't bring them back! How is it possible to go back?'

He screwed up his face in annoyance at the holes she had found in his suggestion and fell silent. They walked back into the town and sat in a restaurant facing each other, ordering a meal which was placed before them.

'Did you receive my letter?' he asked fervently, toying with the food on his plate. 'I hope you weren't offended.'

'Of course not,' she replied easily. 'I was pleased to receive it. You're my friend in Agadir. People have so few friends… real friends… in life I regard you as one of mine.'

'I'm happy you think so,' he added solemnly, 'but you still consider me as a friend and nothing more. I've been thinking a lot about you lately. You have such a beautiful face… such a wonderful mind… and a remarkable calm attitude to life. I can't get you out of my head.'

'I'm flattered,' she returned modestly, 'but I'm a married woman.' She had never thought that not getting divorced from her husband would be something to her advantage.

'I know… I know and I'm a Muslim… you're a Christian but there are lines which can be crossed between a man and a woman when chemistry aligns them closely together however remote the circumstances.'

'What are you saying, Ahmed?' Her tone was sharp and direct.

'I don't really know,' he admitted gloomily. 'I'm scared to say it but I've fallen in love with you.'

'Ahmed!' she admonished. 'You're so many years younger than me. I'd be more like a mother to you than a lover.'

'No… nothing like that!' he snapped. 'I'd treat you in a way no other man would. I'd love you, caress you, take good care of you… … … … … '

She raised her hand to interrupt him. 'You don't realise what you're saying,' she chided gently. 'For one thing, I'm too old to have children. There would be no family and I know how important family is to Muslims. That's just the starter.'

'I don't care about children,' he retorted swiftly. 'I just want you!'

'Your comments are appreciated but you fail to realise that I'm still a married woman. In any case, I don't think I want to be the first of four wives,' she told him with a lilt of laughter in her voice.

'There would be no others!'

'You say that now but you might feel different in the future. I also don't think your family would condone my divorce from my husband.'

'I don't care what they'd say. It's my business!' He was certainly laying his cards on the table.

'And what happens after the honeymoon when your ardour has faded? What happens then?'

He hardly needed time to answer the questions. 'My ardour will never fade as far as you're concerned.'

They finished the meal and he led her back to the Hotel Sahara.

'Think about what I said,' he told her finally, taking her hand and kissing it gently. 'I'll wait for you however long it takes.'

On that note he departed leaving her bemused by their conversation. He had clearly fallen in love with her but she felt that he was more like a friend than a lover. After all, he was so much younger to say the least. And there were all the other matters to take into account. Yet he still said that he loved her. What a thing to say? She really had no idea how to deal with his sudden display of ardour. If she took him on board as a lover it would provide her with too many problems none of which she intended to handle at this point in her life. And then came the image of that awful hovel he called a home. No... she simply wanted him as a friend. There was nothing more than that between them!

*****

When she arrived back in England, she found a letter on the doormat which stated that Gloria had been sent to a hospice. Without delay she went directly to see her and was shown into a small room where her friend was resting. Gloria had lost at least two stone in weight in a very short time and she was looking dreadfully ill.

'This is a fine kettle of fish,' began Diana, taking hold of her friend's skinny hand. 'How are you feeling.'

'How do you think?' snapped Gloria with a wry expression on her wrinkled face. 'I'm dying... probably just a few days or weeks to live.' She paused to gaze out of the window. 'There are so many thing I wanted to do in life and I put them aside to do later. Now it's too late. You never realise it until it's too late!'

'Is there anything I can do for you?' uttered Diana softly.

'You could cure me but you don't have the power,' came the caustic reply.

'But I do, Gloria,' confided her friend boldly. 'I had a friend in Agadir... an English woman who was cured of cancer by this brilliant scientist. Every doctor in England had given up on her. I'm under the same man... he treats me. I could take you to Morocco and he might be able to cure you.'

'Go abroad... to Morocco!' savaged her friend in disbelief. 'I think I'd rather die. I'm not letting those foreigners get their hands on me... no way!'

'Forgive me for saying this,' continued Diana bluntly, 'but you will die if you just stay here and let it happen.'

'I'm not going abroad!' cried Gloria adamantly with tears running down her face. 'I can't stand foreigners. It's bad enough that some of the staff here come from Africa or the West Indies. Can't stand them!'

'This has to be the time when you dispense with these crazy ideas!'

declared Diana curtly. 'It's only a short flight. You could be there tomorrow morning having the treatment that might save you.'

'Look at this wig,' stated her friend ignoring the recommendation. 'I lost my hair through chemotherapy. It was terrible!'

'You're not listening to me, Gloria,' persisted Diana firmly. 'Come with me to Agadir!'

'Leave me alone and let me die in peace,' bleated Gloria lamely. 'I'm going to die so let it be in peace.'

Diana sat back in the visitor's chair exhaling loudly. 'I remember something that you said about me,' she rattled angrily. 'You said there's none so deaf as those who don't hear. Well you're the one not listening now. I'll ask you one more time. Come with me to Morocco and let my good doctor treat you. I ask for nothing more.'

'Let it go, Diana,' came the response. 'I'm not going abroad… not for any reason.'

Diana shook her head sadly. 'I'm sorry to hear that, Gloria. I'm sure Dr. Mahmoud would be able to help you.'

'I've got a fourth person to play bridge with you, Samantha and Jane,' she managed to say in a squeaky voice. 'It's a doctor from the hospital where I was being treated. Her name's Valerie Martin. She'll be the fourth.'

'Don't tire yourself, Just rest!' cautioned Diana, deeply concerned for her friend but unable to help her. The woman was so determined not to travel abroad or be treated by any foreign doctors that it was against all logic. Anyone else would have leapt at the chance and taken the nest plane to Morocco in a desperate attempt to be cured. But not Gloria… no not Gloria!

She left the hospice deeply upset and four days later she received a telephone call to say that her friend had passed away. Maybe it had been too late for the woman to be treated by Dr. Mahmoud but one thing was certain… it didn't matter anymore. She attended the funeral at the local crematorium with Jane and Samantha and they watched the coffin on the tracks slowly disappear behind the curtain. It was a case of ashes to ashes, dust to dust and Gloria was no more in this world. As the prayers were being said, Diana sat back in her seat with her eyes closed. It was all too awful to contemplate.

Sometime after Gloria's body had been reduced to ashes, Jane took the urn and they drove some distance away before distributing them into a lake.

'She had no family,' related Jane simply. 'She asked me to throw her ashes into this lake. She had an illegitimate son, you know, and he drowned while swimming here. I suppose she wants to join him.'

‘She was a very good friend,’ said Samantha with a sad expression on her face. ‘We’ll certainly miss her at bridge.’

‘I understand a Dr. Martin’s going to take her place.’ ventured Diana recalling the last conversation she had with the dead woman.

‘Yes... Dr. Valerie Martin,’ concurred Jane. ‘She’s arranged for us to play all future games at the hospital.’

‘Well,’ commented Diana, ‘at least we’re in the right place if any of us falls ill.’

The words were found to be less than amusing on this occasion and she found herself to be the only one laughing.

The three women and the doctor continued to play bridge at the hospital thereafter but it was never the same... the atmosphere was too clinical. Apart from that, the feeling of friendship and animosity that sometimes aroused themselves between partners who played bridge seemed to be missing. Without Gloria and her famous caustic remarks, as well as the expensive biscuits and cakes she provided, bridge evenings were never the same again.

CHAPTER FIFTEEN

Days, weeks and months went by and Diana continued to take the tablets given to her by Dr. Mahmoud. They seemed to have no effect on her body now and she wondered whether the experiment was actually working. She had to admit that she felt extremely well so it hardly made any difference. One thing she did notice was the fact that everyone around her had aged but she still looked young and beautiful. Her face remained remarkably smooth and there were no wrinkles around her eyes or any puffing which normally affected women approaching their middle fifties. Furthermore her body was still slim and lithe with no evidence of ageing at all. One night she went to bed falling asleep shortly afterwards At last she began to dream! She could see herself drifting in a mist but then the images began to become more tangible. Although she lay flat on her bed she believed that she was laying face down with her body stretched out at full length… her eyes staring downwards. She was flying high up above, soaring like a bird free on the wing, experiencing a sensation of exhilaration which surged through her as she hurtled across the open sky. She could feel the clouds, caress the wind, glide, float and move closer to Heaven. Below the ground remained hazy but she could see tall mountains all around, with their craggy slopes and chasms occasionally interrupted by numerous cluster of trees and bushes. At first she traversed on invisible cross-currents, progressing forward steadily, then she yawed and swerved high above the terrain enjoying every moment of her flight. Her body felt as light as air and she could manoeuvre in any direction at will. This was an experience she would never forget; the last area of opportunity denied to mankind… to fly by himself. Since time immemorial, it had been possible for homo sapiens to walk, run, climb and swim but never to be able to fly without the use of a machine. Yet it could be achieved in dreams… it could happen beyond reality. During the dream, she felt as light as a feather, cruising above the clouds without tiresome or troublesome trivialities. Suddenly she saw someone else flying towards her. It was a man but she could not readily recognise his face. Someone else had achieved the art of flight by his own power. The man flew nearer but she was unable to determine whether it was Greg or Ahmed. The dream she was having appeared to allow her to make the choice. Greg or Ahmed? Then, without warning, her body seemed to become much heavier and she began to fall from her great height rather fast… very fast... much too fast... and the adrenalin began to flow through her body waking her up from her deep slumber. When she opened her eyes, she realised that she was drenched with perspiration almost as though she had actually been flying every minute of the dream. It had given her no clues to the way she felt in real life. However later that day, she picked up a book of crosswords and started to solve the puzzles. She was dwelling on the idea given to her by the therapist, Vivien Williams, on word association. If she could find words within the confines of the book of crosswords that triggered images in her mind she would be well on the way to recovery. However, after trying the experiment for two days she realised that it had no effect on her. Word association might be helpful to some people but it showed no signs of doing the same for her... so she swiftly ended her relationship with the idea.

* * * * *

The next time Diana visited Dr, Mahmoud he looked much better. He was bright and cheerful, and it was clear he no longer succumbed to sleep. She was delighted to see that he had recovered but she wasn't certain how he would continue his relationship with her as doctor and patient. He was a scientist yet he acted exactly clinically like a physician but he experimented all the time on animals, transferring any cures that he found to aid the plight of human-beings. Without doubt he had cured Betty Naylor of cancer and almost certainly was successful with other patients of whatever diseases they had contracted. If he hadn't, the hospital would never have built the annex so that he could work there. On the other hand, his association with her seemed to be much closer than that of a patient. He was like a father figure towards her in a way that she was unable to explain to herself. Indubitably he was using her for his experiment as well as himself and she firmly believed that she was his sole subject with regard to ferradil-x. Nonetheless, a relationship of father and daughter was slowly beginning to emerge and she was quite happy to go along with it.

'You're looking so much better than the last time I was here,' she said opening the conversation.

'I took your advice, my dear,' he said affectionately.' I reduced the dose of ferradil-x tablets. A person can be too ambitious in the quest for success. You made me see the light and the reduction steadied my metabolism. For that I thank you. Sometimes a scientist can fly too close to the wind.'

'What about the animals?' she ventured expecting to hear a positive reply. 'Are they all well?'

The tone of his voice showed that he was somewhat disappointed and he tugged lightly at his goatee beard staring directly into her eyes.

'There's good news and bad news,' he responded slowly watching her chin drop slightly on the adverse information. 'The bad news is that a hamster died recently but that's only one part of it.'

She appeared unnerved by the revelation. 'Oh my God"' she uttered miserably. 'Don't tell me it's been all for nothing!'

'No, no, no!' he remonstrated waving his hands wildly in front of him. 'The good news is that although the hamster died there's another important matter to consider. Hamsters usually live for only two years. This one lived until he was twelve. That's six times the normal lease of life for a hamster. If you work out the equation to its end and say that the life of an average human-being is seventy-five years… multiplying that by six means that a person might live to the age of four hundred-and-fifty years. I am so pleased by the result that I can hardly contain myself. Can you envisage being over four hundred years old. It blows the mind.'

'It works that way on animals maybe,' she cut in smartly, 'but you've yet to be certain it works on human beings.'

'If it does work, I shall be around for a long time with laurels resting on my head. I don't know how it will affect the population of the world because it will grow and grow. Maybe Malthus's theory that there will be insufficient food to feed everyone if the population grows to enormous proportions. But that's not my problem.' He paused to bring his mind back to the current day. 'Tell me, do you have any regrets about your involvement in the experiment?'

She shook her head slowly. 'Not at all. I can't say it's been great fun but it's had little effect on me except for the side-effects which disappeared a long time ago. I must say I still look as young as I did when we started. How about you?'

He shrugged his shoulders. 'For me it's part of my life. As your Oscar Wilde wrote: "We are all in the gutter but some of us look up at the stars." I can see a whole galaxy out there.'

She stared at him as he clenched his hands before him. 'I know you're dedicated to your work but I've been curious about you,' she advanced boldly. 'Do you have a family? What do you do for relaxation and fun?'

He looked at her bleakly. 'I have no family,' he told her candidly. 'I work here day and night. I have a bed in the next room and there is a door which leads to a quadrangle within the confines of the hospital. I haven't been out of this hospital for sixteen years or more.'

She gasped at the revelation. 'Are you telling me you've been cooped up in here for sixteen years and you've never been outside?'

He nodded his head unashamedly. 'My work is all I live for. Provisions and supplies are brought to me each week. It's all I need to keep myself alive and to treat patients. You may think it's strange but I only want to carry on with my research.'

'You're a remarkable man, Dr. Mahmoud,' she managed to say. 'I think you're remarkable.' She thought of the workaholic syndrome suffered by her husband in England musing that it was inherent in the scientist as well.

Dr. Mahmoud continued talking but she didn't listen to a word that was being said. She tried to grasp the concept of a man undertaking treatment of patients and research during the day and simply going into the next room to sleep in his bed every single night. He probably only went out into the hospital quadrangle for twenty minutes occasionally. Such a person, she thought, ought to be treasured and given the highest awards possible from the authorities for such dedication. He was an institution in his own right asking for nothing more in life than to be allowed to continue his research. She felt that he ought to be honoured in the highest degree as someone willing to lay down everything of value in life to help others. There were too few people of such calibre in the world... extremely few!

He handed her a further supply of tablets and she said her farewell and left. There was a fair amount of time before her flight back to England and it was in her mind to visit Ahmed but for some strange reason she decided not to do so. There would only be an element of embarrassment in meeting him whereby he would ask whether she was still dreaming about him. She didn't feel that she need to keep providing an answer, neither did she want him to keep handing out flattering compliments of one sort or another especially as she didn't feel drawn towards him. No... she allowed her head to rule her heart and returned to England without seeing him this time. She hoped that he wouldn't discover that she had visited the scientist in Agadir and had deliberately avoided seeing him but it was a chance she had to take. A strange feeling came over her as she boarded the aircraft at Agadir airport. As her conscience cut in, she realised that he was a true friend and she knew that she should have gone to visit him. However she was now on a aeroplane... it was far too late for her to change her mind!

CHAPTER SIXTEEN

The monthly bridge game continued at the hospital with Jane, Samantha and Dr. Valerie Martin. The atmosphere was extremely clinical with the strange aroma of surgical spirit permeating the room. The four women seemed to get on quite well while the doctor proved to be an adept bridge player. Gloria's name was mentioned occasionally but gradually her memory faded away into the past. She was dead and cremated… nothing was left! It was a sad thing for those who had departed but the people they left behind had to get on with their lives. In effect, the doctor was warmly welcomed by the others and on one occasion during the tea break she turned to Diana.

'You went to Morocco recently,' she started. 'I hear that you go there every six months. Do you visit friends or is it simply a place you like to travel to?'

Diana inhaled deeply willing to answer the question. Gloria had been so xenophobic that the doctor's attitude was quite refreshing. 'I go to see a scientist who's treating me for loss of memory,' she explained. 'Yes I do have a friend there. He's a young lawyer but there's nothing more to it than that.'

'Why do you see a scientist instead of a psychologist?' demanded the new bridge player. 'You've had this loss of memory for many years I understand. What kind of treatment does he give you?'

'I take Beotag and ferradil-x tablets,' she replied throwing caution to the winds.

The doctor's face turned into a frown. 'I've never heard of those tablets before. Which company manufactures them?'

'They're made by Dr. Mahmoud himself.'

There was a pause as the doctor's frown deepened. 'I would be very careful,' she warned. 'Private medical treatments could prove to have very nasty results.'

'This man's a genius,' boasted Diana openly. 'He cured a friend of mine who had incurable cancer. All the doctors in England gave up on her but he cured her.'

Dr. Martin shrugged her shoulders. 'Just be careful.' she advised finally. 'Some people can be cured and some cannot.'

Six weeks later during another card evening, the four women began to chat about trivialities in the tea break when destiny struck with its mysterious force to turn Diana's life upside down. At first, the suggestion was innocuous but no one knew the extent of how things would change for her in the long term. The doctor leaned across the table towards her to suggest an idea that she had formed in her mind.

'I understand you're a lady of leisure. You have time on your hands, don't you?' began the physician seriously.

'My husband refused to allow me to work. He had Victorian ideas about a wife but we've separated so I can do what I like. You obviously have something in mind. What is it?'

The doctor's face took on a serious expression. 'Have you ever thought about volunteering for the Red Cross?' she ventured. 'It's a well-known established institution which does some excellent work.'

Diana shook her head instantly. 'I'm afraid I know nothing about first aid or hospital treatment. I'd be pretty useless.'

'It's not about first aid or hospital treatment,' rattled the doctor blandly. 'I'm talking about serving in one of the Red Cross shops. They sell all kinds of clothing and bric-a-brac and I'm sure you'd do very well there. As I said... it's voluntary. You could decide to work one or two days a week or even just three hours a day. It'll be something to fill up your time and it'll help the Red Cross do their good work. Why not try it? You can always opt out if you don't like it. No one will blame you.'

After they had finished the game, Diana returned home. She thought about the doctor's suggestion, ruling it out of mind instantly. What use would she be to the Red Cross when she couldn't remember her own past. She would be a milestone around their neck. Someone would look at an item and ask about its provenance and she wouldn't be able to remember. It would be a hopeless task. However, despite her reluctance, she went to the Red Cross shop on the following day to learn how it operated. She was surprised to note the simplicity of the work and the friendship shown to her by the staff. Perhaps she had been too hasty to reject the idea and she started to change her mind about her original decision. Subsequently, she approached the manageress and told her of the conversation with Dr. Martin.

'Dr. Martin!' exclaimed the woman. 'She's on our local Red Cross board. She's a real live wire... and she doesn't stand for any nonsense.'

'Perhaps I could work here for a few days a week,' offered Diana readily.

'Of course,' returned the woman delightedly. 'Welcome to the fold! I'm Jennifer. As it happens, Elsie rang this morning to say she had a migraine. If you want, you can start now.'

Diana was ushered behind the counter and she stared around the shop looking at the goods. There was clothing and bric-a-brac everywhere.

Paintings, crockery, toys, books, clothing of all kinds for men and women, and a cabinet with special items of jewellery and small statues.

'Everything has a price tag on it,' explained the woman, 'so you have no problems there. Plastic bags are under the counter… small and large ones. All you have to do is to wrap up the items sold and take the money for them.'

The operation seemed to be simple enough and shortly a customer came to the counter with a colourful teapot which Diana wrapped in flexible cellophane before placing it carefully into a plastic bag.

'I'm buying this for my daughter,' stated the customer taking the money from his pocket. 'She'll love this one. She collects teapots of all kinds. Has some thirty of them.'

Diana made a brief comment and took the money from the customer, placing it into the wooden cash register. She felt that she would find this work very pleasant especially as it was all for a good cause. She had intended to spend only a few hours in the shop but, within the wink of an eye, the whole day passed. This was work very much to her liking and she intended to go back to the shop to assist. In fact, she thought, tomorrow would be a good time to start again.

When the four women met to play bridge some months later, Dr. Martin asked her protégé how she was getting on in the Red Cross shop. Diana told her broadly how she enjoyed working there and meeting all the customers.

'I'm pleased you suggested it,' she replied with enthusiasm. 'I go there six times a week. It's taken over my life.'

'I heard about some of the things you've done to improve the shop,' returned the doctor seriously. 'Over the past month, you've rearranged everything and increased the turnover by twenty per cent.'

'I know. I've got lots of new ideas on how to increase it even further. Next week I'm going to work on window displays. That's should draw in more people. Why have goods in the shop and nothing in the windows to attract them?'

'You know I'm on the local board of the Red Cross,' continued the doctor. 'I'm so impressed by your efforts I want you to take over the running of the shop. Jennifer's leaving… she's moving to the Midlands… and I can't think of a better person to step into her shoes. How about it?'

Diana rose to the occasion. 'I'd love to do it!' she said excitedly. 'When do you think the transfer will take place?'

'How about tomorrow?' She knew instinctively that her protégé would jump at the chance.

Diana was over the moon and she rose to the task. She had managed the shop for the last few months putting into effect various new ideas which proved to be successful. Now she was top dog capable of doing anything she wanted within reason without having to ask permission all the time. The promotion went slightly to her head for when one customer bought a microphone with speakers, she tested it out, going outside the shop announcing all the goods available for sale. Anyone who failed to realise that a Red Cross charity shop existed in the area must have been deaf.

It was a year later when Dr. Martin made a surprised visit to the shop. Diana was arranging a display of dresses in the window and she stopped to greet the physician when she arrived.

'Valerie!' she greeted warmly. 'To what do we owe this pleasure?'

The doctor came straight to the point. 'You've done exceedingly well since you became the manageress here, Diana. I'm very impressed with you. The ideas keep flowing and I believe that other retailers are copying you to increase their sales.'

'It's no problem,' returned Diana easily. She was concerned at the unsolicited arrival of her bridge partner. After all, a visit from a local board member of the Red Cross had to be serious. 'Has someone complained?'

'No one's complained. I've been watching all our activities with regard to fund raising for the Red Cross. You arranged a local marathon which brought in a great deal of money from sponsors. There was also the sky jump and the garden visits, the sponsored walks, the many coffee mornings. I could go on. You made a real change in our progress and brought in a lot of funds.'

'It's something I like doing... for a worthy cause. But why are you here today?'

The doctor paused for a moment. 'The Red Cross has been invited to provide a speaker for a television programme entitled 'Say Your Piece' It does a run-down on various organisations and institutions. After all the work you've done with your brilliant ideas, I've recommended you to represent us on the programme.'

'Me?' gasped Diana breathlessly. 'But I've had no training to talk on television!'

'You seem to have a very easy intelligent manner to me,' came the reply. 'You'll easily promote our cause on television. There's no doubt in my mind about that. I'll provide all the necessary information for you.'

Diana felt her heart pounding as her head went into a spin. 'When will this take place?'

'In two months times... in the London studio of the television network. You'll have more than enough information. Can I count on you to do it?'

The manageress nodded as if in a dream. It would appear that she had no choice. What could she say to millions of viewers watching the programme? All eyes would be on her, especially the people in the Red Cross. If she made a mistake, or stuttered, or paused for a long time, everyone would notice and point the finger at her for being inadequate. It was a daunting task to undertake and it took a while for it to sink into her head. Why had she agreed to do it? She was completely satisfied with her work as manageress of the Red Cross shop. Why do something to upset the apple cart? It was the stupidest thing she had done for a long time!

* * * * *

Some time later, Diana received another letter from Ahmed. Although the words were simple she felt the anger behind them. He was furious of her treatment of him and he made it quite plain in the letter.

Dear Diana,

I was very disappointed to learn that you visited Dr. Mahmoud but you never came to see me. I thought that we were friends, happy to be in each other's company, but clearly you don't think so. You know how I feel about you even though you don't feel the same way of me but to be snubbed when you could have come to see me on your arrival at Agadir is very hurtful. I beg you to please write or come and see me the next time you come to Agadir. I do not wish to lose your friendship.

Yours sincerely,
Ahmed.

He was clearly very annoyed with her. The last letter had ended 'Yours affectionately and sincerely'. This time it was far less amorous. She was angry with herself for not seeing him on her last visit and she wondered how he had discovered that she had seen Dr. Mahmoud. He knew that she came to Morocco every six months and he had probably gone to the scientist to find out why she hadn't come. He was obviously very dismayed when he learned that she had been there and had left ignoring him completely. It was not a thing friends did to each other! He told her that he had fallen in love with her and she treated him very badly even though the feeling was not reciprocated. She would have to be sure to visit him the next time she flew to Agadir otherwise he would give up on her. Although she told herself that she didn't love him, her heart told her that he was a friend and she still wanted him to be there for her. She could not expunge from her mind that he was so much younger in years than her. However, if the experiment with Dr. Mahmoud proved to be successful, he would eventually become older while she remained young. After all, she still looked to be twenty-eight years old and very youthful and he was thirty-three. The difference in their ages in the concept of time had diminish. He had technically overtaken her. Certainly she would need to think positively about age because everyone around her would progress in years while she remained the same.

CHAPTER SEVENTEEN

Diana and Simon Younger sat side by side in comfortable chairs in the television network's make-up room. She closed her eyes remaining silent as she realised what she was about to do. The make-up artist attending her began a sonorous monologue relating to contentious issues in the previous programme, his voice being the only one to echo throughout the room. Eventually he stopped and stood back to admire his work before putting down his make-up materials on the basin in front of her with complete satisfaction showing in his face.

'There you are,' he told her frankly in an affected voice. Remember they take no prisoners in this programme. You've got to be forthright and say your piece. That's what the programme's called... that's what you've got to do! What do you think?'

Diana stared at her face in the mirror. 'I think there's too much lipstick,' she criticised tentatively.

'No, no, no!' he countered vehemently. 'Your face will look fuller in the camera. Too little would mean your lips will appear dull. It's essential to over-compensate. Don't worry... you'll look fine with a pretty face like yours.' He pulled the cloth from around her neck prompting her to stand up.

At that moment, Shaun O'Brien entered the room. He glanced at Diana and smiled. 'Good!' he said sharply. 'You're ready.' He turned to the television presenter in the next chair. 'Nearly ten minutes to go, Simon,' he warned with a degree of urgency. 'You'd better get your skates on!'

Younger opened his eyes momentarily and then closed them again as if nothing seemed to matter and he had all the time in the world. O'Brien stared at Diana more closely before leaving.

'You look a real stunner,' he flattered sincerely. 'You're gonna knock 'em dead on that screen.' He turned to Younger who had just stood up and was staring at himself in the mirror. 'Less than ten minute to go, Simon!'

'Take it easy,' challenged the television presenter. 'There's no need to panic. We've got plenty of time.'

Diana, O'Brien and Younger moved into the corridor. Technicians raced to and fro as though their lives depended on it, cables littered the pathway, while voices could be heard at all levels barking orders and relating terms of confirmation accompanied by whirrs, bleeps and other noised emanating from the technical equipment. The studio buzzed like a beehive although the staff who, despite their total dedication, performed their duties with an unmitigated air of complacency. Diana could feel the surge of adrenalin surge through her veins as they prepared the programme before it went live to the public.

'Come on!' urged O'Brien, guiding them through the labyrinth of corridors until they reached the main studio.

They waited in limbo temporarily as Simon Younger explained the situation to her more fully. 'There are three seats on the stage,' he informed her flatly. 'You take the one on the far side. I'll be in the middle. The journalist will be on the near side. Don't come on until I announce you... then you sit down. There'll be an audience of about a hundred-and-twenty people... just ignore them. Never forget that the programme's being broadcast to millions of viewers. They're the ones who count. Keep your eyes on me all the time... don't look directly at the camera. Pretend it isn't there. Concentrate on what you have to say and keep looking at me at all times. Have you got that?'

She nodded dumbly hoping to be able to remember all that he told her. Suddenly she felt very vulnerable at having to walk onto the stage in front of millions of viewers. However before she could dwell on the matter, the lights began to dim. Younger walked on to the stage holding a sheaf of notes in his hand and he sat down in the middle chair. Within seconds a red light started to glow on one of the cameras and he faced it breaking into his opening dialogue.

'Good evening, Ladies and Gentlemen. Welcome to another edition of Say Your Piece... the show which brings you inside information on organisations, associations and institutes of repute. This evening we have Diana Templeton of the British Red Cross who has come to tell us of the great work undertaken by them.' He turned slightly and put out his arm in a welcoming attitude. 'Diana Templeton!'

Diana hesitated in a moment of panic only to be pushed in the back by O'Brien so that she almost fell on to the stage. She retained her poise and walked across to the chair on the far side and sat down. One of the cameras moved closer which unnerved her a little and there seemed to be a frog lodging in her throat preventing her from speaking. Although she had read the notes given to her by Dr. Martin through and through, her mind seemed to have become completely blank.

'Also here today,' continued Younger easily, 'we have an eminent journalist form the Daily Record newspaper... Elvis Jones!'

Jones emerged on to the stage and took his seat on the near side of the presenter.

'We'll start with Diana,' Younger began shuffling the notes in front of him. 'Tell us a little about the British Red Cross and what it does.'

There was a long pause as Diana fought to retain some poise and then looked up as she found the courage to speak. One of the cameras moved in very much closer but suddenly everything she had studied in the notes came to light in her mind.

'The work of the British Red Cross is wide and varied,' she began, ignoring Younger's earlier instructions to stare directly into the camera. She stopped in her flow for a moment and turned to the cameraman. 'Can you come closer. I want you to read my lips. What I have to tell you is unknown to the general public who simply take the Red Cross for granted. I want them to be able to understand all the good work we do. ' She paused as the camera moved closer still.

Younger fumed at her command. No one on his programme had ever done anything like this before. Despite his anger, he put on a weak smile for the viewers.

'We work closely with a large number of organisation from Social Services to homeless charities,' reported Diana picking up momentum as she went on. There was fire in her voice and sincerity in her heart. 'One scheme, for example, supports people over a twelve-week period after they come out of hospital. At that time they're extremely vulnerable and their families live far away or they're at work. We provide help by shopping for their food, obtaining their prescriptions, looking after them and keeping them company at a time when they would be left in difficulty if no one helped them. Can you imagine how vulnerable people are when they leave hospital to fend for themselves? They're wounded in body and mind and only the Red Cross will help them. We have many volunteers who cope with this operation. They help people in crisis throughout the United Kingdom every day, every week, every year.'

She was amazed at the words which poured from her mouth so effectively. She was in her element. At the same time she managed to ignore the weight of responsibility which rested on her shoulders as a representative of the Red Cross in their single opportunity of appearing on television before a very wide viewing public. As she spoke, she wondered why she had been chosen for the task.

'Let me give you a few more examples of the good work carried out by the Red Cross,' she went on fervently. 'We make ourselves available in all road accidents and train crashes. You may think we're not there but we're always on hand. We're there for people isolated at home or those who become separated from their family by way of war or disaster. There's a scheme for the homeless or someone who has nowhere to go after a hospital stay as well as helping refugees who have HIV but are too afraid to talk to anyone for fear of deportation. After all, these people in need are human-beings.'

At this point, Younger tried to interrupt her but she brushed him aside callously. 'You asked me a question, Mr. Younger so kindly allow me to finish.' There was no doubt which person was in control of the programme and Diana was beginning to enjoy herself. All the fears and blankness she had suffered had gone. She was suddenly a woman in her own right.

'We help people in crisis with a host of volunteers who give up their free time to assist those in need,' she went on staring directly into the lens of the camera. 'There's a transport and escort service to and from hospital as well as escorts for patients to and from London hospitals for people living in the Midlands and the north. We provide first aid classes with the distribution of free kits and CDs to every secondary school in the country and we'll play a vital role in the event of a flu epidemic sweeping the United Kingdom.'

Younger tried to interrupt her again but Diana rode over him as though he wasn't there.

'Although we undertake a number of schemes at home there are some we carry out abroad. We're tackling tuberculosis across the world in partnership with a major pharmaceutical company. In addition, the British Red Cross has built homes for almost three hundred people in Indonesia following the tragedy of the tsunami there with planes to build over two thousand more. At the same time supplies are being sent to thousands of people in camps in Uganda. There's also a cash distribution to Niger in West Africa where millions of people are starving to death. although all the news items have ignored their plight.' She paused for breath at that moment before going on. 'You realise I'm only skimming the surface of the actions being taken by the Red Cross. We work wonders in helping thousands of people at no cost to them at all for work not available from any other source.'

The presenter finally managed to stop her in her tracks. He turned to the journalist quickly. 'Mr. Jones... there's no doubt that the British Red Cross is a great institution. What do you have to say to that?'

Jones looked down his nose and stared briefly at Diana. 'It does do some very good work,' he said begrudgingly, 'but it definitely lacks transparency. There are too few cogent details... so few details offered to my liking. For example, they never explain how many people have help with their home from hospital scheme. They say it lasts for weeks but does it? No one knows. How many road accidents or train crashed do they attend? Not very many I would suggest. And how many people become isolated from their families by war or disaster? Very very few. And what are they going to do if a flu epidemic becomes widespread? Furthermore, why should they help refugees with HIV before they're deported? It doesn't really make sense. The Red Cross needs to produce information in much greater depth.'

Diana fumed at the way the journalist denigrated all that she had said and she burst into action fiercely like a virago. 'Really!' she snarled angrily. 'Is that your opinion in your ignorance! Thousands of volunteers dedicate their live to our cause. Do you expect us to name all of them and record every single thing they do. We would need an army of clerical staff to cope with that useless information. You tell me who would provide the assistance to people. Would you be willing to help out. No… I didn't think so. You sit in your chair criticising. That's all you're capable of doing! I suggest you come along to the Red Cross headquarters and spend one day… only one day… to see exactly what good we do before you attack us with a campaign of criticism. We're a well-known highly respected institution which raises funds of its own accord. We have shops and sponsorships to help with our finances and I challenge you to go into any school and ask the students about first aid. The first thing they will tell you is that they get it all from the Red Cross. We work from the roots upwards to save lives and produce a unique service to those in need, preventing a great deal of suffering. Who else does that?'

The venom that came forth used up all the frustration which had built up inside her and the half-hour programme ended with the journalist reluctantly retreating with his tail between his legs. When she came off stage, Diana found Dr. Martin waiting for her. The physician threw her arms around her and hugged her tightly.

'Wow, Diana! she told her with awe. 'That was some performance. I didn't dream you had it in you. I am so proud of you!'

Diana felt humble but the adrenalin still made her feel on top of the world causing her heart to beat faster.

'I rather enjoyed it,' she said simply.

'You're a natural,' declared the doctor proudly. 'You took hold of the programme and made it your own. Everyone was glued to what you were saying and the way you handled that journalist was magnificent. He won't talk about the Red Cross like that in a hurry. You'll have to come to the National Assembly and talk to us there.' She paused to take Diana's arm on impulse. 'I don't suppose you've had anything to eat. You were probably too nervous.' Diana shook her head. 'Good… well I'll treat you to dinner. It'll be my pleasure after that performance.'

They left the studio much to the acclaim of the doctor. It had been a wonderful evening even if the programme only lasted for half an hour. 'Speak Your Piece' mused Diana thinking of the title of the programme. Well she had certainly done that effectively. Yes indeed… she had certainly done that!

* * * * *

Over the next few days, scores of ovations arrived at the Red Cross shop. Some of them with letters and postcards, others by the way of flowers. Diana had become a heroine for the cause overnight and she blossomed with pride at the accolades. The income raised with shop sales soared as people flocked there to see her and bought goods. She arranged a number of raffles which enhanced the funds with guessing the weight of a cake, naming a teddy bear… there was no end to the ways she increased the amount of money she made for the Red Cross. Her life had changed very much for the better and it was improved by articles in the local and national Press. Her feisty attitude, ease of argument, and the volley of information she had provided took the country by storm. She had become famous… a woman of distinction… even though such renown was not required by her.

When her next visit came for her to see Dr. Mahmoud, she flew to Agadir and went to Ahmed's office directly from the airport.

'I am so sorry,' she apologised profusely as she entered the room staring at him as he pored over some documents on his desk. 'I really am. It was unforgivable. I don't know what got into me.'

He looked up surprised at her presence. He had never expected ever to see her again after sending the second letter.

'You don't have to apologise,' he told her excited that she had come. 'To tell you the truth, in all this time I haven't been able to get you out of my mind.'

'If you're going to ask whether I dreamed about you the answer is no,' she countered in advance of the question.

'I wasn't going to ask you that,' he countered moving to the other side of the desk to change the position of the chair. 'Please sit down. How are you?'

'Fine,' she replied smiling broadly at him. He was so handsome. No one could deny that. She couldn't understand why she felt so unemotional towards him. Maybe it was the thought of him being so much younger than her in the past when she felt that she was more of a mother to him. But he had caught up with her in years. She was still young-looking and beautiful and he was handsome and older.

'It's been a whole year since we last met,' he went on. 'What have you been doing in that time?'

'Nothing in particular,' she responded modestly. 'I do some voluntary work for the Red Cross. I'm the manageress of one of its shops.'

'You actually work in a shop,' he retorted with surprise. 'Why do you do that?'

'I don't have to… it's voluntary.' She was startled by his response. He obviously thought of her as a lady of leisure, someone who didn't have to get their hands dirty by working in a shop. 'I do I to help people in difficulties.'

He stared at her lovingly, his face lighting up as he changed the subject. 'I am so pleased to see you,' he told her, his expression suddenly changing to sadness.

'How about you?' she ventured. She stared at his face but there was no love… no chemical reaction.

'It's been a sad period for me,' he related slowly. 'My mother died six months ago. I've had to look after my brothers and sister every since.'

'My condolences,' uttered Diana sympathetically. 'I'm sorry to hear that. What happened?'

'Organ failure… her kidneys.' It was clear that the details were too painful for him to discuss.

'Couldn't Dr. Mahmoud do anything to help her?'

'I went to see him,' the lawyer told her, 'but he was asleep most of the time. There was something wrong with him. Anyway, my mother died shortly afterwards.'

Silence prevailed for a short while with neither of them knowing how to continue the conversation, then Diana broke the ice.

'How's the firm doing? Do you have many clients?'

'It's a little slow. People in Europe are buying up properties in all the countries there. No one has yet decided to buy any property in Morocco. Once that happens, we shall be inundated with requests from buyers to conveyance their properties.'

'Maybe I should buy a place here,' she ventured thoughtfully. I mean I come her often enough. It might be cheaper in the longer run at current prices for property.'

'I don't think so,' he advised. 'Your treatment with Dr. Mahmoud must come to an end eventually.' He stared at her face like a forlorn lover, his eyes fixed and glassy. 'You are so beautiful,' he uttered, 'and I'm so much in love with you. You know, you look exactly as you did all those years ago when we first met. How do you do it?'

‘It’s the cosmetics I use,’ she lied blatantly unwilling to reveal her secret.

‘You’re the one I want to marry,’ he proceeded to tell her. ‘You are definitely the one.’

‘But I’m still married to someone else,’ she laughed.

‘Divorce him. Set yourself free,’ he countered irately. ‘One day, you shall be mine… I know it.’

She burst out laughing at his ardour which he didn’t appreciate and, after drinking coffee together, she bade farewell and left. Such meetings were doing neither of them any good. He was in love with her but she regarded him solely as a friend.

After leaving Ahmed’s office she went directly to the office of Dr. Mahmoud who seemed to look a lot younger.

‘Are you taking tablets other than Beotag and ferradil-x?’ she asked him point-blank.

‘Why do you say that?’

‘You’re looking so much younger. The last time I saw you, you’d lost a lot of weight and could hardly keep your eyes open. What happened?’

‘I’m experimenting with another extract which I’ve decided to call Apollo-y. It also comes form North Borneo but it’s extremely scarce. I’ve been taking it over the past three months and I do seem to be getting younger. If you wish to join me in the experiment I can let you have some of the tablets.’

Diana shook her head. ‘I really don’t want to look any younger,’ she retorted quickly. ‘If I stay as I am for the next twenty years I’ll be more than satisfied.’

He pulled on his goatee beard fiercely. ‘I should think you’ll do so far longer than that,’ he expressed. ‘Let me know if you change your mind.’

‘I’ll do that,’ she returned slowly with no intention of agreeing to do so. ‘How are the rest of the animals? No more deaths I hope,’

‘No more deaths,’ he echoed calmly. ‘They’re all alive and well.’ He pulled again on his goatee beard becoming serious. ‘There’s something I want to talk to you about,’ he advanced solemnly. ‘People have been clearing the rain forest in North Borneo to establish farming land and it’s been getting harder to find the plant from which I extract ferradil-x. I have enough supplied for the next ten years and I’m working on a chemical substitute but I thought you ought to know of the situation.’

‘What will happen to me if I ran out of them.’ she asked with a tinge of concern in her voice.

‘That’s the sixty-four thousand dollar question,’ he replied. ‘It is possible that your body has built up its own immunity from ageing over the past years but I don't really know if that's true. It's early stages in the experiment as yet. Let's hope that the plant remains available before we concern ourselves too much. As I said, I may be able to find a chemical substitute before the supplies run out.'

He handed her another supply of tablets before she left the office. She was only a little concerned about the situation but Dr. Mahmoud still had years of supply and was working on a substitute. The Wizard of Agadir would probably come up trumps in due course. She felt certain of that. She took a taxi to the airport and boarded the aircraft without delay. There were important matters to deal with in the Red Cross shop. She may have been a lady of leisure but all that was behind her now. She had burdened herself with responsibilities and they came before anything else.

CHAPTER EIGHTEEN

One bright morning some two months later, Diana arrived outside the Red Cross shop with the front door key in her hand to open that large glass doors when she felt the presence of someone hovering behind her. She turned to find Carol Hemsley, a young woman with long blonde hair, dressed in a smart grey suit, holding an executive briefcase.

'Can I help you?' asked Diana believing that the woman had seen something in the shop window and wanted to purchase it.

'Good morning, Mrs. Templeton,' greeted Carol casually. 'I'd like a word with you if you don't mind. It won't take long.'

Diana frowned as she opened the glass doors, moving one of them inwards before securing it with a bolt in the floor. She entered the shop and turned on the lights before going behind the counter. She faced the caller wondering why she wanted to talk with her so urgently in the early hours of the morning.

'I'm Carol Hemsley,' began the woman in earnest. 'I want to talk to you about something which might interest you.'

'If it's to do with insurance, the Red Cross takes care of it,' stated Diana plainly. 'It's not in our remit.'

A smile appeared on the other woman's face. 'It has nothing to do with insurance. It's to do with your future.'

'My future? What do you mean?' The remark was so intriguing that it gained the manageress's full attention.

The caller stared at her directly before she spoke again. 'Have you ever considered standing as a Member of Parliament?'

The words seemed to echo around the room interrupted by a horse-laugh.

'Parliament?' No one was more surprised than Diana. Was this some sort of confidence trick or what? 'I think you're talking to the wrong person,' she uttered in disbelief. 'I know nothing about politics. Mrs. Robertson, one of my staff…'

'It's not Mrs. Robertson I want… it's you!' interrupted Carol moving to a chair at the side of the counter and sitting down on it. 'I don't know what you're political persuasion is but I'm counting that you vote for the Conservatives.'

'I'm not particular interested in politics,' retorted Diana smartly, taking the float from a cupboard and putting the coins into the cash register. 'My husband's Deputy to the Minister of Health for Labour. If you're Conservative you really need to know that.'

'I know,' admitted the visitor calmly opening her briefcase an removing some papers.

'Why have you picked on me?' demanded Diana slightly annoyed at being interrupted in her work.

'We were influenced by your performance on the television in the Speak Your Piece programme,' the woman informed her. 'You were outstanding. You spoke your mind and you did it so well. We're always on the lookout for female candidates with fire and spirit who speak clearly and solidly. You're definitely made to measure for a role in Parliament, there's no doubt about that.'

'I don't think so,' rattled Diana, flattered at the accolade placed upon her.

'Well I have to tell you that there's good news and bad news,' the visitor went on regardless. 'The good news is that although you've been vetted in your absence by the Conservative Area Board to become a candidate, there's every reason you'll be voted in. They've had the advantage of seeing the video of the television programme before they interview you finally. The bad news is that, as a brand new candidate to the Parliamentary scene, the consistency allotted to you will be a Labour stronghold. I'll be honest with you. There's practically no chance of you winning the seat.'

'Then what's the point of me having to go through all that rigmarole if I've no chance of winning?' declared Diana bluntly.

'Politics is a strange affair and these days there are more floating voters than ever before. They swing one way and then the other is according to whim, television programmes and the Press. But we all know that you're a fighter. I've watched that television programme video half a dozen times and I wouldn't like to be your opponent. I've spoken to Dr. Martin on the Red Cross board and she tells me you're full of ideas. That's the sort of person we want on our side.'

Diana sat back on her stool behind the counter with her head in a whirl. She had been simply a housewife for such a long time, bringing up two children, until becoming influenced to manage a Red Cross shop. Now someone was offering her a different opportunity in a much tougher league. Destiny was striking again with full force and she could do little to resist it. She knew in her heart that if went into this battle she would certainly lose. No one, certainly not a novice in Parliamentary procedure, could ever win the seat for the Conservatives in a Labour stronghold. She would simply be wasting her time and effort. But it was clear… the plan of her life was rolling out before her.

Did she really want to change the course again? After all, she was currently satisfied with the way things were going.

'How do you feel about the prospect?' asked Carol lightly. 'I have some instructions for you if you agree. Places, times and information about the Area Board as well as answers to a few questions they'd like to ask you.'

Diana blew out her cheeks to exhale as she thought about the offer. 'Will one of the questions be why should I want to stand as a candidate for the Conservatives when my husband's the Deputy to the Labour Health Minister?'

'Yes... questions like that I presume,' came the reply hoping to be able to influence the manageress. 'We need more women in Parliament. You could be one of them.'

'Except that I wouldn't win the seat,' returned Diana swiftly. 'I'd never win for your Party in a Labour stronghold.'

'That might be the case this time round but at the next election you'd get a better prospect. It would be a marginal seat that you could win.'

'That means I'd have to wait another five years. When will the next General Election take place?'

'Not for about four months or so,' Carol informed her briefly. 'The polls are very much in our favour at present but the Government will be forced to hold the election when their term is up.'

Diana caught her breath as she viewed the prospect in a calm light. She was determined not to put her life on the line without thinking long and hard and in that moment she decided to turn down the offer.

'Thank you for coming to see me, Miss Hemsley, but I'll be honest with you. I'm not politically-minded. I can't see myself standing up in the House of Commons and talking. It's out of the question.'

'Of course you could,' countered Carol smartly. 'Watch your video on teevee. You carried that programme all by yourself. Think about it.'

Diana had made up her mind. Politics were for people like her husband... dull, dry workaholics with the gift of the gab. Worst still they never answered questions directly. It was always a political response avoiding anything asked. They wormed themselves out of salutations with semantics. No... the role was definitely not for her.

Carol Hemsley left the shop disappointedly. Despite her best efforts she was unable to influence the manageress. Diana felt very sad herself that politics was not her forte and that she was well out of it. That evening, she had just finished dinner when the telephone rang.

'My name's Horace Weaver,' announced the caller, 'and I'm talking to you from the House of Commons.'

'Horace Weaver,' repeated Diana dumbly. 'Who are you?'

'I'm the Deputy Shadow leader of the Conservative Party. I understand Carol Hemsley called on you this morning suggesting that you stand as one of our candidates at the next General Election.'

'That's correct,' she managed to say in awe of the person at the other end of the line. She had seen him on television a few times attacking the Government on one point or another.

'It may be an old cliché, Mrs. Templeton,' he went on in a sonorous voice, 'but your country needs you. It needs you badly. I know that you have no chance of winning a seat this time round but it will be good preparation for the next time. You'll be helping us out even if you aren't successful.'

'You mean you need cannon fodder. Someone who'll stand in a constituency they have no chance of winning. You say you need me badly... well give me a better constituency... a marginal seat,' she reproached.

'Sadly there's a system operated by the Party,' he informed her. 'We need to line up people we think are suitable for the future. You're brand new on the circuit. If you don't succeed this time, you'll be in line for a seat next time.'

Diana weighed up the pros and cons in her mind swiftly. If she agreed, the Conservatives would be off her back. As she was certain not to win the seat she really had nothing to worry about. She would be involved in a few weeks of work in the hustings before the General Election took place and then her task would be over. The situation was very simple really and, in that moment, the die was cast.

'Very well,' she returned curtly. 'I'll stand for your Party, Mr. Weaver. Please arrange for details to be sent to me about when your Area Board wishes to see me and inform me what I need to do.'

'By the way,' he added finally. 'I saw the video of your performance on Speak Your Piece. I have to say you were excellent. If only some of the members in our Party had as much spunk we might have a great chance of winning the next election.'

The line went dead and Diana smiled to herself. It was indeed a compliment from someone so eminent in politics. She had been honoured by a major politician.

Later on that evening, after thinking about it, she was annoyed with herself for having agreed to a no-win situation. She wasn't a very good loser and it went very much against the grain. She would need to leave the Red Cross shop and spend a great deal of time and energy in the hustings, talking to hundreds of people and distributing leaflets containing the Party's manifesto through countless doors in the constituency. It would take her away from everything that made her comfortable and she now regretted it. Entering the political scene was going to be a mighty task to perform… a mighty task… and in the end it would be all for nothing!

CHAPTER NINETEEN

Jane, Samantha, Diana and Dr. Martin met once again at the hospital to play their regular game of bridge. By this time, Gloria was long forgotten… a relic of the past… her name was never mentioned. The four women sat down at the green-baize table preparing to play and Diana was highly delighted on this occasion for some of her memory had returned. It had been quite sudden, almost as though she experienced a click in the head, and everything began to fall into place. Within an instant, she began to feel quite normal again. All the fears and trauma which had dogged her for so long were gone and her mental attitude improved immensely. She could remember all the incidents which had occurred in her past life without effort and she knew that she was ready to face the world as she had done before. She recognised the images of her husband, Charles, as he looked in the past, but despite that she still didn't like the look of him.

'I understand you've been approached by the Tory Party to stand in one of their constituencies,' began Dr. Martin as Jane began to shuffle the cards.

'Yes,' returned Diana dryly. 'They asked me and I agreed but there's no chance of winning the seat… it's a Labour stronghold. It was last won with a majority of twelve thousand votes.'

'Things change over a period of five years,' commented Samantha wisely, trying to give her friend some element of hope.

'And pigs have wings!' retorted Jane still shuffling the cards. 'Twelve thousand votes in front means you've got a great hill to climb. I'd say it's impossible.'

'Nothing's impossible,' snapped Samantha curtly. 'We even got a man on the moon!'

Surprisingly Diana took umbrage at Jane's remark. 'I see,' she countered irately. 'You're the expert, are you? You think it's impossible!'

'A mission impossible,' stated Jane adamantly. 'I'm surprised you let yourself go in for it. You haven't got a dog's chance!'

'Well I'm going to give it my best shot, I've a number of ideas I could put into place…'

She stopped as the doctor burst out laughing. 'I'd be surprised if you didn't have a few things up your sleeve. Do you know, Diana, you're so refreshing… you're a marvel. I'm really glad to know you.'

‘Well there’s been quite a change over the past five years in that particular constituency. Immigrant have been flooding into the area… Poles, Pakistanis, Bangladeshis, Czechs and so on. Most of all are the people from those countries joining the European Union. There must be a way to influence their votes.’

Jane should her head refusing to relent. ‘Twelve thousand votes,’ she muttered. ‘That’s a really big swing!’

‘Many people were swayed at the last election because the Conservative Government had been so weak. Now Labour seem to have made a mess of it. Who knows what will happen this time?’

Jane placed the cards down on the table and Samantha cut them, then the four women carried on playing bridge. During the tea break, Jane looked into a mirror fixed to one of the walls to examine her face closely.

‘I must be getting old,’ she said almost in a whisper. ‘Look at the crow’s feet round my eyes. I’m getting old.’

‘Aren’t we all,’ concurred Samantha sadly. ‘They say that death and taxes are inevitable but they forgot about a woman’s good looks.’ She stared at Diana’s face as she sipped her tea and became thoughtful. ‘I’ve known you for many years, Diana,’ she went on, ‘yet you never look a day older. Do you know something that we don’t? How do you do it?’

‘I apply the make-up advertised on television,’ came the reply. ‘You know, the one that makes you look years younger.’

‘I’m not buying that!’ retorted Jane sharply, looking more closely at Diana’s face. ‘You’re not wearing make-up. I’d like to know how you do it. I mean you’ve been looking about twenty-eight years old forever.’

‘Yes,’ cut in Samantha suspiciously. ‘Your face is as smooth as a baby’s bum. You’ve no sign of wrinkles at all. It’s as though you’ve remained young for all these years.’

Diana’s heart beat a little faster when she realised that she would have to come up with a realistic answer.. What better than the truth? ‘I’ll let you into a secret,’ she advanced cautiously. ‘In Morocco, I go to a scientist who gives me these special pills and they keep me young.’

‘What pills are these?’ demanded Jane sharply, hardly believing the story.

‘They’re extracted from the essence of exotic plants in North Borneo,’ continued Diana frankly. There… the secret was out and she could have bitten her tongue for revealing it. God only knew what Dr. Mahmoud would say when he discovered that she had betrayed him!

‘Yes.’ snapped Samantha. ‘As Jane says, pigs have wings I don’t believe a word of it but it’s a good story. I only wish such tablets were available.’

Diana felt very relieved that they hadn't believed her even though it was true. However Dr. Martin looked at her in a strange manner. She knew that her bridge partner took tablets made by a scientist in Agadir and her suspicions were aroused when Diana told her story. It was clear in her mind that an experiment of some kind had been taking place. She hadn't known Diana for all that long but the comments made by the two other women started her thinking that something odd was going on.

'Let's get on with the game,' insisted the doctor realising that further discussion on the subject would get them nowhere except to embarrass Diana.

They finished their tea break but failed to continue playing cards. Instead they sat facing each other across the table discussing their colleague's strategy and tactics for winning the seat in her constituency. Diana sighed with relief that no one mentioned her youthfulness again although Dr. Martin decided she would watch her much closer in future. If Diana had stumbled on to a process which would keep women looking younger she wanted to be in on it. There was a fortune to be made and, as far as she was concerned, the centre of it was focussed in Agadir.

CHAPTER TWENTY

Two weeks later, Diana faced the Conservative Area Board. The interview was a done deal and it became obvious as that from the start. All the previous candidates had been dismissed and she discovered that she was the only person to be interviewed.

'Your husband is the Deputy to the Minister of Health,' began one board member who could have done with a measure of dieting to reduce his obesity. 'Do you have any concerns that he's in the Labour Government... in opposition to the role you wish to undertake?'

'I can't see the problem,' she responded candidly. 'We've been separated from each other for many years. I haven't seen him in all that time.'

'How do you feel about standing in a Labour stronghold?' asked another board member bluntly. 'You have very little chance of winning.'

'You think that, do you?' she retorted feistily, her anger rising swiftly. 'What kind of a Tory Board are you to be so defeatist? Every seat is there to be won. Why do you think so negatively? Why should you suggest that I won't win? An eight per cent swing will clinch it for the Party. My task is to overturn a majority of twelve thousand votes!'

Her vehemence took all the board members by surprise. They were used to people cowing before them in the hope of being chosen for a constituency. This woman was a virago!

'Will you support the policies in our manifesto without question?' asked another member. She was slim and looked very smart but her face was covered with wrinkles. Diana considered that the woman would have benefited greatly from the experiment with Dr. Mahmoud.

'Not necessarily,' she retorted fiercely. 'If I think your policies are against the British people I'll oppose them with all my will.'

It was not the kind of answer they expected but the woman continued undaunted. 'None of our policies are against the British people,' she countered sharply. 'Quite the contrary. Our aim is to make Britain a better place in which to live.'

'I hope so,' rattled Diana. 'What are your policies on crime, immigration, the National Health Service, wars and the country's finances?'

The board was astounded to be attacked with such a question from a brand new candidate who knew little about politics. It was as though the roles had suddenly changed. Instead of them questioning her, she was challenging the board!

As the interview ended, they told her that she had been selected, although two members of the board indicated that they were reluctant. Diana went home thinking that it was the end of the road until the hustings. If she thought that she was in for a big surprise. The next morning, just after she had opened the Red Cross shop, one of her staff came bounding in excitedly waving a national newspaper in his hand.

'You're famous!' she shouted continuing to wave the newspaper. 'Famous!' She placed the journal on the counter in front of the manageress to allow her to read the item. 'Look at this!'

Diana turned her attention to two photographs on the front page. The heading was "Husband and wife: Labour or Tory!" and the photographs were of her and her husband. It was clear that the Press were excited that they were on two different sides… contestants in the forthcoming election. Husband versus wife! It made a good story. Too much of a sensation not to hit the front page. There was even an editorial about the issue on one of the pages inside. Indeed, now that her photograph had been advertised to the general public she was famous. However the publication did not bring much joy for that evening Templeton visited her at her home. She hadn't seen him in years and it was quite a shock to see how much he had aged.

'How are you?' he began politely, pouring himself a drink from the cocktail cabinet.

'Fine,' she responded uneasily. 'My memory's returned.' She paused to reflect for a moment. 'I know why you've come.'

He sat down in an armchair before replying, sipping at his drink. 'You've seen the newspapers no doubt. How could you think about going into politics with the Conservatives? Why not Labour?'

'The reason for that's simple,' she explained easily. 'No one in the Labour Party asked me.'

Her response set him back for a moment. 'You can see my position, can't you? You'll have to withdraw your nomination. There's nothing else for it.'

She resented his remark strongly. 'I don't think so,' she told him angrily. 'I've a right to do anything I want! Why shouldn't I stand for the Tories?'

'You'll embarrass me greatly if you do,' he uttered with a tinge of anguish. 'I'm already being ridiculed by some of my colleagues. It can't go on!'

'Well I'm not changing my mind!' she told him adamantly.

'You have to,' he insisted. 'I've worked so many years to get where I am. You're going to ruin my reputation overnight.'

‘Look,’ she reasoned. ‘I’m standing in a Labour stronghold. My chances of winning the seat are zilch. After the election, everyone will have forgotten about me.’

He chewed on an olive thoughtfully. She was right but he was still uncomfortable with the issue, especially as the newspapers had got their teeth into the story. ‘I’d like you to reconsider,’ he pressed firmly, even though he knew that his wife wouldn’t comply with his wishes.

They discussed the matter for a while longer without him changing her mind. When he left, Diana felt that she had made the right decision to separate from the man. Whatever had been between them in days gone by had disappeared completely. They were two separate people leading different lives that set them worlds apart. They were far better off without each other.

* * * * *

Carol Hemsley presented herself at Diana’s house two months later. She had been appointed as the main support to her protégé by the Area Board and she was ready to set to her task. It was going to be disappointing to lose the seat at the election to the favourite Labour candidate but it was necessary for the Party to provide someone in the contest regardless of the end result.

‘The Government’s just announced the date of the General Election,’ she informed the manageress. ‘It’s in just over two months time. I’ve been appointed to support you although there will be limited funds at your disposal. How you want to proceed is entirely up to you.’

‘I don’t suppose any well-known names will come to my constituency to support me.’ Diana was not hopeful of any help to her from the Tory hierarchy.

‘They’ll be going to all the marginal seats,’ came the reply.

‘Well I’ve worked out a strategy,’ declared Diana simply, staring at the other woman. ‘I want to tour the area talking in different districts every day. All you need to supply is a wooden podium for me to stand on, a microphone and speakers, a white cloth with the Conservative logo, a British flag, and leaflets and badges. I want you also to find some musicians.’

‘Musicians!’ retorted Carol with surprise in her voice. ‘What are they for?’

‘The Americans find them very useful in their political campaigns. So why not us? People usually pass by the speakers but they’ll always stop to listen to music. If you could manage a brass band all the better.’

Carol stared at her strangely. ‘You’re going down fighting this seat, aren’t you? You think you have a chance of winning.’

'Of course I am. What do you take me for? I hate losing… even more I hate time-wasting especially when it's my own time.' Diana's attitude was very definite. 'If I go into battle, I want a strategy to help me win. Remember the story in the Bible about David and Goliath. Now you know where I'm coming from.'

Carol stared at her in amazement. 'I don't think the Board knows what it's taken on. You're the Minotaur in the Labyrinth. My God… I'm glad you're not my opponent.'

'We'll start each time with me on the podium, the white sheet with the Conservative logo behind me so that everyone knows who we are. Leaflets will be available on a nearby table together with the badges. The musicians will start to play, the audience will be attracted, and when the music stops I shall speak. After ten minutes or so, the musicians will start playing again… something like the Battle Hymn of the Republic and we'll finish with You'll Never Walk Alone. Everyone knows that one. I'll talk to them for another five minutes and then the musicians will play something again. I envisage each performance will last half an hour. After that we move on to the next place. There's no point in ramming politics down their throats for any longer than that.'

'Wow!' exclaimed her supporter in awe. 'How many talks do you think you can get through in one day?'

Diana shrugged her shoulders. 'Probably about eight. I think you should contact the supermarkets asking their permission if we can use their car parks for half an hour. That's give us the edge to speak to crowds of people. Once they hear the music, they'll come in droves.'

Carol stared at her in wonderment. I think you're brilliant. How is it we never picked you up earlier? ' She paused to stare at Diana's face. 'That's a silly question. You're only about twenty-six or seven.'

Diana laughed at the comment. 'No one's asked me for my curriculum vitae yet. I'm fifty-seven.'

Carol's face dropped as she stared at Diana's face again. 'You're kidding me, aren't you!' she managed to say.

'It's the truth. That's my age.'

'You must have a fantastic secret you're not telling anyone else,' retorted the other woman. 'What is it?'

'You wouldn't believe me if I told you,' stated her protégé tiredly. 'Come on. We've got a lot to get through if we're gong to make a real fist of it. To tell you the truth, I was dreading the idea of going into politics but now I've got the bit between my teeth I'm going hell for leather.'

They worked out the strategy together for the next half hour with Diana introducing a number of new ideas. They were now on track to fight like tigresses for the seat in the constituency. However there was some concern when Carol reported back to the Area Board. They were used to running their own mundane programme in the hustings relying on the speeches made by candidates on doorsteps, handing out leaflets containing details about the manifesto and television appearances by the leaders of each major Party. The idea of using American methods using musicians, speaking on street corners and car parks on a podium, using a large sheet with the logo and numerous opportunistic ideas did not go down well with them. At first they resisted making comments such as "we don't want a circus!", suggesting that Diana should resort to normal standard practices but Carol persuaded them to let her protégé have her head. Consequently, Diana's garage was soon filled with literature and other items to be used in the battle. The problem remained concerning the musicians. When Carol approached some bands, they saw the opportunity of making pots of money and wanted to charge sums way above the budget. However she eventually found five musicians willing to join them for one month in the task. There was one who played the tuba, one with a trumpet, another on the saxophone a drummer and a guitarist. They were an unknown band but they hoped that by their performance during the month someone would recognise their talent. As far as Carol was concerned, they were playing for her for free.

Diana was exceedingly nervous on the first day of the hustings. All this was very new to her. She had never done anything like it before and she reckoned that her husband had been right… she should have withdrawn from the start. Yet she had foolishly agreed and now found herself in the forefront of that decision with only Carol to support her. What was she to say to the public? She held the Tory manifesto in her hand but most of it was gibberish to her. Yes… there was mention of the main items affecting the country but nothing to say what they truly intended to do about them. It was all gobbledegook! How could the Party expect to deal with such important matters in a tiny leaflet the size of a foolscap envelope? It was utter nonsense!

The first of her speeches was scheduled to take place in a busy square in the town centre. People were going in and out of the shops and some were sitting on wooden bench seats basking in the sunshine, enjoying a rest from the busy pace of life. The Conservative van arrived shortly and two men removed the podium which was quickly put into place and secured the microphone with the speakers in front of it The white sheet with the name and logo was fitted up at the back between two metal poles while the musicians formed themselves in the front. A small table was set to one side with the leaflets and some badges. At last they were all set to go.

The musicians started playing a stirring tune and, as the noise wafted across the square, the public turned their attention in that direction. Shortly, a fairly large crowd gathered which increased in size in a very short time. When the band stopped playing, Diana climbed on to the podium.

'Ladies and Gentlemen,' she began in a hesitant tone before her adrenalin started to kick in. 'I come here as your Conservative candidate but I'm not like the usual politicians who talk to you.' People began to take notice as her commanding attitude shone through. Clearly she was going to say something of interest although some of the crowd doubted that she would do so. In their fixed opinion, politicians were all the same… to be tolerated not listened to.

'Parliament is comprised of over six hundred politicians who are supposed to represent the constituencies all over the country. But what do they do? They toe the Party line whenever they're ordered to vote on a one, two or three-line whip. This means they represent the Party's views and not those of the people. Why should we stand for that? There are no referendums on major issues so they don't really know what we want. They say we're too dumb to decide on matters of such great importance. What a load of codswallop! Don't they realise we have brains… that we have intelligence! Of course we can decide if the country should go to war. After all, who will be the soldiers? We will! And why don't we have a say in domestic matters which affect us? If I'm elected as your Parliamentary candidate at this General Election I make this solemn promise… not a politician's promise which is practically worthless… but one of my own. I shall fight tooth and nail against any person or Party… even if it's my own Party… who moves against Britain or the British people. You are the people who count and I am here for you. I want to be sure that you're not simply voters at the election but the people I represent in Parliament. I shall hold surgeries each week in this constituency and if anyone has a problem or an opinion I want them to come and see me. I warn every other politician and every Party that if I should win this seat they will have a virago on their hands… someone who will fight against poverty, red-tape, unemployment and utter foolishness!'

'What about all the immigrants?' yelled a man at the back of the crowd.

'I'm a member of the Red Cross and we treat immigrants who have contracted HIV, finding food for them before they're returned to their own countries. For those who have claimed asylum, they have just as much right to stay here as any Briton living on this island. As for Europe, well the gates are open. Another political faux-pas by the people you probably voted in at one time or another. But there has to be a limit to the number of people coming here from abroad. We're only an island with limited space and facilities. Action must be taken sooner rather than later.'

'What will you do about crime?' demanded a woman near to the front. 'How do you think you can control it?'

'Very simple, madam.' Diana was beginning to get into her stride. 'I intend to make that one of my priorities. We cannot allow gangs to operate in major cities carrying guns or young people threatening others with knives. This Government has done absolutely nothing to quell the number of crimes committed each year. If I'm elected, they will be so sick and tired of me bringing up the subject that they'll be forced to do something about it. I have some definite ideas how to increase the police force without straining the Government's purse and to reduce crime to its lowest level for a hundred years.'

She went on under the watchful eye of Carol Hemsley who stared at Diana in disbelief. At the last election she had supported a dull wimpish man who's ambition was simply to become elected to Parliament. He had no new ideas and Carol believed that he couldn't even write properly. This time she was supporting an exciting brand new move in politics. Her protégé was articulate, confident, putting our a completely new message even though it was contrary to the normal political practice undertaken by all the other Parties. Nonetheless, the strategy appeared to be highly successful. The audience which swiftly grew into a mighty crowd lapped it up.

Diana stopped speaking after ten minutes for the band to play another stirring tune and then she continued with her oration. The musicians ended the session by playing 'You'll Never Walk Alone' to which the crowd joined in by singing at the top of their voices. They then dispersed on a happy note taking away some of the leaflets and a lot of the badges. Many of them had never voted at elections through apathy but Diana hoped they would do so in her favour when the time came.

It was an initial triumph for her. So much so that Carol intended to report the progress back to the Area Board without delay. She had taken a tape-recorder to ensure that her superiors could hear exactly what her protégé was saying to the public. However, this was only the start of the operation. The two men bundled the podium and the other items into the back of the van and drove a quarter of a mile down the road to the next venue before putting it all out again in another square. Diana stood on the podium as the musicians played and a new crowd began to build up in front of her.

'I'm Diana Templeton... your Conservative candidate for the General

Election,' she reiterated. 'I don't intend to talk politics to you but merely to say that if I am elected I'll do a number of things which will benefit you as well as the rest of the people in this country. That is my sincere promise. I shall fight against all other members of Parliament and their Parties if they do not agree with my terms. I shall be the cat amongst the pigeons… the spanner in the works! I want to ensure that all pensioners receive an additional payment of ten pounds each week and be completely free in having to pay any income tax. That will allow most pensioners a chance to lead a more decent life. Then I intend to press for Council Tax charges to be reduced by twenty per cent. There is too much slack in the current arrangements. Cuts need to be made, Why should you… the people… have to fork out all the time for other people's inadequacies. Most of you just have your rubbish removed and pay through the nose for it. That has to stop!'

'How can you find the money for that?' demanded someone in the crowd. 'You're talking of billions of pounds.'

Diana moved closer to the microphone. 'I'll tell you how it can be funded' she related boldly. 'I would close down some of the useless quangos that suck up so much money. Every year, over twenty-five billion pounds is spent on committees which include the Apple & Cider committee, the Clean Air Act agency, the Freewheel Cyclist committee, and dozens of other useless committees. I could save fifteen billion pounds at the wink of an eye. It'll mean that all those fat cats making money in this way will no longer be able to do so. Why should the Government be allowed to waste your money? You work hard enough for it, don't you? At the same time, we can stop the Ministry of Defence spending the public purse on new aircraft, tanks, ships and weaponry. Who knows how many billions are wasted in that way. Does that answer your question?'

Carol Hemsley stood on the sidelines in wonder. Diana was so refreshing but she still didn't believe that she was in her late fifties. Where did the woman get all this information? There was only a couple of sheets of information that had been given to her… nothing on them like this.

'In addition,' continued Diana authoritatively, 'I intend to bring all out military personnel back from foreign countries. We're just a small island in the Atlantic Ocean. We have no responsibility to other countries in terms of military action.'

'What are you going to do with all the soldiers, sailors and airmen then?' asked a man at the far end of the crowd.

'Turn them into policemen to fight crime in this country,' rattled Diana without hesitation. 'Crime is one of my main priorities. People living in communities should be allowed to live in peace but in some areas they are too scared to go out at night. Youth gangs vandalise cars and properties and they have no compunction but to harm innocent people who stand in their way. This has to stop! That kind of behaviour in a civilised society must cease and the addition of, say, a hundred thousand more police will put an end to it.'

Her audience were fascinated by the way she spoke and the things she said and they were spellbound when the music started to play. The band ended the half hour session with the same final tune and shortly everything was packed away with remarkable efficiency.

'How are you holding up?' asked Carol smiling. 'Are you sure you're okay to carry on?'

'I'm fine,' returned Diana clearing her throat. 'As long as I don't lose my voice I'll keep going.'

At the next part of town, in the car park of a large supermarket, the van arrived and the two men repeated the process. By that time, Diana was raring to go again.

'I'm Diana Templeton, your Parliamentary candidate for the General Election and I've come to talk to you about crime. Our cities are rife with criminals of all kinds who carry guns and knives and who deal in drugs, gambling, prostitution and blackmail. There are gangs of youths terrorising neighbourhoods making innocent people's lives sheer misery. It has got to stop! What can be done you ask? Well we'll have to change the rules. We're far too soft on criminals in this country. Community service is not the answer. I shall approach the Prime Minister to build prisons on islands surrounding Britain. These will be devoid of any facilities such as television, pool, football, darts, card games and so on. They will be hell holes for prisoners. But that's only the start of it. The rules must change. With violent crimes, the criminals will be sent to prison for twenty years. Medium type crimes will attract a sentence of ten years while minor criminals will suffer five years in jail. Three time offenders will remain in prison for the rest of their lives. And there will be no remission for good behaviour. Within one year of such laws being passed, crime will be reduced in Britain by seventy-five per cent... either because the perpetrators are all behind bars or that they realise the serious consequences of continuing with crime. Every prisoner will be required to break up rocks and, as I said, no amenities will be available.'

'What about the human rights of prisoners?' ventured a woman in the crowd.

'Another do-gooder!' scoffed Diana cynically into the microphone. 'Let me tell you the only people with any rights are the victims not the perpetrators! I want to rid Britain of crime and this is the only way forward. I shall press the Government very hard to draw their attention to my ideas and I'll find supporters in this cause to set the plans into action.'

Diana was a whirlwind on the podium. Carol had never seen anyone so powerful, so vehement before. With the band playing tunes every ten minutes, the audience stood stock still waiting for the next pearls of wisdom to fall from her lips. It was a performance they had never witnessed before… a woman of command setting out new ideas for a better Britain. The unit carried on in the same way at the end of the half hour to move to another site. By this time, Diana's voice was beginning to sound hoarse so she decided to call it a day. Carol hastened to report back to the Conservative Area Board that evening with the tape-recorder in her hand.

'How's the three-ringed circus doing?' mocked the obese member, Dennis March.

'That's a little harsh, isn't it?' challenged Carol sharply.

'Well,' he replied casually, 'it's not very British, is it? Doing the hustings with a band of musicians. It just isn't done.'

Carol smarted at his words. 'You ought to be out on the circuit watching her,' she criticised firmly. 'That woman's a marvel!'

'You're really taken with her, aren't you?' The question was tinged with ridicule.

'Do you know, if she continues the same way, I reckon she might even win the seat.'

'Oh yes,' guffawed March sceptically. 'And I'm going to sprout wings! How can she possibly overturn a twelve thousand majority in a Labour stronghold? Not a chance! She hasn't got a hope in hell!'

'Just you wait and see!' came the swift response. 'You may be surprised. I don't suppose you'd like to put a bet on it.'

March's stared at her greedily with dollar signs appearing in his eyes. 'You want to bet on the result? How much are you willing to gamble?'

'Name the amount!' She became fired up by the man's negativity.

'No… you name it,' he said, counting his winnings in his head even before the bet had been placed. 'It's like taking candy off a baby.'

Carol thought for a moment. 'Let's say a hundred pounds.'

March laughed aloud, his fat body shaking all over like a jelly. 'I'll take that. Shake on it!'

They shook hands and Carol wondered whether she had been foolish or wise after the event. How she would love to wipe the grin off the man's face by winning the seat. However the bet was on and it was up to Diana to pull it off.

* * * * *

On the following Saturday afternoon, a week before the General Election. Diana took a flight to Agadir. It was her intention to arrive there in the evening and return the next day in advance of the last few days of the hustings. She wasn't feeling particularly well in herself and the malaise worried her. She needed to see Dr. Mahmouod to ask whether he had made any changes in the structure of ferradil-x that might have caused it but when she arrived at his office he wasn't there. She called out his name and opened the door to his private room. It was extremely Spartan… a tiny chamber with a simple single bed, an old wooden chair and a large cabinet with shelves filled with volumes of medical books… but there was no electronic equipment of any kind, no television, no hi-fi, nothing! To her dismay the scientist was not there yet he had told her that he never left the hospital. She looked around and discovered a door leading off, opening it to find herself in a small square quadrangle within the hospital. She shuddered to think that the scientist had actually lived in such menial conditions for the last sixteen years. He had dedicated his whole life to his work and then a terrifying thought came into her mind… where were the animals? Was the experiment all an elaborate hoax? If so, she didn't think she could bear it. With that in mind, she went to the reception desk in the hospital to ask whether they knew the whereabouts of the scientist.

'He fell ill,' stated the desk nurse dryly. 'He's in Room Sixteen undergoing treatment.'

'Can you tell me where he keeps his animals… those that he experiments on?' she asked with her heart beating faster.

'They're kept in a separate room not far from his office,' came the reply.

Diana relaxed as the tension in her body slowly subsided, Well at least he was telling the truth about that part of the experiment. 'Room Sixteen,' she repeated thanking the desk nurse for the information. She went directly there, knocked on the door and entered. Dr. Mahmoud lay in the bed with a drip in his arm and an oxygen mask over his face. 'What happened to you?' she asked sitting in the chair next to the bed. He looked so ill that she feared she would find herself in the same situation in the near future if this was the effect of the experiment.

He peered at her through half-closed eyes. 'Don't worry, my dear,' he managed to say. 'It won't affect you.'

'Can you clarify that for me please?' she demanded in a soft tone for she felt great pity for the scientist.

'I injected one of the monkeys with an experimental does of Apollo-y and he bit me. You see me now as normal. You ought to have seen me last week. My face swelled up at double the size.'

'I'm sorry to see you in this condition,' she told him sadly. 'Is there anything I can do for you… anything you want?'

'No,' he returned, his body shaking as he coughed loudly. 'I don't need anything.'

'Are you taking ferradil-x tablets every day?' She envisaged that he might not be able to take them while in this condition but he assuaged her fears.

'Yes… yes,' he replied slowly. 'I insisted I have them every day. I can't let the experiment lapse on account of a monkey bite.'

She spent half an hour with him until he fell asleep and she returned directly to her hotel. There was really nothing for her to concern herself about the experiment. She returned to the hospital the following morning to visit the scientist and he seemed very much improved.

'You've come on in leaps and bounds since yesterday,' she told him with a smile on her face.

He smiled back at her weakly and nodded. 'The pain has gone and so has all the swelling,' he rattled. 'You must have waved a magic wand that cured me when you left last night.'

'If only I had one,' she laughed 'I've had a word with the nurse and they'll discharge you tomorrow. I suppose you can't wait to get back to your work.'

'I can't,' he told her candidly. 'But your visit's not for a while. Why have you come?'

Her face puckered up as she spoke. 'I've been feeling a little low lately. I came to ask you about it. But after seeing you in hospital, I'm sorry I came.' '

'I know you now, Mrs. Templeton. You use up all your energy on one action or another wearing yourself out. It creates stress in you and the one thing that ferradil-x hates is stress. You must slow down in your activities. Then you'll feel better.'

'Huh!' she guffawed. 'I'm right in the heart of a General Election in Britain… contesting a seat in Parliament and it's tough going. I'm talking to hundreds of people every day asking them to vote for me.'

'How long will it go on?' He shifted uncomfortably in the bed.

'Not much longer, thank God!' she replied swiftly. 'Not much longer.'

'When it ends you must slow down. Come back and see me again.'

She left the hospital much happier than when she first arrived in Agadir. It was sad to see the scientist in hospital but she was satisfied with his explanation. Now she wanted to see her friend Ahmed. There was no point in going to his office on a Sunday because he wouldn't be there. She wandered into the public square and sat down for a moment in the hot sunshine. Ahmed wasn't anywhere to be seen and, after a while, she took a taxi to his home address. It was the hovel that always made her shudder when she thought about the night she had stayed there.

She knocked on the door and one of Ahmed's young brothers answered.

'Is Ahmed at home.'

The boy failed to respond but immediately went inside., There was a torrent of Arabic dialect and the eldest sister came to the door.

'He ees not een today,' she uttered closing the door rudely in Diana's face.

There was still the same resentment she had felt during her stay in the hovel. It was something that would never be resolved within the family... a Christian becoming involved with a Muslim.

She caught the aircraft back to England that evening. She could feel stress building up inside her. Dr. Mahmoud was right. She had to slow down but there was her commitment to the Conservative Party with regard to the General Election. For the moment, it would have to come first but at least there would soon be an end to it after the voters had made their decision.

* * * * *

The last week of the hustings was frantic. Candidates from all the parties urgently tried to get their messages across to the public within the next few days and the door to door canvassing increased in intensity. Diana was performing eight sessions each day, together with the musicians, and the effort began to take its toll. She wished with all her soul that the day of the General Election would come so that she could go home and sit in the comfortable armchair in her lounge and forget all about it. The newspapers had become fully aware of her remarkable campaign and they printed details of her speeches daily. It was definitely a bull-point in her favour. Meanwhile, her opponent, Roger Spooner, the entrenched Labour candidate with many years of Parliamentary experience, ran his campaign from a van with a loud-speaker fixed to the roof. He drove around the streets shouting at people to vote for him. Which candidate would win in the end? One with a van and a loud-speaker or one with a musical band? The hours were fleeting by and all would soon be revealed.

Carol was delighted with the situation, thinking hard about winning her bet with Dennis March. It wasn't the money that inspired her, although the sum of a hundred pounds would be welcome. She simply wanted to wipe the smile off his face and make him eat humble pie.

The day of the General Election finally arrived and Diana stood outside the polling station dressed in a light blue suit, holding a schedule which contained the names and numbers of all the voters. It was a very exciting day; one in which she could relax without having to speak although she did pass the day talking to voters as they came and went. She was so tired at the end of the day that she didn't really care about the result for, despite her great effort and brilliant ideas, she considered that she had no chance of winning. At nine o'clock that evening all she could think of was relaxing at home with a drink in her hand watching a film on television. She closed her eyes when she thought about the Red Cross shop. Although she had some excellent volunteers, she knew that when the cat was away the mice will play. She really wanted to get back there to check that everything was in order. Even more important was that she had entered a date in her diary to attend the Red Cross National Assembly. Her fame from the television programme and the latest newspaper reports caused the organisers to ask her to address the assembly. After all she had done to influence the people to vote for her, it would be refreshing to talk to a large group of people who were willing to listen.

That evening, the ballot boxes were delivered to the Town Hall and the people hired to count the votes began to stack them into boxes. Each standing candidate had a box with his or her name on the front and, as the voting papers were opened, they were placed in the appropriate candidates' boxes. Roger Spooner, dressed in a sporting jacket, stood at the back of the room looking very confident. He firmly expected to return with a majority over ten thousand votes. He was annoyed at Diana's intrusion into his territory believing that her attempts to oust him were simply a legend in her own mind. He watched the boxes on the table like a hawk becoming a little concerned that Diana's container was filling up quite well... only a little behind his own. The other candidates fell well behind the two leaders and Spooner believed that Diana's votes would soon run out. However he was in for a big surprise because it didn't turn out that way. Suddenly they were neck and neck in the count with just a few hundred votes left. Diana's started to feel the hairs on the back of her neck stand on end. Could she possibly have turned the tide in her favour to achieve a fantastic victory?

Shortly after all the votes had been counted, Diana was called to the officiating table together with Roger Spooner.

The Recording Officer cleared his throat. 'The situation is this,' he stated plainly. 'The votes for Mr. Spooner are twenty-one thousand four hundred and sixteen. Those for Mrs. Templeton are twenty-one thousand four hundred and seventy-nine. As the margin is so close, do you wish to demand a recount?'

'I certainly do!' muttered Spooner angrily. At the last election he had a majority of twelve thousand... now he faced defeat. It was inconceivable to him! The votes were recounted and the ordeal continued for both candidates. Diana really wanted to get home and sleep but she was forced to wait until the recount was over. Eventually the Recording Office was satisfied with the conclusion and he climbed the rostrum to address the few people who were there.

'As the Recording Officer for this constituency,' he related, 'the votes recorded are as follows: Peter Grimes, New Liberal Democrats, two thousand three hundred and six. Angela Hendrey, National Loony Party, eight hundred and seven. Roger Spooner, Labour, twenty-one thousand four hundred and eighteen. Diana Templeton, twenty-four thousand four hundred and ninety-two. I declare Diana Templeton the Member of Parliament for this constituency.'

A roar went up from Carol Hemsley while Roger Spooner looked very down in the mouth. The impossible had happened... he had lost his seat in a Labour stronghold. Diana didn't seem to take in the fact that she had won but Carol was over the moon at the result. She hugged her protégé so tightly in her excitement that Diana was almost unable to breathe.

'We did it!' she cried loudly caring little that other people could hear her delight. 'We did it!' She could now collect the hundred pounds she had bet with Dennis March and make him eat humble pie. She could hardly wait to see him again. Her protégé had triumphantly won a seat in the House of Commons when all the signs were against her. She had accomplished a mission impossible coming out a winner and she had done it all by herself.

The newspapers made the most of the story. Conservative woman in Parliament with a husband who was Deputy to the Labour Health Minister. It was too good a story not to print.

The party held on the following day was outstanding. It was an auspicious occasion and the wine flowed as well as the provision of an excellent buffet. No one could believe that Diana has won the seat in a Labour stronghold the first time she ventured into politics and Dennis March paid Carol the amount he lost on the bet very reluctantly.

'So... the three-ringed circus won the day,' gloated Carol rubbing salt into the wound.

'Maybe we should revise our operations for the next General Election,' submitted March indelicately. 'She's certainly the right woman to take us through this century. I've seen her curriculum vitae. There's an error with her age though.'

'She looks so young for her age. It's hard to believe.'

'I reckon someone made a typing error and put in fifty seven instead of twenty-seven,' he muttered.

'You should have heard her,' continued Carol enthusiastically. 'She spoke with such force, such vehemence, such strength and it all made sense. She's going to do great things for the Party.'

March nodded and moved off to a group of other people. Diana was listening to a few successful candidates, each of whom held a glass of wine in their hands, when the door opened and Robbie and Karen entered. She turned toward them in surprise placing her glass on the table before greeting them. They both hugged her, congratulating her warmly on her success.

'My, my!' exclaimed Robbie in wonderment. 'I thought Dad was brilliant getting his appointment but you really take the cake. First I thought you were going to be a great film star. Now you're an MP. What next do you have up your sleeve?'

'We followed your progress in the newspapers,' related Karen delighted with the success of her mother. 'They put you on a high pedestal.'

'Higher than the podium on which I stood,' joked Diana taking hold of their hands affectionately. 'I'm so pleased to see you. Would you like a drink?'

'I don't think you have the time, mother,' stated Robbie blandly. 'The Press is waiting outside for you to give them a statement. It seems, mother, that you're the dish of the day.'

'You'd better get out there,' urged her daughter smartly, 'while you're in their good books. You know how quickly a person can fall out of favour.'

Diana went outside to face a volley of newspaper reporters and photographers. They jostled about taking photos of her and shouted out questions.

'Your Party didn't get in, Diana,' called out one reporter informally. 'but you managed to get a seat with a mighty swing. What do you say to that?'

'I told the public the truth... not political clap-trap. I meant every word I said with sincerity. If the policies of either of the major Parties doesn't suit the British public, I shall oppose them and strike out for change. I'm patently aware that I'm not only responsible for my own constituents but for every person in this country. They need to know that!'

The photographers continued to take pictures of her with flashlights going off all over the place.

'How do you feel about your husband being on the other side?' asked another newspaperman.

'I'd face the Devil if needs be to do my job properly regardless of any counter situation. Come to think of it, now we're in opposition that's exactly what I'll be doing.'

There was a titter of laughter and then a female reporter posed a question.

'Are you serious about your plans for crime?' she demanded.

'Wouldn't you?' exclaimed Diana tartly. 'How much longer can we tolerate the situation? The police are busy with paperwork which takes them away from doing their job, while the gangs maraud all over the place with guns and knives. I've outlined the plan how we can reduce crime in Britain. It's simple really. It's up to the Government to implement it without delay or it will remain a yoke around their neck and never go away. I'm going to press hard. I'll not let them get away with it. They'll soon know where I'm coming from. If nothing's done, the public will eventually make its own feelings known. Vigilante groups will form and then we'll have trouble. They'll be worse than the gangs. The lack of commitment by the Government will create a ridiculous situation and they have to realise it. If vigilante groups are formed, the public will have more effective powers to resolve the situation than the police. Is that what they want to happen?'

The questions continued for about twenty minutes and then Diana thanked them for their interest and went back inside to the party. She was on top of the world. Her photograph and comments would be printed in the national newspapers on the following day in all their glory. What other politicians would make of them was another matter. In her opinion, many members of Parliament were arrogant, selfish people, who only stood as candidates for the salary offered to them if they won a seat. Many of them had little experience and were totally inadequate for the task. They simply made up numbers for their Party and, on most occasions, voted as they were told by the Chief Whip. Blind sheep came to mind when she thought about them. Well someone had to intervene to protect the rights of the public and get things straight!

* * * * *

Although the Press made great play on Diana and her husband, she knew that she would come face to face with him on occasion. However it did not happen because the day before she took her seat in the House of Commons, she received a message to say that Templeton had suffered a serious heart attack and had been taken to hospital. At first, she thought about sending him a

'Get Well' card with a basket of fruit, then emotion set in and she changed her mind deciding to visit him. After all, they had been married for many years and had brought up two children together. She felt that she owed him that much in his hour of need.

'This is a fine kettle of fish,' she greeted on entering the private room afforded him by the hospital. 'What happened?'

He smiled weekly, clearly uncomfortable in the bed. 'I had a severe pain in my chest and collapsed in the street,' he informed her miserably. 'You didn't have to come but I'm glad you did.'

'I know I didn't,' she affirmed. 'Robbie and Karen will be here soon to cheer you up.'

He took hold of her hand and she flinched for a moment but didn't pull away. 'I've always loved you,' he told her amorously. 'There was never any other woman in my life… just you. When I look back, I realise I was such a fool but now I've come to the end of my life I know I lost my greatest treasure… you!'

'The end of your life,' she guffawed although a feeling of dread passed through her mind. 'Don't be so morbid!'

A tear rolled down his cheek as he closed his eyes. 'You look so beautiful. Do you know you haven't aged a day in all these years. Your skin… your eyes… your hair…' He tailed off tiredly.

'Now that's enough!' she chided gently. 'We mustn't get melancholy.'

'I mean it,' he went on undeterred. 'I gave up everything for my work. What did I really achieve in all that time? How much did I sacrifice for it?'

'Hold on, Charles!' she cut in swiftly. 'You're the Deputy to the Minister of Health!'

'A lot of good it's done me now my health is failing. Someone else has already stepped into my shoes. So what was it all for? All those hours, days, weeks, months, years I could have spent with you and the children. Wasted… all wasted! When you were in hospital in Morocco, I couldn't wait to get back to my office. What kind of person would do that when his wife had been attacked and needed him?' He moaned weakly as more tears rolled down his cheeks. 'All the years have passed and I've got nothing to show for it. Nothing!'

'You have two wonderful children. Robbie and Karen.'

'Children whom I've hardly ever seen. I don't even remember them as children. I was never there.'

His head lolled to one side and the bleeper started on the electronic machine behind him. Within a few seconds, a nurse hurried into the room and then ran out to find a doctor. Diana was asked to move into the corridor and she waited there for a while before the doctor and the nurse came out.

'He's not too good,' revealed the doctor with no expression on his face. 'He suffered a severe heart attack and we'll need to operate on him tomorrow.'

'Will he recover?' She felt extremely sad at the thought of her husband undergoing a major operation.

'It's far more complicated than that,' the doctor informed her. 'He has about a thirty per cent chance of survival. I don't think he should have any more visitors today.'

Diana sat in the hospital cafeteria sipping coffee. She still didn't like the man, even though he was her husband, but he was someone with whom she had lived within the past and they had brought up two children together. There was a lot in that to say the least. Yet other problems began to form in her mind. First of all, Charles would need a place to stay. He couldn't live alone in his apartment. He would have to come and live with her. She wasn't too pleased about that. If he did stay in his apartment and had another attack there would be no one to help him. Secondly, if he lived with her, he would need a nurse to take care of him on a full-time basis. It was all so inconvenient yet she felt helplessly bound. The problem spun around in her head making her more annoyed as she thought about it. After all those years of separation, she didn't really want him interfering in her life in that way.

She went home and returned to the hospital the following day. Templeton was undergoing surgery while she waited and two hour later the surgeon emerged from the operating theatre. He saw Diana sitting on a seat outside and approached her.

'Mrs. Templeton,' he said, placing his hands in his pockets. 'I recognise you from your photograph in the newspapers.'

'How's my husband?' she asked with hope in her heart. 'Was the operation successful?'

The doctor moved his head from side to side as if unsure. 'In a way,' he informed her uncertainly. 'Clinically the operation was successful but I'm not sure he has enough strength to pull through. We shall have to wait and see. In the meantime, they'll take him to the Recovery Room. You can see him there.'

She thanked him and made her way along the corridor. The doctor didn't give her husband much chance of survival but he had come through the operation even though the doctor had told he that he had only a thirty per cent chance. Templeton was shortly wheeled into the Recovery Room and they connected him up to the electronic machine behind the bed. He seemed to be wide awake but at first he didn't seem to recognise her.

'I'm dying, Diana,' he managed to say weakly. 'They probably think the operation was successful but I can feel myself slipping away.'

'Don't be so melodramatic, Charles!' she challenged boldly. 'The operation was a complete success. The surgeon just told me so.'

As her words faded into the distance the bleeper on the electronic machine sounded loudly and the image on the screen flat-lined heralding his death.

Diana raced out of the room to find a doctor but it was far too late. Despite all the efforts to revive him, Templeton had passed away. Five minutes after his death, Robbie and Karen arrived. They had no idea of the severity of their father's condition and were devastated to hear the news. They hugged their tearful mother, then asked to look at the body of their father. They entered the Recovery Room to stare at the corpse and tears flowed down Karen's cheeks as she saw her dead father.

'Bye, Dad!' uttered Robbie, offering a posthumous farewell to his father. 'Rest in peace!'

Karen took her father's hand and pressed it firmly. She was devoid of talk or emotion, staring at his body vacantly.

They were all shocked at his sudden demise which had been so unexpected and they fought to absorb the fact of his departure in their minds. During his life, he had not been the perfect father in any sense of the word but he was the man at the head of the family regardless of his faults. The sad fact was that, despite all the hard work he endured over such a long period of years, no one would really miss him. He was an important person in his high rank in the Government when he was alive Now that he was gone he was a past nonentity. All he had done during his lifetime would be carried on by someone else who had filled his shoes and the name of Templeton would vanish into infinity.

Contrary to how she thought she would feel, Diana was extremely sad that he had passed away. He had made provision for her in his will, but that was an ancillary action as far as she was concerned. When people are young, she thought, they don't fear death for it's only what happened to old people. It's very remote and distant from their minds. And yet, when it comes, as it is destined to do, it buries sadness in the heart for death, at any time, always comes unexpectedly. The philosophy was true!

* * * * *

After Templeton's death, Diana became very thoughtful. His words on his deathbed had been perfectly right. A person could get sucked into the work ethic unwittingly and end up like her late husband... ruining his life for the sake of ambition. It had happened to Templeton and now she realised that its tentacles were beginning to encroach into her life. Firstly there was her volunteer work as the manageress of the Red Cross shop which had crept up on her slowly. Now it was the winning of the seat in the House of Commons. Little by little, her life was being taken over by events somewhat beyond her control. Was there some kind of Cosmic Joker in the firmament who played such tricks on people's lives? It definitely seemed to be the case. Well she refused to allow it to happen to her. Something would have to go!

The funeral was held four days later in a cemetery in the countryside. Two plots had been purchased by Templeton many years earlier for both of them and, as she stared vacantly at one of the gaping plots, she wondered how long it would be before she filled the other one. If Dr. Mahmoud was right, it would be the best part of another one hundred-and-fifty years before it happened. A hundred-and-fifty years! Her mind reeled at the idea. Everyone she knew would be dead by then… all the people in her life… her son, Robbie, Karen, her friends Jane, Samantha and Dr. Martin, her supporter Carol Hemsley… everyone! It was a daunting thought that preyed on her mind.

The attending priest uttered a prayer over the coffin after it was wheeled out on a trolley into the field. The sexton arranged for it to be lowered into the cavity as those attending watched mournfully. More prayers were said and then the priest threw some dirt on to the coffin before the mass of earth interred it forever.

Not surprising, as Templeton had been so high-ranking, many people attended the funeral, mostly Civil Servants and politicians, and, from the look on their faces, some of them were delighted that Templeton had passed on to the next world. Diana imagined there would be a great battle amongst them as they fought to be appointed in her husband's place.

After the burial, most of the mourners entered the vicarage where wine and sandwiches had been prepared. One person Diana recognised was Alan Greenfield, the man who had come to her house with a large bouquet of flowers after she had separated from her husband. He had told her that he had admired her from afar for a long time and he tried to proposition her to have an affair with him. It soon became evident that he was undaunted by her rejection of him. He was a horrible creep and she stared at him bleakly noticing that he was well over the limit having already imbibed five full glasses of wine. After eyeing her up and down

blearily, he plucked up courage to sidle up to her causing her to feel sick to her stomach.

'Hi, Diana!' he slurred with a stupid grin on his face. 'Nice to see you again.' She ignored him and started to walk away but he followed her like a sheep dog moving so the he could face her. 'Why don't you and me let our hair down?' he ventured staggering slightly from right to left. 'Come and have dinner with me. Yeh... why don't you have dinner with me? And afterwards we could have a good time.'

'You ought to be ashamed of yourself!' she castigated irately. 'You're a married man with a family. Go home to your wife and stop making a fool of yourself by trying to play the field. You're not cut out for it!'

He smiled completely undeterred by her criticism, swaying slightly as he reached for another glass of wine. 'Charles is gone,' he muttered whimsically. 'You have to get on with your life. Why not give me the chance? You know how I feel about you. Don't let the opportu... opportune... opportunity pass you by.'

She looked down her nose at him in disgust. 'I wouldn't get involved with you if you were the last man on earth and that's a fact. You're disgusting and I despise you!'

'Ah, he said, regurgitating, waving his glass in front of her face. 'I like feisty women. I like the ones who say no when they mean yes,'

'Get out of here!' she snapped angrily in a whisper so as not to attract the attention of the other mourners. 'If you don't I'll have you thrown out!'

'Huh!' he laughed drunkenly. 'Thrown out by the widow of the dead man at his funeral. That must be a first. Why don't you call the police and have done with it?'

She moved away from him and launched herself into a group of Civil Servants on the other side of the room. It was sufficient to stop Greenfield from pursuing her. The gall of the man, she thought to herself, trying to proposition me at my husband's funeral! What a horrible man! What was the world coming to when senior Civil Servants acted in such a manner?

After she arrived home, she realised that her sister knew nothing of the incidents in her life so she rang her to appraise her of the news. Laura was overwhelmed to hear of her sister's success at the General Election but her voice saddened as she learned that Templeton had died. She hadn't known the man for long but the fact was that he had been one of the family and his passing caused her an element of grief. She would have been far more concerned had Diana and Charles not been separated for a number of years. It somehow softened the blow.

'Why don't you come over here for a while?' she invited helpfully. 'Just until you get over the loss.'

'It's very kind of you,' returned Diana mildly. 'I've only seen Charles once in the last decade and that was when he asked me to withdraw my name from standing for Parliament so there no sense of loss really.'

'Why not come for just a week? The change will do you good. You can surely spare one week. Mac and the kids would dearly love to see you again. And I want to hear everything that happened to you in detail. You've got to come over here and tell me.'

Diana screwed up her face as she thought about it and then made her decision. 'I'm sorry,' she told her sister point-blank. 'I'm expected in Parliament tomorrow. There's an awful lot going on and I really mustn't miss it. If I can persuade the Chief Whip to let me go for a week I'll come... but it'll be for one week only that's for sure.'

'Well you're always welcome,' continued her sister. 'Let me know one way or the other. I'll have your room ready.'

The line went dead and Diana pressed her lips together. She couldn't really spare the time to cross the Atlantic Ocean again, not with her new career. If she could only split herself in two it would have been easier. Then she thought 'strike while the iron's hot!' You have only one life. Make the most of it!

The following day she met Duncan Redfearn, the Chief Whip, in the entrance of the House of Commons, seeking his permission to travel to the United States for one week.

'I can't see the problem,' he advised her. 'Members of Parliament are at liberty to come to the House or stay away. It's entirely at their discretion. For obvious reasons, when there's a major vote on an issue, they must come but I can't see any objection to you being absent for one week. Have a good time there.'

'I will,' she told him delighted at the freedom. 'I'm going to visit my sister and her family in Los Angeles.'

'An interesting city,' he responded amiably. 'By the way, now that you're here. I understand from some of your speeches in the hustings that you don't intend to follow the Party line on some issues. Is that true?'

'It is Mr. Redfearn,' she told him bluntly. 'If the Party tries to do anything I think will harm some or all of the British public you can expect me to challenge it fiercely. I'm a woman of my word.'

'I understand where you're coming from,' he retorted firmly. 'We're a hundred per cent for the British public and everything we do is intended to benefit them but we can't be all things to all men.'

'You do nothing with regard to crime and taxes,' she countered strongly. 'They should be your top priorities. Nothing is being done to curb criminals who carry guns or knives. Parliament simply stands back and lets it happen.'

‘You must understand we’re not in power so our hands are tied. We haven’t enough seats to press strongly enough to introduce legislation to prevent such things happening. It’s entirely the province of the Government.’

‘I don’t buy that for one second,’ she snapped. ‘Why don’t we pester the Government non-stop to do something about it? If you don’t then I’ll do it. You can bet your life on it.’

He stared at her in dismay. ‘You have no idea how politics work, Mrs. Templeton. It can’t turn on a sixpence. There are so many matters to discuss and put into legislation. Everything takes time. It has to.’

‘Why?’ she demanded tersely. What’s wrong with changing the crime laws in, say, three months time? It doesn’t need a genius to work out what needs to be done. I’ve set it out myself in a ten minute speech. It calls for a massive revision of the law in Crown Courts. Surely that would be simple enough to arrange. People should be punished according to their crimes. Five years, ten years, twenty years and life with no remission. We have to eradicate crime. As such we would need less policemen and women to establish the peace.’

‘I agree with you wholeheartedly,’ he concurred, ‘but I’m relatively powerless to keep pressing the Government on the single subject of crime. There are hundreds of other matters which need urgent attention.’

‘So you’re willing to let crime prosper in Britain with no help for the victims! I think that’s shameful. We must do something about it!’

He was clearly defeated in the argument and decided to put an end to it. ‘I hope you have a very pleasant time in America,’ he said finally and quickly departed into the main chamber of the House of Commons.

Within five hours, Diana was on an aircraft travelling to the United States. It was a welcome relief to sit back with a drink in her hand after all the work she had done in the hustings and the death of her husband. Robbie had met her to see her off and she was soon on her way for a short visit to see her sister and the rest of her family.

When she arrived there, Laura was waiting outside the airport. The two women hugged warmly before they climbed into the car.

‘Is there no end to your talents, sister?’ joked Laura exceedingly proud of her sister. ‘I don’t know how you do it,’ she laughed. ‘You could be a film star, you were a manageress in a shop and now you’re a real high-and-mighty member of Parliament. Gee I don’t know what you’re taking but I wish I had some of it. You must tell me all about it. Everything. I want to hear it. Every single word.’

‘You’re a hard taskmaster,’ laughed Diana easily. ‘By the way, how’s Greg… the amorous Greg who so wants to marry me?’

Laura burst out laughing. 'You're too late sis. You had your chance. He got married a day after his divorce came through. Married a boopy blonde who's taking him for a ride. She shops every day buying expensive dresses, shoes, hats, handbags and a whole host of bling, and he's having trouble keeping up with the finance.'

'Does this mean another divorce is in the offing?' asked Diana with a broad grin on her face.

'I don't think so,' came the reply. 'You see people like the luscious blonde Estelle have good looks and a terrific figure and they only go for the money. Well she's spending all of his so there's no point in going for a divorce because she'd get nothing.'

'My God!' exclaimed Diana. 'Hasn't the man any sense at all?'

'You know what he's like with women. He's in love with every one of them... short, tall, blondes, brunettes, whatever.'

Poor Greg, mused Diana unable to stop smiling. 'He'll never learn.

When they arrived at Laura's house, Diana met Mac, Rusty and Chuck once more. She realised how deeply she felt for her family relishing the fact that she had now become a part of their lives. That evening, when the children had gone to bed, they sat in the lounge drinking and talking, mainly about the campaign waged by Diana at the hustings. Mac had imbibed a few too many beers and he became quite light-headed. He stared at his sister-in-law and unwarrantedly made a comment about her age and appearance.

'Say, Diana,' he began in an America drawl, slightly slurred by the drink. 'I've seen some photographs of you about twenty years ago in Laura's album and you don't look a day older. Laura now looks like the older sister instead of it bein' the other way round.'

The comment was incisive and Laura reacted swiftly to it.

'Hey!' she chided with a tinge of anger in her voice. 'Lay off , will you! Of course she's my older sister.'

'But she looks so young,' continued Mac shrugging his shoulders.

Diana smiled although she felt embarrassed. It was true. Laura looked so much older but what could she do? It was impossible to reveal her secret to her sister especially as the words of Dr. Mahmoud rang in her ears. Laura would definitely believe her and soon there would be thousands of women banging on the scientist's door begging for treatment. She couldn't do it. In the ensuing silence, Laura turned to Mac.

'Stop drinking and go to bed,' she commanded. 'I want to talk to Diana about Charles.'

Mac staggered to his feet and left them to go upstairs to bed. Diana turned to her sister and related the details about her husband's operation and his ultimate death. To Dian's relief, the matter of age was quickly forgotten. Nonetheless, Laura's attitude towards her sister became a little tepid after that evening. She seemed unable to accept the fact that she looked much older than her sister. She kept looking at Diana's face and then examining her own in a mirror. Mac was right. Laura was looking older with crow's feet forming slightly around her eyes and the start of puffy bags under them while Diana hadn't aged one iota over the years… still looking as young as she did when she was twenty-eight. It was not without relief that Diana left the United States at the end of the week. Triumph had a way of suddenly turning into disaster at a moment's notice in life and although the sisters contacted each other fairly regularly by telephone, Diana was never invited to stay in Los Angeles again.

CHAPTER TWENTY-ONE

As a result of the trip which should have been delightful, Diana returned home to England with a troubled mind. The last thing she wanted was estrangement from her sister yet Mac's comment seemed to have upset the apple cart. She opened her front door to discover a large amount of mail and eventually sorted through it to find another letter from Ahmed. His message was loud and clear.

My dearest Diana,

I send my most humble condolences on the loss
of your husband. I read about his death in the news-
paper and I know how shocked you are by the event.
My sister told me that you had visited me on your last
trip to Agadir but I wasn't here. I'm so sorry because
I would dearly like to see you again. Dearest Diana,
my heart bleeds for you. You know how much I love
you and now you are free to come and see me. I want
to be with you all the time. I'll buy you a new house
in the best part of Agadir to live with you for ever.
Please come and see me soon.

Affectionately,
Ahmed.

The envelope that he sent felt thick and she looked inside to find a photograph of him. He looked much older now that the years had passed by and she thought about the situation for a while. There were two barriers which had been demolished in double quick time. The first was that he now looked older than her, so age was no longer a consideration. The second was the fact that she was no longer married but a widow. Ahmed was definitely the man in her dreams but she didn't dream any more. The rest of her mail was divided into bills, junk mail and letters of congratulations on her success at the polls. She now had her own bills to pay although she benefited greatly from her husband's Will mostly from the sale of his apartment in London. She was now a rich widow capable of affording anything she wanted to do in life except for the fact that she had committed herself to five years of work in Parliament. Furthermore, with the reticence that she had already faced from politicians, she knew it was going to be a hard slog. However on reflection, she now had all the money she would ever need with at least another hundred-and-forty years of youthful life. There would be plenty of time for her to enjoy it.

One of the letters that she opened made her smile. It was from a national cosmetic company which manufactured skin cream for women, inviting her to a meeting at their headquarters in London to discuss her appearance in an advertisement for television. They intended to portray a gorgeous-looking woman to influence others to use their product. How false was that advertisement because she never used any make-up whatsoever. When was all this deceit and folly going to end? Without hesitation, she tore up the letter with a wry expression on her face. She refused to lie to anyone for any reason. She realised, however, that the demands on her were increasing all the time and she began to dislike it intensely. It was so easy to be twisted and turned by fate in order to serve the needs of others. She needed to sit back and think more about herself.

Despite her fatigue from jet-lag, she arranged to meet Jane, Samantha and Dr. Martin that evening for another game of bridge. At tea time, Jane approached her to make conversation.

'How's your memory holding up,' she asked casually. 'Are you remembering everything from your past now?'

'It's normal again,' replied Diana sipping her tea. 'No problems at all.'

'Funny thing about the brain,' intruded Samantha. 'It's a computer inside our heads working away all day. It even works at night in our dreams.'

'Dreams!' repeated Diana slowly. 'I used to dream but since my memory returned I don't anymore.'

'It's your brain's reaction,' stated Dr. Martin. 'You will dream eventually. Your brain is catching up with events.'

'I look forward to that time,' returned Diana hopefully. 'I used to enjoy my dreams. They were really good.'

'Really good?' echoed Samantha with interest. 'What were they about?'

'That would be telling,' came the reply.

'You little devil, Diana Templeton!' reproached Jane laughingly. 'You have dreams of love and romance and I bet there's a lot of intimate activities.'

Diana appeared to be somewhat embarrassed by the remark but she laughed it off. 'If only,' she lied. 'Chance would be a fine thing.'

After a while, Jane and Samantha discussed the play on one of the hands that evening while Dr. Martin sidled up to Diana to whisper in her ear.

'I'd like to talk to you in private after the others have left,' she told her quietly.

Diana stared at the doctor vacantly. Why did she want to talk to her privately? Could it be something to do with the Red Cross? Or was it something to do with her new role in Parliament?

When the other two women left, Dr. Martin invited her to sit down. She looked directly into Diana's eyes and placed her hands down flatly on the green-baize table indicating her nervousness.

'I want to know... ... ' she began firmly ending the sentence in mid-air.

'Want to know what? Diana was confused at the remote approach.

Dr. Martin hesitated for a moment before continuing. 'How have you managed to stay so young and never aged?'

'I thought we went through all that a while ago. Who said I never age?'

'Come off it!' challenged the physician. 'Jane knows it, Samantha know it and I know it. There's something you're not telling us. How do you keep so young. It's uncanny. You're nearly sixty and you look in your twenties. You have no signs of wrinkling... no crow's feet... no bags under your eyes... your skin is perfect. There's obviously something going on that you're not telling.'

Diana was rocked back on her heels. 'I don't have to tell you anything, Valerie,' she countered sharply.

'I think you do, Diana. Yes you do!'

'What do you intend to do about it if I don't?' Diana was beginning to rally her thoughts, annoyed with herself because her reply indicated that there was something to reveal.

'It has to do with your trips to Morocco, doesn't it? You go there every six months. Why?'

Diana's resolve began to crumble. She found herself painted into a corner. She could refuse to answer any further questions and go home or face the consequences. 'Very well I'll tell you but if you repeat any of it to another soul I shall deny having told you. You must understand that. What I told you was true. I've been involved in an experiment for the best part of fifteen years with tablets taken from the essence of two exotic plants which grow in North Borneo. I told you all this before but you didn't believe me.'

'What effect do these tablets have on you?' The doctor was becoming very interested.

'It keeps one looking young but there's another benefit which you might find hard to swallow. I expect to live for two hundred years. It's all in the experimental stage but it's been proved to work on animals. The scientist and myself are the only two human-beings involved in the experiment. Neither of us knows the full outcome. Maybe we will in a hundred years time or so.'

The doctors stared at her in amazement. 'That's a most fantastic story,' she retorted. 'I don't think you'll need to wait that long. If it works on animals it will probably work on you. So he uses animals in his experiments.'

'A hamster with a life expectancy of two years lived until it was twelve. On that calculation, a human-being would be expected to live until he or she was four hundred-and-fifty years old.'

The physician gasped at the comment. There was a long pause as she thought about the prospect. 'Can you get me in on this experiment?' she asked with an element of hope.

Diana pursed her lips in thought. 'I can ask him,' she replied solemnly. 'The name of the scientist is Dr. Mahmoud. I call him the Wizard of Agadir. He has an office in the annex of the hospital there. He's cured people of cancer and other diseases. One of my friends had terminal pancreatic cancer and he cured her after all the British doctors had given up on her.'

'I'd appreciate it if you'd have a word with this scientist of yours,' continued the doctor.

'In the meantime,' pleaded Diana looking at her directly, 'not a word to anyone. I've already exceeded my remit by telling you. It has to be kept a secret or everyone will want to get in on the act. Is that clear?'

You have my solemn promise on that,' declared the other woman sincerely. 'You're right. The less people who know about it the better.'

Diana went home that night with a heavy heart wondering if she had done the right thing. There was no getting away from the fact that the doctor had been most perceptive and followed her instincts through. Well she was determined not to mention anything to Dr. Mahmoud about it. He would be furious with her for revealing the secret to another person. He had insisted on secrecy. She needed to fob off Dr. Martin in stages, playing for time, letting her down slowly. After all what could her bridge partner do about it? No one would believe her if she told such a tale. They would think she was out of her mind.

CHAPTER TWENTY-TWO

There's an old adage which says that a week in politics is a very long time and Diana learned that to her cost. She took her seat on the back benches in the House of Commons to be alienated by some of the other politicians. She had no idea why they had adopted such an adverse attitude towards her, assuming that she had failed to make any real ties with them having missed the first session of Parliament due to her trip to America. However their dislike of her soon became apparent when Duncan Redfearn, the Chief Whip, stood up in relation to a question on finance during Prime Minster's Question Time.

'Prime Minister,' he began in a sonorous tone. 'How do you intend to pay for the increase in Civil Service staff as stated in the White Paper you have just produced. You seem to have avoided that issue.'

Before the Prime Minister could reply to the question in his usual gobbledegook language used by politicians to avoid a direct answer, Diana rose to her feet without the permission of the Speaker with a suggestion.

'I have the answer to that one,' she shouted from the backbenches to everyone's astonishment. 'You cease the activities of many of the quangos. The Government spends twenty five billion pounds every year on committees that do practically nothing for the nation. End the activities of most of them and you'll have enough funding to reduce the rate of Income Tax and Council Tax charges and leave a sum to benefit pensioners.'

The Speaker stood up in amazement at the interruption. He had never witnessed anything quite like this before. 'You are out of order, madam,' he reproached angrily. 'Please sit down. As you're a new member, I'll overlook your outburst but you should be well aware there are procedures which operate in this House. Make certain you understand them in future!'

Diana sat down extremely angry at being rebuffed. If this was the way they ran Parliament was it any wonder the country was always in a mess. Procedures in the House! That was part of the problem. No wonder very little was ever done about the important matters that needed changing. Why didn't they tell it as it is? She really didn't want any part of it. Her mind reverted to the Red Cross shop where she had been so happy. She didn't need to stand for this nonsense! Without hesitation, she stood up to deliver a tirade causing other members in the House to groan and give way to their impatience.

'I cannot understand why a person can't speak freely in a country where free speech is supposed to prevail.' she ranted loudly to the calls from other members to sit down. 'If it is not, then this House is in conflict with the unwritten laws in this country which insists that it happens. But not here I notice. I demand the right to say my piece in relation to this question. If not, then I challenge this House to revise its procedures because they are contrary to the law.'

The House was in an uproar with members waving notes and shouting for her to sit down. The Speaker went red in the face and stood up demanding silence.

'Madam… will you kindly take your seat or I'll have you removed,' he barked irately. 'I will not tolerate such conduct! If you persist I shall arrange for your eviction from this chamber!'

His ruling was plain enough. She would be thrown out if she interrupted the proceedings again even though she was trying to help the Government in its quest. It was a cross too much to bear. After the session, Duncan Redrfearn came to see her, intending to advise her on proper conduct in the House.

'You must observe the code of conduct or the procedures in the House will fall into disarray. Much of the good work we do is carried out behind the scenes with committees. What you see here is the tail end of the situation. It's really all a game. We argue and poke fun at each other but the main work has already been done.'

'Well forgive me if I don't join in your game, Mr. Redfearn,' she retorted angrily. 'I want to do my duty as a politician not fool around nonsensically in an old boy's club. What use is my presence here if it's all a game?'

'When you've been a member for some time and you've learned the rules, it'll make more sense to you.'

'How long will that take?' she riposted. 'Elections come every five years!'

'There you have it,' he told her politely.

'I really can't wait that long to represent the people,' she reacted. 'You can keep your seat in Parliament. I've got better things to do than be one of your sheep.'

'If you refuse to come to the House, I suggest you report in sick every month,' he uttered seriously. 'We can't afford to fight a bye-election so early after the General Election. It's not on!'

'Do the hell what you want,' she snapped curtly not wishing to have any part of it. 'I'm finished with politics!'

She stormed out of the chamber, furious at the harsh way she had been treated. It was a ridiculous situation whereby new politicians had to be silenced. It was the symptom of the problems facing the country that only experienced members ingrained with the procedures and rules were allowed to speak. Fancy having to fight two more elections to get a foot in the door. It was unspeakable! No wonder her late husband had to work day and night to get somewhere in the political scene. It wasn't worth it! She had achieved great heights, far more than most other women of her time but now it was over. When she next saw Dr. Martin she asked whether it was possible to go back to the Red Cross shop as the manageress. At worst she might be accepted back as a volunteer staff worker now that she had abdicated from her political career.

'There's a problem, Diana,' related the physician. 'We appointed a new manageress when you won your seat in the House of Commons and we have a full staff of volunteers at the present time. To be frank, we thought we'd seen the last of you. I'm sorry but I can't do anything for you at the moment.'

Disappointed at the rejection, Diana went home to reflect on the situation. Destiny was a two-edged sword. It had offered her some wonderful opportunities to change her life and then had taken them away almost as quickly as they came. She had burned her bridges with the Red Cross... she had given up on politics... and she had disposed of the letter from the cosmetic company for a chance to become involved in a television advertisement. Not very clever for a woman who thought she was intelligent! One moment it was all going well for her with a little too much to control and then suddenly it was gone. Well she could relax now and lead the life of a lady of leisure... cruising around the world in a liner... taking exotic holidays in far distant countries... doing anything she wanted! Perhaps after all that had happened, fate had decided the best way ahead.

* * * * *

After a month had past by, Diana realised that the stress she had suffered had vanished. She felt as free as a bird, excellent in health as, as Dr. Mahmoud had predicted, it had been the stress which had cause her the malaise. She was visited by Robbie one day who seemed to be rather distressed.

'What's the matter?' she asked. 'Is something wrong with Stella or the my grandson?'

'No, they're perfectly all right,' he responded, sitting down heavily in an armchair. 'If the schedule's correct she'll be having our second baby in a week's time.''

'You haven't answered my question,' she pressed stolidly. 'What's the matter?'

‘I don’t know whether to laugh or cry,’ he told her.

‘About what?’ She was becoming frustrated at his prevarication. ‘Will you stop faffing about and tell me!’

‘I’ve just seen a photograph of the two of us taken outside the Conservative Party’s headquarters when you talked to reporters after you won the seat in Parliament.’ he continued.

‘What about it?’ She was puzzled as to what he was going to say.

‘Someone made a comment at the time which surprised me,’ he went on. ‘You look so young in the photograph they thought you were my sister.’

‘Well,’ she laughed shrugging her shoulders uncomfortably knowing where the conversation was going. ‘It’s a mistake any one might make.’

‘I didn’t think anything of it at the time. And then I saw a photograph of the time I graduated from college. You and Dad were standing behind me in it. I compared the two photographs and you’re the only one who looks exactly the same in both of them. Don’t you think that’s strange?’

‘Many people retain their good looks until late in middle age,’ she countered. ‘I’m happy to be one of them.

He shook his head slowly. ‘It’s a good thing really but you’re almost sixty, mother, and you look so young… so perfect. You look younger than I do. I don’t understand it. You really did look like my younger sister outside the Tory’s headquarters.’

‘You’re very flattering. Thank you for that but shouldn’t you be with Stella in case she goes into labour.’ He thought about her remark for a moment and then stood up. ‘By the way,’ she went on. ‘You father’s Will has been approved by the Probate Office so you’ll soon be receiving the money granted to you. Together with your new baby, you should be over the moon.’

‘I could do with it,’ he muttered. ‘Now that the baby’s coming we’re thinking of buying a bigger place. We’ll need it.’

He left the house with Diana slightly concerned about her son’s comments. It was something she hadn’t foreseen when she began the experiment… people realising only too well that she wasn’t ageing. Ostensibly, they were all moving ahead of her in years. She didn’t know how long she could keep the secret to herself before everyone prised it out of her.

That night she lay in her bed reviewing the latest features in her life, cursing the fact that she had acceded to the whim of Carol Hemsley to stand for Parliament. Yet looking back, she could not help but smile at the interest she had created, especially with those poor musicians seeking fame and fortune. Nonetheless, despondency raged through her mind in relation to the Red Cross shop. She had been so happy there. Now the gift had been snatched away from her so quickly she had difficulty getting her head around it. There was a lesson to be learned. If a person is happy at their work, they should never be distracted or spoil it to be lured away to pastures green. You have only one life... enjoy it! What a fool she had been to give up something worth fighting for! She had gone for gold and had ended up with her feet in the mud!

In a while, she drifted into an uneasy sleep and for the first time in many years she began to dream. At first it was mysterious in its content without any rational meaning but eventually it became clearer and an old scene returned to her. Once again she stood on the edge of the Sahara Desert staring at the sandy horizon at the side of Ahmed. On this occasion he looked so handsome ... so good-looking... so much older. She put her arms around his shoulders and he clasped her tightly around the waist. Then his face moved forward and he turned kissing her tenderly on the lips. She found it warm and refreshing as she reciprocated.

'My dearest Diana,' he cooed into her ear. 'I love you so much. .I adore you... I need you... I want you!'

She felt her body go limp as he kissed her softly on the lips once more.

'I'm not sure,' she told him in her dream. 'I'm not sure I really want you. It's all a matter of love and I don't love you.'

'Of course you do, my darling,' he responded calmly. 'You've loved me and wanted me all these years but you refuse to overcome your inhibitions. Let yourself go and feel the warmth of romance. The time will come for us to make perfect love together and we will both be ready for it.'

She gazed into his dark brown eyes with an element of love forming in her mind. He was right. She had to let her inhibitions go. She looked at him directly, running her eyes over his handsome face, feeling her legs weakening as passion built up insider her with a vengeance.

'I think now is the time,' he told her, kissing her on the neck which caused her head to jerk back slightly as a force of erotic nature surged through her body.

Suddenly the chemistry between them began to spark into life. He was lithe, attractive, energetic and filled with love for her. It excited her so much that she felt couldn't delay serious intimacy with him for a moment longer. Desire overcame her so badly that her body became moist with passion as he led her back inside the tent. In the dim light that existed, he lowered her gently on to the mattress and began to remove her clothing erotically, touching her softly in places which made her feel as though she was high on drugs. She began to experience feelings of high passion that she had never felt before in her life. Undressing himself, he moved forward so that their bodies closed fast together and he began to kiss her tenderly on the neck, the shoulders, her breasts and her abdomen. It was a wonderful exciting feeling that surged through her and she moved herself closer to his body in the expectation of serious intimacy taking place. Within a very short time, they were tightly united in ecstasy and Diana moved her body up and down in the bed as though being seduced physically by a fantastic lover. As the sensuousness began to reach its zenith she cried out in her sleep: 'More… more! Don't stop now! Don't stop!' And then breath spouted from her mouth in a series of short gasps as the continued action of the intimacy caused her to reach a sensational climax in the dream. Thereafter, her body relaxed completely satisfied and she woke up with every fibre of her body alive and burning with passion. She was bathed in perspiration and truly believed that what she had experienced had been an act of wholehearted sexual intercourse… except that it was all a matter of make-believe. Yet the sensitivity of her body and the actual climax she experienced proved that she was sexually satisfied. She now considered Ahmed in a different light and the photograph he had sent her appeared in her mind. He was a great lover… of that she knew from her dreams. The only segment missing from the equation was that none of it was real. She recognised from the imagined intimacy that she needed to strip herself of all her inhibitions in order to enjoy a relationship with him to the full… but that had to happen in real life! She glanced at the clock on the table beside her bed. It showed that it was four-thirty in the morning. How was she going to get to sleep again after such a fantastic dream? She lay back in bed trying to make some sense of her life when, to her surprise, the telephone rang.

'Hi, Mom! It was the excited voice of her son, Robbie. 'Sorry to wake you up so early but I can hardly contain myself. Stella's just given birth to a bouncing baby girl. A sister for Jack!'

'Congratulations!' uttered Diana in a gruff voice as though she had a mouthful of cotton-wool. 'Well done, Robbie! How's Stella?'

'Both she and the baby are fine. She was eight pounds six ounces. We're over the moon… both of us!'

'And what's the baby going to be called?' asked his mother beginning to wake up fully.

'Evangeline Gwynneth,' replied Robbie boastfully. Evangeline Gwynneth Templeton. How's that for a name?'

'Well she's your child. You can call her what you like.'

The conversation ended almost as quickly as it had started and Diana replaced the receiver tiredly and lay back in the bed. She had another grandchild. Well good for Stella and Robbie but where did it leave her as a twenty-eight year old looking woman just on the right side of sixty. By the time she was a hundred years old, the new baby would look older than she did. What would people say to that? It was a thought that really concerned her at four-thirty in the morning.

CHAPTER TWENTY-THREE

The next time she travelled to Agadir, she took a taxi directly to the office of Dr. Mahmoud. To her dismay, he wasn't there but another man sat in his chair with his feet on the desk reading a comic book.

'Where's Dr. Mahmoud,' demanded Diana puzzled by his absence. He was always in the hospital at his desk. He lived his life there.

'You're Mrs. Templeton, aren't you?' advanced the man. 'He told me you'd be coming. I'm Hamid Arran. I'm standing in for Dr. Mahmoud while he's away.'

'Away?' Alarm signals began to cross Diana's brain. 'Where's he gone?'

'To North Borneo. He's gone there to bring back some plants.'

'Any idea which ones?'

'Not sure. There's a problem with people clearing the rain forests . I think he wants to preserve some plants and grow them here.'

'Those are be the ones from which he gets Beotag and ferradil-x I presume,' she went on.

' I don't know,' he replied blandly. 'He's out there now but he'll be back in a few days' time.'

Diana sat down in the chair opposite him trying to get her mind into gear. A few days! She could stay in Agadir for as long as she liked. There were no longer any pressing engagements requiring her attention in England. The only matter of prime importance was to see her grand-daughter but there was nothing else of importance on her agenda. 'I'll wait to see him,' she told the man.

'You can't stay here in this office,' he retorted believing that she would remain in her chair until the eminent scientist returned.

'Not here, you fool!' she rattled sharply. 'I'll be staying at the Sahara Hotel. I'll come back in two days' time.'

The man nodded and rudely returned his attention to his comic book ignoring her entirely. She shook her head and rose from the chair.

'I don't suppose it would be too much trouble to make a note of what I've told you to show Dr. Mahmoud. It would be helpful if he rang me at the hotel when he returns.'

'I'll tell him when he comes back,' muttered the man continuing to read his comic.

‘Right, Mr. Arran,’ she snapped finally with contempt in her voice. ‘Don’t let me interrupt your erudite reading!’

Two days passed by and there was no telephone call from the scientist. Diana went to his office to ask Arran whether the doctor had been delayed to discover him sitting behind his desk.

‘I left a message with your deputy to telephone me,’ she bleated in annoyance, ‘but he obviously was more interested in the comic book than to deal with my request.’

‘I received no message,’ Mahmoud informed her sombrely.

She sat down opposite him. ‘You gave me quite a scare. I thought something had happened to you.’

He laughed out loudly at her remark. ‘Didn’t you know,’ he joked, tugging at his goatee beard. ‘I’m going to live forever.’

She ignored his comment as idiotic. Forever! The man was surely becoming over-ambitious. It wasn’t possible for anyone to live for ever… even with organ transplants… or was it? ‘You travelled to North Borneo I understand.’

‘I was concerned about the clearance of the rain forests,’ he told her solemnly. ‘As you know, the plants from which I extract Beotag and ferradil-x are extremely rare. The actions of the clearers could eliminate them entirely. So I went there to pick up a hundred plants which are now growing in the hospital. They remain in darkness in the forests which is their natural environment and they are so placed here. The temperature is established by the heaters in the hospital. I have secured an abundant supply for the future regardless of how much rain forest is cleared in North Borneo in the future.’

‘That’s a relief,’ returned Diana delighted at the outcome.

‘There is one problem however,’ he went on sadly.

‘The hospital will not fund the cost of the room in which the plants have been relocated. They refuse to pay the heating bill required to keep the tropical temperature. I don’t know how long they can keep going.’

‘No problem,’ she retorted smartly. ‘I’ll pay the bill. You can leave that to me.’

His eyes lit up and he stared at her brightly in appreciation. ‘My thanks to you, Mrs. Templeton. You’ve ensured that the experiment will continue.’

‘It’s in my own interest after all,’ she told him delighted to be able to assist financially. ‘You’re looking well. Are there any further developments with the animals?’

‘Everything’s fine,’ he replied. ‘They’re all fine. Arran took care of them while I was away.’

Diana paused before venturing on her next mission. 'Dr. Mahmoud,' she began tentatively. 'I'm very much aware that there are just two of us involved in the experiment. How do you feel about introducing a third person?' She was thinking of Dr. Martin but was unable to tell the scientist that she had revealed the secret to her.

To her surprise he nodded his agreement. 'If it's the right person,' he uttered briefly. 'I'm currently writing a paper on the subject which I shall send to all the medical authorities in major countries. In that case, our secret will be out.'

'Is that wise?' she countered seriously concerned. 'Won't you have every woman in the world knocking at your door to obtain the tablets?'

'Truth is, no one will listen to me. They'll all consider me to be a mad professor. My address and location will not be told to anyone so I've no problem on that score. No… no one will believe me so we're relatively safe. I'll be branded as a charlatan out to make money from unsuspecting people. It's to be expected… par for the course.'

'When do you intend to present this report?'

He smiled at her tugging at his goatee beard. 'In about six months time. It'll be filed or lost, no doubt, so I don't expect to hear anything about it again. I'm in no hurry. In a hundred years time I'll be able to prove my point. My longevity will influence all the sceptics.'

Diana saw a means by which she could bring Dr. Martin into the fold but it was quite clear that her bridge-playing friend would have to be patient. She discussed a number of minor matters with the scientist and then left. Her next priority was to see Ahmed. After having experienced the exotic dream, she felt much warmer towards him and the light of love began to invest itself in her mind. It was the most important thing in her life that was missing… the warmth and sensation of true romance. Since the dream, her mind was filled with thoughts of love and Ahmed was the only man to whom she could relate. He was a person who had declared his undenying love despite all the problems which stood in their way… the only lover in her life about whom she dreamed. She went directly to his office and entered without warning. His face lit up as he saw her and he leaned forward readily to kiss the fingers of her hand gently.

'Diana!' he exclaimed jubilantly. 'You've made my day coming here! What a wonderful surprise. Oh… you look so beautiful… so young!'

She stared at his face closely. 'No!' she remonstrated puckering up her face. 'I don't like that moustache!'

He touched the hair which adorned his upper lip and shrugged his shoulders. 'If you don't like it, it will disappear overnight,' he said assertively. 'You can be sure of that.'

There was a pause as they stared into each other's eyes. He looked so much older now than when she first met him, maturing over the years while she had remained exactly the same. Due to her involvement with the experiment, the age-gap had changed between them considerably.

'I dreamed about you the other night,' she revealed openly. 'I had a fantastic dream about the two of us.'

'Snap!' he retorted. 'I dream about you almost every night,' he exclaimed. 'I can't get you out of my mind and I'll tell you one thing, we've got to do something about it. We can't go on like this!'

'I agree,' she concurred, throwing all caution to the winds. 'But what do we do? You have a firm in Agadir. Your family live here. I live in England What can we do?'

He was surprised at the sudden turn of events. She had rejected his love for so long but now the chemistry between them was different. Diana was clearly willing to lose all her inhibitions and start a new life with him... if only they could think of a way to overcome the obstacles in their paths.

'Why don't we capitulate,' he suggested, staring at her face with a loving expression.

'In what way?' She couldn't find a solution herself but he seemed to have found the means.

'We could live in England together. We could live in your house.' He was hesitant in advancing the idea believing that she would never agree to it.

She was taken aback as it appeared that he was ready to give up everything to be with her. 'I've no objection to that,' she remarked, 'but what about your firm... your business... your family?' The questions ran off her tongue like the rain falling heavily on trees in a tropical forest.

He paused to reflect for a moment on her agreement for him to live with her in Britain. 'I could sell my business,' he advanced thoughtfully but we would have to be married in order for me to stay in England.'

'And your family?' she countered considering that to be the biggest obstacle in their path. However she was stunned by his reply.

My uncle can take care of them. I mean my brothers and sister are old enough to look after themselves now. My sister will soon be married to a man chosen for her and my brothers are on the point of going out to work. I can't see it's any problem.'

'So be it!' she told him wondering what her son and daughter would think about the arrangement. Then another thought came into her mind. How would he react when he discovered that she was almost sixty years old. Would he be such an ardent lover then? It was yet another hurdle she needed to overcome. Of course she could keep it a secret from him but as the years went by and she remained the same he would realise that something was strange. But that was really not a serious problem for if he loved her enough and their intimate relationship continued to flourish she need have no worries on that score. For a while she fought in her mind whether or not to tell him her secret then she decided against it. There was an old Chinese proverb which went: 'A wise head keeps a still tongue.' It was sound advice. After some degree of examination, she decided it was a saying she needed to follow.

* * * * *

There were many things Ahmed needed to settle before he came to England and Diana passed the time leisurely on her return. She spent a day talking to her friends in the Red Cross shop but the opportunity for he to work there again had long gone. She was bemused by the fact that she had once been so important to the institution that they had asked her to represent them in a television programme. Now she was a forgotten entity… a relic from the past. How strange was life that people forgot so quickly… especially about people who had served them so well. Shakespeare was right when he wrote, in Julius Caesar: 'The evil that men do lives after them; the good is oft interred in their bones!' It was a betrayal of loyalty but would never be recognised as such.

One morning, she was relaxing at home reading a book when Duncan Redfearn, the Conservative Chief Whip, called to see her. She was very surprised and invited him inside. He was handed a drink and sat in one of the comfortable armchairs to face her.

'Have you made up your mind finally what you intend to do about your seat in the Commons,' he asked amiably, although he was burning with anger inside at her reluctant attitude to conform to Party procedure.

'I'm definitely not continuing my role in Parliament,' she told him adamantly. 'In my opinion, it's all a sham. I regard it as pointless in the long run. No one has any intentions of resolving the serious problems of this country. They're all white-washed.'

'Why should you say that?' he enquired becoming more angry at her response. She was a loose cannon in his mind.

'I've just told you!' she fired back at him. 'My presence in the House is simply one of cannon-fodder. You tell me how to vote and I do it. Well I'm not one of your sheep simply following orders. I became a politician to get things corrected in an imperfect Britain. No one in politics seem to be bothered about it. So what are we all doing there?'

'You realise you're letting down your constituents,' he went on dramatically. 'They voted you in. They depend on you for support and guidance.'

'I've a friend who uses a term quite often. 'And pigs have wings!' What support can I give my constituents? No one's ready to listen to me in Parliament. It's a sheer waste of my time and theirs. When I agreed to stand for election, I made a promise to the voters to get Britain back on its feet and protect them. How stupid I was! Do you know who would suffer mostly if my crime laws were put into place. Firstly it would be the criminals themselves with very long harsh sentences. Secondly, would be the lawyers and barristers who make fortunes out of the fees they charge for cases. I would limit every case to a maximum of five days. I've just learned of one that's lasted for nine months at a cost of thirty million pounds to the taxpayer... the man in the street works hard for that money! No... lawyers and barristers would soon realise the situation. The laws of the country for criminals must change and quickly.'

'You're talking about matters which take many years to change,' he challenged incisively. 'The whole of our legislation grinds very slowly.'

'Far too slowly and very little to benefit the people of Britain,' she attacked strongly. 'What you all need, if you'll pardon my French, is a kick up the arse! Members of Parliament draw huge salaries and a mass of expenses but they do nothing for the public.'

'You need to regard these issues over a period of time,' he defended. 'Look at the advances we've made since Victorian times. Life is quite different now than then.'

'Despite the slow grinding nature of Parliament,' she said sarcastically. 'I'm going to resign. I understand I can apply for the Chiltern Hundreds which will be accepted as my resignation.'

He had tried his hardest to persuade Diana to return to the House of Commons but she was not to be moved. After a while, he could see that his visit had been futile so he rose and went to the door turning to make a last plea.

'Diana,' he began seriously, 'are you going to come back to the House? I have to know. The Government have a majority of fifty-two. We need every vote we can muster to oppose them. Your vote will be vital in a Division.'

'My vote!' she muttered angrily almost under her breath, turning her attention rudely back to the book she had been reading.

He stared at her solemnly and then without speaking further he left, his body language indicating his annoyance at her refusal.

Diana was proud of her resolve. The newspapers would probably make a meal of her resignation so soon after the General Election but she imagined that Redfearn would wait a few months to let some time pass. Then, after the bye-election, everyone would have forgotten about her. That was exactly the way she wanted it to happen. And if she lived to the ripe old age of two hundred, everyone alive today would be dead and buried. Her actions would be lost in the multitude of events which had occurred in the flurry of the past.

CHAPTER TWENTY-FOUR

Jane, Samantha, Dr. Martin and Diana met once again to play bridge at the hospital. The doctor could not take her eyes off Diana's face waiting patiently for the moment when they could speak again in private. It seemed to cloud her mind for her skill at bidding and playing was seriously impaired that evening.

'Wake up, Valerie?' snapped Jane, as the doctor made another poor decision in the bidding. 'What's the matter with you this evening? Your mind's clearly on other things.'

'Yes they are,' reported the doctor uneasily. 'It's been a very hard day. We lost two patients on the operating table. That's two too many. I'm sorry but I don't think I want to continue playing.' She pushed away the cards in front of her to the dismay of the other players. 'I'm just going to freshen up.' She left the card table and disappeared from the room.

'It's not like her,' commented Samantha as she turned on the electric switch to heat up the kettle. 'I think there's more to it than that.'

'Perhaps it's her time of the month,' added Jane, pulling a face as she set out the tea cups.

'Maybe,' continued Samantha, 'but I still think there's something else that's troubling her.'

'Well it's none of our business,' uttered Jane solemnly. 'All I'm concerned with is the game. It doesn't look like she's in a fit state to continue.'

'It doesn't seem so,' intruded Diana.

Shortly, Dr. Martin returned and drew Diana away to one side as the other two busied themselves with the tea.

'You've been to Morocco,' she said in a low tone to avoid the others hearing what she wanted to say. 'Did you ask him?'

'I did,' replied Diana flatly. 'He's writing a paper on the subject which he'll send to all the major medical authorities in the world and then he'll include you in his experiment. You'll be one of us.'

'When will this paper be completed?' she asked tentatively. The question was fired like a bullet from a rifle.

'In about six months time,' related Diana. 'You'll have to be patient.'

'I can't wait,' echoed the doctor.

Diana's face took on a wry smile at her bridge partner's anxiety but there was nothing she could do about it. Dr. Mahmoud had agreed to include another guinea pig but was in no hurry to do so at the present time.

'You'll provide me with details in due course, I hope'

'Naturally, Valerie. You have my promise.'

Jane moved across with two cups of tea staring at them suspiciously. 'What's going on with you two?' she asked.

'We're just talking about Morocco,' lied Diana.

'I've given up trying to look as young as you,' declared Samantha joining them. 'I've had some success with a product called Evangeline but it's clearly not enough.' She reached for a biscuit waiting for a response.

'Evangeline,' repeated Jane, staring at Samantha's face to determine any improvement. 'What's it supposed to do?' '

'They say it rejuvenates the skin and makes one look younger. That's what it's supposed to do.' She turned to Diana. 'Do you use it?'

'No,' came the reply. 'I was approached by the company that makes it some time ago. They wanted me to appear on television in one of their commercials. I refused. Those products aren't really any good and I didn't want my name associated with it. I think it works when it's first applied but the wrinkles come back the next morning.'

'I know exactly what you mean,' agreed Samantha.

'They tell you how wonderful it is just to make you buy the stuff,' criticised Jane. 'Well they're not going to get my money!'

Diana rolled her eyes to the ceiling at the remark as though asking for help from a higher authority. At the same time, Dr. Martin became angry at the trend of the conversation, unable to keep her temper under control.

'Why does everyone keep talking about good looks?' she ranted. 'Can't we find something else to talk about?'

'You know that last hand we played,' cut in Diana, changing the subject quickly. 'Jane played it in four hearts but it should have been in three no trumps. What went wrong with the bidding there?'

The atmosphere changed immediately as Jane and Samantha explained in detail what had happened and Dr. Martin sat back in her chair with an irritated expression on her face.

It was quite clear to Diana what was on the doctor's mind. She fervently desired to look young and live a long life but the situation was not going to be offered to her for at least six months… or even longer by the time the medical authorities reviewed Dr. Mahmoud's findings, if they ever accepted the paper. Indeed it would be some considerable time before she was accepted to take part in the experiment.

* * * * *

It was Shakespeare who wrote the immortal line 'When troubles come they come not single spies but in battalions.' So it occurred with Diana who sought a peaceful life for herself with no outside interference. The Cosmic Joker was still controlling her destiny and it decided to work its magic again. It shook up the kaleidoscope of her life to produce a picture totally unexpected. She was sitting in her lounge one evening with a glass of sherry in her hand, and nothing of particular importance in mind, when the telephone rang. A new era was about to invade her life as she answered the call after placing the glass down on the coffee-table.

'This is Greg,' announced the caller. 'You remember me. I was at your sister's house in Los Angeles. We went out to dinner. You know, the film producer who took you for a screen test.'

A smile appeared on Diana's face as she heard his voice. 'Greg,' she echoed cheerfully. 'How could I forget you. You wanted to marry me.'

'I still do,' he retorted openly. 'You're a beautiful lovely lady and I love you,' he expressed in amorous tones.

'I understand you married again,' she countered smartly. 'How's that panning out?'

'Yep, I did,' he admitted, 'but it's not worked out well at all. I've filed for divorce. We've arranged to go to Reno to do it. You see, I've found the right woman but you won't marry me.'

Diana shook her head in disbelief. He was certainly a Casanova marrying and divorcing at a rate of knots. 'To what do I owe the pleasure of this call,' she demanded tiring quickly of the conversation.

'I'm coming over to your country in a day or so,' he informed her. 'I'm making a movie at Pinewood Studios. You don't live far from there, do you?'

'No… not far at all.'

'Well I know this is an imposition but I wonder if I could stay with you while I make the movie.' He was really pushing his luck with the request but she could understand his situation.

'How long will the film take to finish?' She was concerned at having to face the brunt of months of unappreciated amorous approaches.

'About three months,' he replied. 'The rest of it will be on location in Switzerland. It's a remake of 'I Remember Mama' the 1948 movie with Irene Dunne and Barbara del Geddes.'

'I recall the film vaguely,' confirmed Diana, lapsing into silence.

‘Do I have a yes or a no,’ he asked eventually. His voice sounded more in hope than expectation.

‘I’ll think about it,’ she told him wisely. ‘Leave your phone number and I’ll get back to you.’

‘There’s just one more thing,’ he went on in an attempt to win her over. ‘There’s a part in the movie for you. It’s a fairly sizeable role’

After the call had finished, Diana sat back thinking about the request. Did she really want to get into films as an actress again? The ten second shot she had performed in his previous film had been amusing but did she really want to go headlong into another one? He had told her it was a sizeable role so it was certain she would have lines to learn. She recalled her school days when she had been a fairy in a pantomime shortly before the Christmas break with a few lines to relate to the audience. She had come on to the stage in a glittering outfit holding a wand which she waved about wildly. However when it came to her turn to speak the words were lost. She stood up on the stage and froze. Her mouth opened but nothing came out. The experience was horrifying and she never forgot it. Nonetheless she could hardly deny the accommodation he required. She would be inconvenienced for about three months but the time would soon pass albeit she would have to repulse his amorous approaches.

She rang him back to tell him of her decision and, two days later, he appeared at her front door with a large holdall in his grasp.

‘Wow!’ he exclaimed staring at her face. ‘You look more beautiful than ever. How do you manage to look so young. It’s amazing. You never seem to age.’

‘You can drop the compliments,’ she told him bluntly. ‘Save them for your next wife.’

‘It could be you if you agree to marry me,’ he proposed, causing her to smile. ‘I swear if you do so, I’ll never look at another woman.’

She ignored his comments admitting him into the lounge and then showing him upstairs to the guest room. He stared at her with a whimsical expression on his face.

‘There’s no chance of sleeping in the same bedroom as you, I s’pose,’ he advanced boldly.

Diana took the comment as a joke even though he seemed to be serious. ‘Not until Hell freezes over,’ she retorted curtly. It was clear that the amorous Greg was not going to miss any opportunity when it came to seducing women.

‘I’ll take you to Pinewood Studios in the morning,’ he told her.

She nodded sombrely. ‘It’s okay. I hope you don’t think I’m going to learn lots of lines.’

He threw the holdall on the bed. 'I want you to consider the role of Barbara del Geddes,' he said point-blank. 'You can start off as a fifteen year old... don't worry the make-up people can do wonders... and you progress from there. You mature into an authoress.'

'It's too big a part for me,' she responded almost in a panic, becoming fearful at the task.

'Have confidence in yourself. You can do it! I'll make you a film star. Leave it to me.' He paused for a moment. 'Have dinner with me tonight.'

She accepted the offer without hesitation. There was no hardship in dining with the man as long as his approaches failed to continue. He was a clown with a penchant for women. He obviously never saved any money, living day to day from what he earned from the films he produced, spending it all on women. Well it was no skin off her nose if he wanted to be a fool all his life. Her problem was to find a way of opting out of appearing as an actress in his film.

The following day he drove her to Pinewood Studios. It was a vast place with props of all kinds stacked in different areas. She stared in awe at the great rocks that weighed only a few pounds, large Greek columns, parapets of castles and a variety of other features that cluttered the space here and there. To his credit, Greg took control of the situation without delay. Outside the studio, he was a clown chasing every woman in sight. Inside he was monumentous, a completely different character, a master of his profession. He counselled one of the staff advising the man of all the props he needed... where the cameras should be installed, how the lighting needed to be arranged, and all the background scenery he required. There was no hesitation as he rolled out his plans for the forthcoming film and everyone became cognisant of what he intended to achieve. Diana met all the actors and actresses that Greg had cast for the main parts, but she was extremely shy at having been given such a large role he had chosen for her. Now that she was actually in the studio, the idea of acting in the film terrified her. Once again she realised that she was doing it to please someone else and not for herself. She recalled the tale by Aesop in one of his fables about the donkey on its way to market with the owner in the saddle. People started to berate the man because his son was walking all the way beside him. To please them, he alighted and put the boy on the donkey's back. As they went on, other people complained that the boy should give way to his elderly father. Further on, more people grumbled that the donkey shouldn't have anyone on its back. So the man got off again to please them. Then the donkey fell into a stream and died and no one was satisfied. She felt exactly in the same position. No doubt, Robbie and Karen would be delighted to see her in a film but she had never had any training and she didn't know how to act. She became determined to satisfy herself regardless of what anyone else wanted her to do.

Later that evening, as she and Greg dined at a restaurant, he handed her a script of the film.

'You don't have to learn all the dialogue at one go,' he advised her. 'Just one scene at a time. We always start at six-thirty in the morning for make-up. You can read your lines then.'

But I'm no good at remembering lines, Greg,' she bleated. 'You know I lost my memory way back. I can't make words stick in my mind.'

'Look,' he told her sternly. 'You only have to remember them one at a time You can read the lines during make-up. After you've done each scene you can forget the words.'

She shook her head boldly determined to stick to her guns. 'No… I can't do it! I can't do it!'

'Come on, sweetie!' he urged, unwilling to lose her from the cast. 'Stick with it. I'll get you through!'

'I've never acted before,' she smarted. She was now becoming angry at his unqualified insistence.

He huffed and puffed at the rejection. 'Think about it. Sleep on it. That's all I ask.'

'I've thought about it,' she rebuffed without a tinge of conscience. 'I'd rather tell you now before you start shooting, than when you were halfway through. You don't need someone like me putting a spanner in the works.'

He sat back to think about her words, trying to reconcile the situation in his mind. 'I knew something like this would happen,' he moaned bitterly, 'so I advanced the situation by hiring a substitute in case you didn't want the part. It seems that I was right.'

'I'm sorry, Greg, but you kind of thrust it upon me.'

'Don't worry about it, honey,' her returned amorously. 'I thought you'd jump at the chance. You're a sure thing to become a star with a photogenic face like yours.'

She accepted the compliment gratefully breathing a sigh of relief that she had relinquished her right to the film role. She was so delighted she felt that she could kiss her dining companion and then thought better in case he misread the signal. No doubt Greg would have believed that she had changed her mind about him. In that case the action was simply a figment of her imagination.

Three months passed by and Diana saw very little of her American friend.

She was surprised at the way he tackled his work. He was a lion in the fight, working from seven o'clock in the morning until ten o'clock each night. Towards the end of the filming, he had lost almost a stone in weight and looked a very worried man. Yet the film was completed on schedule and within the budget but Greg was never satisfied with the final cut. Whether it would make any money at the box office was an unknown quantity. He needed to earn enough to pay for all the purchases made by his current wife before the divorce took place.

The advantage that lay with Diana was the fact that Greg was missing all the day, every day, and every evening. He was so tired when he came back that romance was non-existent. She had expected him at some time to enter her bedroom in order to make advances towards her but he was too tired to do anything but sleep. The man was a perfectionist in film-making and he had taken on a lot of responsibility borrowing a large amount from banks and investors in order to produce it. And he was the sole producer and director.

When the filming was over, he came down one morning with the holdall in his grasp and hugged Diana as she emerged from the lounge.

'We'll honey,' he said with a sad expression on his face. 'I reckon we have to part, but you can still change your mind about me at any time. The offer to marry you is still on the table. I mean it. It's there any time you want.'

'Thank you,' she returned calmly. 'It's been a pleasure having you here even though I haven't seen much of you.'

'We can always put that right,' he advanced as she moved away from him.

'Why don't you come to LA? You can stay with your sister.'

'I'll take a rain check on that,' she laughed. 'Good luck with your film... and good luck with your divorce.'

He shook his head slowly. 'It's different in the States. We change partners like you change cars. It's easier to do that than be fettered with the wrong partner. All you have to do is to go to Reno. It's over in one day.'

She took him to the front door, waving to him as he climbed into a taxi. There was one thing about Greg... he was an interesting eccentric person to say the least. She closed the door shutting her eyes as she thought of the horror of being married to him. It was too terrifying to contemplate. Far too terrifying!

CHAPTER TWENTY-FIVE

Although she was unaware of it, Diana's journeys to Agadir were coming to an end. This would be the last one to see the scientist. Over the years, he had always been there for her, supplying tablets and giving advice. On this occasion, she sauntered into his office, her eyes opening widely as she saw Hamid Arran sitting in the chair with his feet up on the desk. As in the past, he was reading a comic book.

'Where's Dr. Mahmoud?' she cried worriedly.

The man's face turned sour and he removed his legs from the top of the desk slowly indicating from his expression that she was going to hear some bad news.

'It's not good,' he told her, trying to ease the pain of what he was about to tell her.

'What do you mean? What's happened to him?' Alarm bells began to ring in her head. Arran's attitude was completely different to the last time she came to see the scientist. He had been in North Borneo… this time it was clearly more serious.

'He's dead!' muttered the man sombrely. 'We received a panther to be used for experimentation. He injected it with a new serum and it turned vicious. It savaged him severing his jugular vein and he died within seconds.

Diana put her hand to her mouth in anguish. 'Oh, my God!' she uttered almost in a whisper.

'I've been working with him for four years. Now I'm in charge,' boasted Arran, putting the comic book down on the desk.

'You trained under Dr. Mahmoud?' she returned in disbelief.

'He taught me all I know,' confided the man. 'I'm quite capable you know.' He saw her eyes drift to the comic book on the desk. 'I do read medical books!'

'What do you know about Beotag and ferradil-x?'

'All there is to know,' he rebounded. 'They help one to retain their looks and physique and extends their lives. We've been working on animals here.'

'He thought he was immortal,' mused Diana sadly. 'He was a great scientist who cured many people. What happens about the tablets in the future?'

'I've been making them for him for the last four years. I'm a qualified pharmacist. You need not concern yourself. We have the plants here.'

‘He was going to write a paper on the experiment and send it to all the major medical authorities in the world,’ she went on heartbroken. ‘I don’t suppose he had the chance to do it.’

‘He started but only got about a quarter of the way through. I’m not capable of carrying it on so the secret of the experiment rests between me and you.’

Diana sat down heavily in a chair trying to make sense of it all. ‘Okay, Mr. Arran,’ she ventured. ‘You say you make ferradil-x tablets?’

‘Yes I do,’ he replied naively not expecting the request from the woman.

‘I want you to make twenty years of supply for me. Do you hear? Twenty years at four tablets a day. You can work it out.’ Her attitude was completely commanding.

He stared at her coldly starting to work out the figures in his mind. ‘That’s an awful lot of tablets,’ he said eventually. ‘I’m not certain whether ferradil-x tablets have a sell-by date. Whew! That’s an awful lot of tablets to produce.’

‘Dr. Mahmoud told me that he already had ten years supply. All you need to do is to double that. I’ll give you two months to make them,’ she told him like a Commander talking to one of his subordinates. ‘I’ll pay you for them. Is that a deal?’

‘How much will you pay for them?’

‘How much do you want?’

‘Let’s say ten thousand pounds and no haggling.’

‘Done… it’s a deal. Two months!’

‘The impossible can be done instantly,’ he responded delighted at the thought of making so much money. ‘Miracles take a little longer.’

‘Two months!’ she repeated adamantly. ‘I want them packaged and sent to my home in England. As soon as they’re received I’ll arrange for an immediate bank transfer to your account in Agadir. Is that understood?’ She took a calling card from her handbag and gave it to him. ‘Don’t lose it or I’ll come looking for you and you’ll be in a heap of trouble. Just don’t let me down!’

He took the card, staring at her like a schoolboy who had been caught stealing and nodded. ‘Two months,’ he repeated. ‘I really see no difficulty.’

Diana left the office extremely unsettled in mind. What a thing to happen? Killed by a panther! Poor Dr. Mahmoud. She had liked him so much and he was always so helpful. They had built up a kind of business relationship and he was a friend to her. In her mind she envisage him staring at her stroking his goatee beard… he always did that… it was a habit. He thought he would live for eternity and it had ended so tragically… so quickly. Destiny certainly had other ideas sending death to him so sharply. She had no doubt that Arran would comply with the order, supplying her with enough tablets to last her twenty years. She would be almost eighty years old by then. There was another matter that disturbed her… Dr. Valerie Martin! What could she say to her except to explain that the experiment had ended with the death of Dr. Mahmoud? The physician would be desolate at not having the opportunity to become involved. Unfortunately, due to the events that had taken place the doctor would be left wanting.

Diana took a taxi to Ahmed's office and he greeted her warmly, kissing the fingers of her hand gently. She realised that she was falling in love with the man slowly and she looked for more than a simple kiss on the hand from him. She knew in her heart that there was a world of romance waiting for her in the near future.

'I'm glad you lost the moustache,' she began easily.

'It disappeared overnight.'

'How are things, Ahmed?'

'It's all happening,' he informed her excitedly. 'My partner's willing to buy me out. He's getting a loan from the bank and I've arranged for the papers to be signed on completion.'

'And your family?

'They're already with my uncle. I shall make arrangements for them to have sufficient money to keep them going but they are now searching for employment. The problem is the dowry to be paid when my sister gets married.'

'I thought it was the men who paid the dowry,' she said slowly.

'Not in this country,' he went on unhappily. 'The father of the bride is expected to pay.'

'How much is a dowry going to cost?

'A lesser price for a pretty woman… a much higher price for an ugly one. My sister's in between. She takes after my father.'

'I could pay it,' Diana told him willingly.

'I'm not sure I can accept that from you,' he told her.

'I could give it to you and you could pretend that it was yours.' she suggested.

'The wedding won't be for some time so we can deal with the matter when it happens.' He paused to stare directly into her eyes. 'I do love you,' he went on, moving into an amorous mode. 'Your eyes are so beautiful. I can't wait to marry you.'

She bridled at the comment. 'Marry you!' she spat. 'Did I ever say I'd marry you? If I did I must have been out of my mind.'

He ignored the fact that she objected so fiercely. He thought that it was a done deal. He would go and live in England with her. Suddenly she had changed her mind. 'Well it doesn't really matter,' he uttered after a short hesitation. 'We don't have to actually get married. I mean what's a piece of paper between two people who love each other?'

'We've already been through all this,' she reproached. 'Marriage would cause us all kinds of problems. In a church… in a mosque… in a Registry Office! I really don't think that's a good idea! What I would dearly love to do is to stand in front of a tent at the edge of the Sahara Desert staring at the sunset… just you and me. You carry me into the tent and we make mad passionate love together. That's my dream and that's what I really want. After that you can come and live with me in England.'

'But how can I stay in England without the statutory immigration papers?'

'We'll have to work through that one,' she told him carelessly.

'It's going to take a lot of thinking if you won't marry me.'

'Kiss me… properly,' she said, waiting for him to come around the desk, taking her hands and kissing her on the lips.

She responded warmly returning the affection. It was the first time she had done so other than in her dream. She suddenly realised that she was falling in love with the man. The chemistry between them was coming together very fast.

A short while later, she left to catch the aircraft, sitting quietly in her seat after she had boarded. She mused over the conversation with Ahmed. Marriage! What was she thinking of? Although she had started for feel differently about him it was the furthest thing from her mind. Living a life in illicit sin was far more to her liking. They were both free agents so it didn't harm anyone else. In that way, if either of them tired of each other, the could go their own separate ways. She realised that if she was true to herself, she wanted him only for romance and love… the touch of his body… the erotic feelings of sensuality. At that moment in time, anything else was beyond the pale!

* * * * *

From then on, her dreams became nebulous… more mystifying and difficult to determine. Ahmed appeared in all of them but they were never the same as the highly sexual dream she loved to experience so much. One night she found herself riding on a horse in a carousel which revolved round and round in a circular motion. She could see Ahmed riding a pony on the opposite side and was desperate to reach him. Yet despite her best efforts she failed to get any nearer. He remained on the other side of the carousel laughing at her. After a while, she ignored the danger and alighted, trying to get to him by walking across but, however hard she tried, the carousel kept spinning at a faster rate and she was unable to keep up with it. A week later, in another dream, she found herself with Greg in a large ballroom with many other dancers. She could see Ahmed dancing with another woman but try as she could she was unable to get near him. She could hear him shouting to Greg but the American took no notice of him, taking her in the opposite direction. She began to shout back at him and suddenly sat up in bed with her eyes wide open realising that she was screaming at the top of her voice. Such dreams were, in effect, mini nightmares and she had no idea why they kept forming in her sleep. Was she, in some strange way, resisting the love of Ahmed? She had been so uncertain of her feelings towards him for so long and now the tide had turned. Perhaps it was a bridge too far. She though about Mohammed, the interpreter of dreams, introduced to her by Ahmed, No doubt he would have definite views on what was going on in her mind.

Two months later, almost to the day, a huge package was delivered to her home. It contained numerous canisters of ferradil-x tablets that Hamid Arran had promised to send. She wondered how hard he had worked to achieve such a massive production… most probably day and night for the whole two months. Nonetheless he had worked the oracle and she had twenty years supply to hand. She shuddered to think that he had probably drained all the exotic plants to fulfil the task. She went directly to her bank to send him the money she had promised him for the tablets. It was necessary to keep in touch with Arran as she was paying for heating the room which housed the plants. The jury was still out on him. He had told her that he was a qualified pharmacist but that was a far cry from being a brilliant scientist. He was a man who read comic books and he certainly didn't have the dedication of Dr. Mahmoud. Her mind went back to the time she had been told about the hamster living until it was twelve years old. Four hundred and fifty years it had lived in terms of man-years. How would she fare if she lived that long? Her mind flashed back a hundred-and-fifty years to the Victorian age. There had been no motor cars, no planes, no television or proper telephones, no computers, let alone all the electronic equipment currently available and modern kitchen appliances… nothing, only railways and steamships. How far would the world progress in, say, three hundred years time? Shrugging her shoulders to help rid of such thoughts, she went to the utility room to store the tablets in a cool dry place.

After pouring herself a dry martini, she went to the conservatory at the back of the house taking with her the letters which the postman had delivered that morning. There was a small packet from the United States which she opened quickly and her face broke into a smile as she removed a video disc from it bubble-covered wrapping. She read the letter that accompanied it from the ever-amorous Greg.

Hi, Di,

You gorgeous dame whom I can't get out of my mind.
I enclose a copy of the remake I made of I Remember
Mama which we shot at Pinewood. Hope you like it.
You would have been great in the part I offered you.
I got divorced in Reno. I'm single now but I've met
this brunette who I think I'll marry. I still want to be
with you for ever so what I'm saying is, give me a call
to say you're mine and we can get married right away.
I love you dearly, you good-looking woman. Come to
Greg now! My arms are dying to hold you. Godammit!
Pick up the phone and call me!

All my love and kisses...
Greg.

She laughed inwardly for he was an incorrigible character... a love-lorn fool. So he had got divorced and was about to marry again. Why was he so obsessed with women? He would have been a real catch for a psychiatrist who would reach back in his mind to his childhood to find the answer. She played the video highly delighted that she hadn't taken the part. It was far too major... far too large. The actress playing the role did so with finesse and sensitivity, far beyond the capabilities of a lady of leisure. Taking a major part in a film required a special talent... a degree of confidence and professionalism after a great deal of training as well as an aptitude for learning dialogue. Diana was forced to admit to herself that such technicalities were far beyond her capability.

CHAPTER TWENTY-SIX

For some reason, Diana missed the bridge game for two months. At first, she considered that her life was busy visiting Robbie and Stella to see her beautiful grand children. In addition she went regularly to the Red Cross shop in case an opportunity arose for her to serve there. In the end, she recognised that the logic for her not meeting with Jane, Samantha and Dr. Martin was because she didn't want to have to tell the physician that Dr. Mahmoud had passed away. Valerie had become so eager to take part in the experiment that she would be bitterly disappointed when she learned of the scientist's death. However Jane rang Diana one afternoon begging her to attend that evening because the person who had substituted for her had fallen ill. Reluctantly Diana agreed and took her place opposite the doctor at the bridge table. Before they started, Jane produced a newspaper with she laid on the table so that they could all see it.

'I know why you haven't been here with us for a while,' began Jane smartly.

'You do?' Diana questioned in her mind what the woman was talking about.

'Yes,' said Jane, pointing to an article at the foot of the first page. 'You haven't read this, have you?' Diana shook her head as her attention went to the newspaper but it was upside down so she couldn't read it. 'The heading's "MP RESIGNS THROUGH ILL HEALTH" continued the woman. 'It goes on to say: "Illness has forced the resignation of Diana Templeton, the Member of Parliament for Torpington, shortly after the General Elections. She was attacked some years ago in Morocco by a man who fired a gun at her at point-blank range damaging part of her skull, causing her to lose her memory. It had been believed that she had recovered but the effects returned and she was forced to apply for the Chiltern Hundreds, the means by which MPs can resign. Duncan Redfearn, the Conservative Party Chief Whip commented: 'It's very sad. Diana had great promise. She'll be greatly missed.' A bye-election has been called for the eighth of September… blah, blah, blah!"

'I think I've heard enough!' snapped Diana sharply.

'Why didn't you tell us you'd lost your memory again,' asked Samantha as Jane folded the newspaper and put it aside.

'That article is untrue. It's a load of codswallop. They're trying to make out that it was an act of God that put me out of action. I resigned because my views on helping the British people were in direct conflict with those of the politicians. They're only in it for themselves, their rules and their Party procedures. The House of Commons is a boy's club in which they all play games. They're more interested in what they earn than helping the people of this country.'

'Are you saying that the rights of the people in Britain are being ignored,' forwarded Samantha with concern.

'Not their rights, Samantha, their needs. The plight of the poor people, those unemployed, the homeless and those who really need help. They're the ones who should be considered but Parliament doesn't agree with me. The rules and procedures don't allow it. They close their eyes and get on with their game.

'That's shameful,' cut in Jane. 'I'm not surprised you didn't want anything more to do with it. They shouldn't be allowed to get away with it.!'

'That's the reason I resigned, Not the clap-trap they printed in the newspaper! I couldn't sit on the sidelines and watch it happen. It's a sad thing when people who are supposed to be represented by politicians are ignored because of rules and procedures.'

'Shameful!' repeated Jane vehemently filled with sympathy for her friend. 'I think you did the right thing.'

'Sadly,' continued Diana, 'it doesn't resolve the problems faced by so many people who live hand-to-mouth day by day.'

Before they started to play bridge, Diana noticed that Dr. Martin had remained silent since her arrival. She sat back turning her nose up at the strong smell of surgical spirit knowing that this was probably the last game she would play with any of them. After she told the physician that there was no hope of her becoming involved in the experiment, she had a feeling that the four of them would never meet again.

The doctor's opportunity to speak with her came during the tea break. Jane and Samantha were on the other side of the room making the tea as the doctor moved towards Diana with only one thought in mind.

'What did Dr. Mahmoud say when you approached him about me?'

Diana swallowed hard before replying, expecting a violent reaction from her colleague. 'Dr. Mahmoud was killed by a panther in one of his experiments,' she told the doctor flatly. 'The beast severed his jugular vein and killed him instantly. I'm afraid that the experiment has come to a very swift end.' She decided not to inform the other woman about the supply of tablets she had accumulated. It would only complicate matters. The physician might have insisted on sharing them and, to her mind, that wasn't a good idea. The problem was that Dr. Mahmoud would not be around to explain the side-effects or even deal with them if necessary. It was too great a risk to take.

'What are you going to do' asked the doctor. 'Will your good looks eventually vanish?'

'We shall have to wait and see,' returned Diana sagely. 'Time will tell.'

On the following morning, Diana received a letter from Duncan Redfearn. It commented that her application for the Chiltern Hundreds had been processed and approved. He went on to say that he regretted her decision to stand down and wished her well in the future. It was too little, too late! She had already been advised of the event in the national newspapers. She was furious at the way things had turned out. Her efforts to win the seat in the House of Commons had been for nothing. All that time, effort and toil had been a waste of time. There was no one looking out for the poor, the homeless, the needy and the helpless. Everyone was in it for the money. She had no option but to resign. It was against her nature to promise falsely or avoid the truth. For her, it was necessary to go for the throat in a contest and Parliament wasn't having any of it.

Her days suddenly became empty and she realised that she needed Ahmed's company. His tender compliments, the promise of romance and the essence of sexual excitement caused her to think about him. He could come to England to live with her as they planned if they could find a way to establish him as an immigrant. He had an old passport from the time he attended Oxford university and she could vouch for him to the immigration authorities. It could be that there would be no difficulty in allowing him to stay in Britain. Then, with the care and attention he would lavish on her, the life she desired would be complete. And, after they started living together, she would assess the situation carefully as time passed by. In the effluxion of thirty years, she would remain looking young while he would be over sixty becoming wrinkled and looking much older. At that moment, an alternative thought entered her head. Was youthfulness and longevity in years the best way forward? She thought about Oscar Wilde's story entitled 'The Picture of Dorian Gray' where a man remained young and youthful in looks all his life but a portrait of him in his attic grew aged as the years went by. Would it be more advisable for her to live a normal life with Ahmed and grow old with him? If she lived for a hundred-and-fifty years, Ahmed would have died long before and she would be left alone. It was something to contemplate. Would she find another lover like him? It was possible. There was another problem. Would her sexual desires fade with age. She might be forced to live a life of hell if she couldn't find love and pursue it to the end. There was a distinct advantage in simply leading a normal life. Normally, at the end of seventy or eighty years it was all over and then there were no problems to face. Her existence and the decision she had to make depended solely on her taking two ferradil-x tablets in the morning and evening every day. All she had to do was to leave them in the canister. It was so easy enough to do that… a sacrifice that might be worth making!

* * * * *

One night, she went to bed in a sombre mood. Nothing in her life seemed to be going right. Everything was way off course. She no longer cared about the Red Cross shop, she had resigned as a Member of Parliament, her relationship with her sister Laura seemed to have come to an end over the senseless remark made by her husband, and Robbie had made her a grandmother… a title of which she did not particularly approve. The ostensible failures made her feel old in mind. All she had to look forward in life was a lawyer in Agadir. As she slept, she suffered another nightmare. She found herself chasing Ahmed through a forest but, try as she could, she was unable to catch up with him. The race went on for a considerable time and suddenly a monster with three heads blocked the way. She tried to avoid it by racing around the trees only to come face to face with a giant snake hissing at her with forked tongue. She hurried on to face another monster which lashed out at her with its tail. All the time, Ahmed kept laughing at her as if he didn't want her to reach him. She woke up startled feeling tired and weary, trying to make sense of the dream. It was as though she had fallen down a black hole and it was crushing her to death.

She wasted no time in travelling to Agadir the next day. Her concern focused on Hamid Arran. She stormed into his office to find that he wasn't there. The vision of him sitting there with his feet on the desk, reading a comic book, came into her mind. She knocked on the door which led to the bedroom and opened it slightly. Arran was laying on the bed fast asleep.

'Wake up!' she demanded vehemently, prodding him in the chest. He opened his eyes slowly and moaned. 'It's just over four o'clock in the afternoon. You should be working at your desk!'

He sat up slowly scratching his head. 'I sent you the tablets,' he groaned. 'What more do you want? Leave me alone!'

'Are you a qualified pharmacist?' she asked point-blank.

He stared at her through bleary eyes. 'You know I am. I told you so,' he muttered half asleep. He yawned loudly laying back on the bed intending to return to sleep.

'Why aren't you continuing with Dr. Mahmoud's work?'

'I am!' His voice sounded as though his mouth was filled with cotton-wool. .'My hours are eight until four. Now leave me in peace!'

She screwed up her face and left the man to continue his slumber. He was a qualified pharmacist but would he be able to step into the shoes of his master? She sincerely hoped so. The experiment had to continue. It had to! Her next task was to visit Ahmed to make the final arrangements for him to travel to England. She now had the bit between her teeth and went to his office, entering without knocking. He was the perfect lover, taking her in his arms and kissing her firmly on the lips. She was delighted at his romantic approach. No longer did he kiss her gently on her fingers...now it was a full blown kiss. He pointed to a chair indicating that she should sit down before informing her of his situation.

'The sale of my half of the firm has gone through,' he told her. 'The funds are in my bank account.'

'And your family?'

'They're well settled with my uncle. I have my passport ready.'

'It all seems to have worked out well,' she went on but there was her secret of ageing that she felt she had to tell him. She feared that when he learned the truth it might cause him to change his mind about her. 'There's something important I need to say before we go any further.' He stared at her bleakly hoping that she wasn't going to turn him down at the last moment. 'You know I've been seeing Dr. Mahmoud all these years.'

'He was helping you to recover your memory.'

'No he wasn't,' she explained with her heart in her mouth. 'We've been carrying out an experiment with the essences of exotic plants from North Borneo.'

'An experiment?' he echoed. 'What sort of an experiment?'

'It keeps a person looking very young and increases the longevity of life. I take four tablets of one kind every day. I'm supposed to look exactly as I do today until I'm at least two hundred years old.'

He paused to consider the situation refusing to believe her. 'You don't want us to be together, Why don't you tell me directly instead of making up such a ridiculous story?'

'It's the truth,' she insisted. 'Do I look any different to you since the first time you saw me?'

He stared at her face thoughtfully to reflect. 'You look very young,' he admitted. 'It never crossed my mind before...' he tailed off as the impact of her words struck him. 'Are you saying you'll look exactly the same in fifty years time?'

She nodded affirmatively. 'Do you want me to stop taking the tablets. It could end the experiment and I would look old. Do you want me to do that?'

He shrugged his shoulders aimlessly. It was all too sudden for him and he was totally confused. 'Are you really saying you'll live to two hundred and look the same as you do today?'

'You'll grow old but I won't,' she told him sadly. 'But I'm willing to sacrifice everything for you. I could stop taking the tablets and grow old with you.'

'It's going to take me a little time to get my head around this.' he muttered. 'How old are you now?'

'I'm almost sixty,' she told him with concern in her voice. 'I'm sorry to throw this at you.'

His head went up as he made a swift decision. 'Keep taking the tablets, Diana,' he told her fervently. 'I don't care what age you are as long as you keep looking as you do today. There... I've made up my mind. Better still, I will join you in the experiment taking the tablets with you.'

She was surprised at his reaction and it warmed her heart that he had accepted the situation so readily. Of course... he had put his finger on the solution. They could grow old together both looking in the future as they did at present. It was a great idea!

'Now that's settled,' he continued as though nothing had happened, 'I have a surprise for you.' He stood up and waked around the desk taking her hand tenderly before leading her outside to his vehicle.

'Where are we going?' she asked him tentatively.

'To the Purple Mountains and further on,' he told her. He drove a few miles outside Agadir stopping the car by the side of a rugged path where a man stood holding the reins of two asses. 'Come on,' he invited. 'We have a journey to complete.'

She sat on the second ass and Ahmed led the way forward striking his animal lightly with a whip handed to him by the Arab owner They rode a short way into the Sahara Desert to a large tent which had been erected there previously and alighted.

'I brought you here to see the sunset over the desert,' he informed her taking her into his arms. 'This evening we shall fulfil your dream and make love together.'

She inhaled deeply as emotion began to overtake her. This was the testing moment in her life. Having been married for many years and given birth to two children, she was now on the verge of starting a completely new life… a second chance for an intimate sexual relationship.

They stood on the edge of the desert watching the sunset in all its glory and then Ahmed took her arm. 'Come into the tent and change into something more comfortable,' he advised. 'I've brought some clothes for you.'

He had become so masterful, so quickly. She had been independent for so long that it was a relief to hand over the reins to someone else. She entered the tent where a mattress had been placed on the sand. She undressed and put on a dressing-gown that was there. Within a short while, Ahmed entered the tent. He stared at her face and took hold of her hands.

'You are so beautiful,' he whispered sincerely. 'I love you so much.'

Diana felt her legs weaken as he held her tightly and kissed her fully on the lips. She moved away to allow the dressing-gown to slip from her shoulders exposing her lovely slim figure. Her long legs moved towards the mattress before she turned to her handsome lover. Then she folded neatly into his arms enjoying the warmth of his lustful intimate embrace. His hand caressed her neck gently moving up and down in an erogenous area. Emotion swiftly welled up inside her. His hands moved slowly to her breasts stroking each one smoothly, touching her nipples gently so that she felt transported to a higher level more than she had ever known before. She felt her body becoming moist as her heart beat rapidly in anticipation and beads of perspiration began to appear on her forehead. It was exhilarating… brilliant … wonderful…

erotic! His hand moved to a lower part of her body causing her adrenalin to begin to flow freely. The difference on this occasion was that it was not a dream. No longer was it a mirage in the figment of her imagination. It was real… now happening in real life making her feel like a perfect woman. Yes… it was sensuous, exciting and erotic. Even better was the fact that it would go on for another one hundred-and-fifty years or more. What in real life could be better than that?

THE END

Lightning Source UK Ltd.
Milton Keynes UK
UKOW02f0204211115

263169UK00002B/32/P